MISS FORTUNE

**Center Point
Large Print**

**This Large Print Book carries the
Seal of Approval of N.A.V.H.**

MISS FORTUNE

AN ALLIE FORTUNE MYSTERY
#1

Sara Mills

CENTER POINT PUBLISHING
THORNDIKE, MAINE

This Center Point Large Print edition
is published in the year 2009 by arrangement with
Moody Publishers.

The text of this Large Print edition is unabridged.
In other aspects, this book may vary
from the original edition.
Printed in the United States of America.
Set in 16-point Times New Roman type.

ISBN: 978-1-60285-437-6

Library of Congress Cataloging-in-Publication Data

Mills, Sara, 1978-
  Miss fortune / Sara Mills.
      p. cm.
  ISBN 978-1-60285-437-6 (library binding : alk. paper)
  1. Women private investigators--New York (State)--New York--Fiction.
    2. New York (N.Y.)--History--1898-1951--Fiction. 3. Large type books. I. Title.

PS3613.I5698M57 2009
813'.6--dc22

2008054306

Acknowledgments

I COULDN'T HAVE written this book, or any other, without the help, support, and encouragement of my wonderful husband, Keith, and my ever-so-patient children, Isaiah, Laura, and Julia. Thank you so much for all the times you let me flake out on laundry, cleaning, and cooking in order to work on the story. But even more, thank you for all the times you dragged me away from the keyboard to play Trivial Pursuit, to walk the land, or even to watch something stupid on YouTube. You guys keep me centered. Or at least kind of centered.

I couldn't have persevered through the tough writing years without the support and encouragement of my family. Thanks to Mom and Blaine, Dad and Sam, and Rowland and Wilma (the best in-laws ever).

Eternal thanks to my agent, Steve Laube, who is one of the most stand-up guys I know. Getting *the* call from you kept me from investing in a lifetime's worth of nylons and going back to school. As that would be a fate worse than death, I'm grateful. I'm also thankful that you put up with my obsessive tendencies without hanging up on me.

Thank you to my amazing critique partner Ronie Kendig; you are a blessing beyond measure. This book would not be, without you. With you, every-thing is always shiny.

Thank you to another amazing critique partner, Sara Goff, whose eye for beauty and simplicity of language changed the way I wrote. Thank you.

Thank you to ACFW, the strongest, most encour-aging, most professional, and most fun writing group on the planet.

Thank you to the wonderful staff of the Claresholm Library. I wrote half this book in "my office" there. It's a wonderful place to hang out.

Thank you to my local Claresholm writer's group. We may not be big, but we're small. Thanks for letting me vent over the years and for keeping me sane.

Thank you to Sheila Gray, who would come by and occupy Julia for the day, discuss books with me, and in general help in any way she could. Thank you.

Thank you to the Fringirlz (Shelly Dixon and Wendy Thompson)—for encouragement, coffee, and group therapy. To many more years on The View. For nonwriters, you guys really seem to get it.

Thanks so much to Andy McGuire for taking a chance on me and to Cheryl Dunlop for fabulous editing.

And most especially to God, who gave me a gift He wouldn't let me give up on.

Chapter 1

TWO THIRTY IN the morning and it was sweltering. The whole city was wrapped in a greyish blanket of twilight and haze. The windows in my apartment were open, but there was no breeze, not even a stir of air to ease the heat.

I should've been sleeping, working out in dreams what troubled my soul. Instead I sat curled into the windowsill of my apartment, staring down at the streetlight, waiting for daybreak. And the stillness made me crazy.

Twelve blocks away, lying on the desk in my second-story office, was a file that could change my life, and it terrified me.

Maybe I should have burned it when it arrived in the mail. Maybe if I'd just touched match to paper, I could have slept tonight.

Maybe, but I doubt it.

Instead, I was wide awake and had to know.

Breaking the stillness, I rose. It took only a moment to dress and get ready for the day. No need to fix my long hair; like so many other nights, my head never touched the pillow. I buttoned the last buttons on the wasp-waisted suit jacket, smoothed down the matching grey skirt, and grabbed my black felt hat from the hall table. I positioned it at

7

an angle and jammed the hat pin through to anchor it, then took a quick peek in the mirror. Dark circles under my eyes notwithstanding, I looked all right. No different than most of the women in this city, but in my line of work I knew exactly how deceptive appearances could be. I walked out the door, closing it with a soft click.

My name is Allie Fortune, and I was the only female P.I. in New York City. Most of the other private detectives in the city referred to me as the P.I. Princess. It was half insult, half endearment, but it made no difference. I didn't care what they called me.

The streets at three a.m. were night-quiet. Which wasn't really quiet at all, just filled with sounds that went unnoticed during the day. The high-pitched tap of heels on pavement, the bark of a dog a long way off, and the hum of streetlights. Dank cement and humidity are the scents of summer in New York. The sounds and smells flittered through my subconscious throughout the ten-minute walk. I stared straight ahead the whole time, avoiding eye contact with the other lost souls out wandering the darkness.

The clatter of my shoes as I climbed the stairs to the office sounded like echoing thunder. I unlocked my office door. Black stenciled letters on opaque glass announced it as the office of A. Fortune, Private Investigator. I pulled my keys out of the lock, tucked them back into my purse, flicked on the lights, and avoided looking toward the desk. I needed just one more minute to get myself ready for the folder lying there.

I removed my hat and placed it on the rack in the corner, crossed the room to run the tips of my fingers along the wooden filing cabinet, and made a pretense of straightening some of the papers on my desk. After another minute I was ready to face it.

I went to the file, took a deep breath, and forced myself to flip open the cover. My breath stalled as I looked at the eight-by-ten photo. It was a clear shot, with no out-of-focus blurriness to make the identification difficult. I couldn't bring myself to touch it, so I leaned closer. The man's height and build looked right. He was in uniform, laid out on the dirt. There were no gunshot wounds that I could see. He didn't look peaceful or angry. He just looked dead. Tears stung my eyes. He also didn't look like David. My shoulders slumped, and I let out a ragged breath.

Shutting the folder, I pushed it away so I didn't have to look anymore. Letting myself slump into my chair, I wondered if I had enough strength to keep up the search, but realized almost immediately that the alternative, giving up, was not an option. I straightened my spine and shored up my resolve once more. I would keep looking at photos and following leads until I found out what happened to him. Reaching across the desk, I swept the file into the trash can. The label on it caught my eye and made me wince. A soldier being reduced to simply John Doe #5435 was cold, even for the bureaucrats at the War Office.

Shoving a stack of files out of the way, I laid my head down on my desk, and the emotions I'd been holding in swamped me. I felt joy at knowing that it wasn't him but also the desperate wish that something, anything would stomp out that last flicker of hope I still carried like a talisman.

For that instant, though, the relief won out and I let myself sink into its coolness for a moment.

The rise and fall of emotion left me drained. I glanced over at the long, hard leather couch, my second bed, and wondered if there was any chance I could get a few hours of sleep before dawn. After a moment I decided it was at least worth a try.

A sudden loud bang on my office door sent my thoughts flying and set my heart thumping. The knock came again, hard enough to make the door rattle and my breath jerk. I tried to make out a silhouette through the frosted glass but couldn't see clearly.

"Who is it? What do you want?" I couldn't remember if I'd locked the door when I came in, so I rummaged through my desk drawer for something to use to defend myself.

"I need your help. Please, I need someone to help me," a woman's voice called through the door.

I set down the five-pound glass ashtray I'd been ready to fling, but I was still cautious. As a general rule, when someone knocks on a door at three in the morning, it means trouble. They are either causing it or being chased by it. I wasn't keen on either.

I crossed the room and spoke through the door. "We're not open for business. You can come in and tell me all about it tomorrow. Business hours are from eight to five."

"I can't wait until tomorrow. I need help tonight. Now. Please, let me in."

I heard the fear in her voice. The silhouette changed as she shifted from foot to foot and hugged her arms to her chest. She seemed genuinely frightened, glancing over her shoulder as though searching for danger. I reached for the knob, turned the lock, and peeked through the crack before opening it all the way to let her in.

She was a small woman. Dark hair, pretty enough face, but nothing special. She was neither a high-class lady nor a chippy. Her dress was at least three years out of style but neatly pressed. Still it had that Rosie the Riveter, cheap, industrial look to it. Her shoes looked tattered around the edges, as though she strode a lot of pavement in them. Her hair was caught up in a roll at the base of her neck, but wisps escaped to curl around the sides of her face. The dark circles under her eyes probably matched mine. Here was a woman who'd had little sleep and less money. Not the type of person who'd likely be able to afford my services.

"Okay, come in. But only for a minute." I didn't bother to hold back a long sigh.

She entered my office, looking over her shoulder.

I motioned for her to sit on the oxblood leather couch that ran the length of the room.

She sat perched on the very edge, as though ready to jump up at a moment's notice. She looked around, and it appeared she wasn't overly impressed by what she saw. I tried to see it through her eyes. The office was small, with windows lining two walls, a battered wooden desk in the corner, and a bank of dark wood filing cabinets. The paint was peeling in places, but the room as a whole was fairly tidy. Papers were mostly put away, with the odd open file here and there. It wasn't luxurious, but it suited my needs.

"Why don't you start by telling me who's after you."

"Why would you think someone's after me?"

Oh, for pity's sake. "Ma'am, you're pounding on my office door at three in the morning, terrified and looking over your shoulder. Either someone's after you or you're loony. Now, I don't care if you don't want to tell me about it, but then you're going to have to find someone else's office to hide in, because you're sitting on my bed." I looked pointedly at the couch and the blanket draped over its back.

She chewed at the edge of her fingernail for a moment before yanking her hand back down and placing it in her lap. She shrugged. "Okay, maybe someone is looking for me. Someone that I'd prefer didn't find me, but they're not chasing me per se."

I wasn't sure if it was lack of sleep or her evasive answers that made me dislike her, but there was something about this woman that I didn't trust.

"Don't you have somewhere else you could hide from this person who's looking for you but not chasing you? Because I think it would be better if you left now." I rose, ready to escort her to the door.

The woman pulled herself up, and ice edged into her voice. "I don't know who you think you are, ma'am, but I'm sure your boss wouldn't like you speaking this way to a potential client." She glared at me. "In fact, I think I'm going to have to sit right here until Mr. Fortune arrives. I'm sure he'd like to know that his secretary is *not* making a good impression." She then turned her face away from me and settled into the couch.

I counted to ten in my head, but it didn't do much to dissipate the annoyance I was feeling. "I'm Allie Fortune, and this is my office. I'm the P.I., *not* the secretary." I reached out my hand to her, giving politeness one last shot.

"Oh. Miss Fortune, I didn't . . ."

I winced. "Call me Allie, please."

"Now, let's try the truth this time. Tell me what's wrong."

"Well, Miss Fortune . . . I mean Allie, I need a private investigator because someone is trying to kill me."

Chapter 2

"OKAY . . . WHY DON'T we start with your name, and then we'll get to who's trying to kill you and why. And don't forget how you ended up at my office in the middle of the night."

The little wrenlike woman nodded and took a deep breath. "My name is Mary. Mary Gordon. I happened upon your office because it's the only one with a light on for blocks. I took the chance that someone was here and knocked."

I was sure my skepticism showed in my expression. "So you're in trouble and you see an office with the light on and it just happens to be a private investigator's office? You sure you want to stick with that story?"

"That's what happened." Mary crossed her arms over her chest and leaned back into the sofa. She glared at me. Obviously this wasn't the way to go about getting information from her.

"Why do you think someone is trying to kill you? Start there and maybe all this will start to make some sense."

"Well . . ." She pulled a handkerchief out of her

dress pocket and twisted it around her finger. "It all started last week. I was walking home from work, and I noticed a man following me."

"Where do you work?"

"I clean office buildings downtown at night. I had just finished and was on my way home. I'm usually done around ten o'clock, so the streets aren't overly crowded just then. Anyway, I was walking down the street, headed for home, when I remembered that I'd left my umbrella at the last building. I turned around right then and there to go back for it. The last time I forgot anything in that building, I never saw it again. I turned suddenly, and I saw a tall, heavyset man in an overcoat go into a doorway a few yards away. It was after ten, but a steamy night like tonight, and I remember thinking how hot the gentleman must be, wearing that woolen overcoat." She stopped speaking for a moment and twisted the handkerchief tighter.

"And you went back to the building? For your umbrella . . ." I prompted her.

"Yes, I got my umbrella and started out for home again. By now it was a quarter to eleven, and I was getting anxious about being out alone on the streets. So I moved quickly. It's about a mile or so." She shifted in her seat. "You know how it is when you're all alone at night in this city. You start to get nervous, maybe a little paranoid. I started looking around me, checking to make sure no one was following me."

Yes, I knew that feeling exactly. "But someone was."

"It was that man again. The one in the wool overcoat. No mistaking him. He was a giant of a man. If I'd only seen him once I wouldn't have paid any attention, but seeing him behind me twice, I started to think the worst."

I nodded. Despite the fact that this was just a conversation and not a case, I grabbed a pencil and a pad of paper and started taking notes.

"So, I did the only thing I could think of. I hailed a cab. It was an awful expense, but I was just so scared. When it dropped me off at home, I let myself in and ran to the window. Sure enough, not a minute later another cab pulled up, half a block away, and the man in the overcoat got out. He went over to a different man, who was leaning against a lamppost across the street, and had a quick conversation. Then he got back into the cab and took off." Mary shuddered. "I didn't sleep at all. I just watched the man by the lamppost smoke cigarettes and stare up at my building all night."

"I can see how that would be frightening." I laid the pencil and paper down and came around to the front of my desk to lean against the corner. "But this happened last week. What happened tonight that got you out and brought you running to my door?"

She got up off the couch and moved toward the window. Looking out, she began to speak again.

"All week I've been jittery, looking behind me, but I've never seen those men again. I tried to convince myself that I was only being paranoid, that it didn't really mean anything. Tonight I had to work very late, and I didn't get out of my last building until nearly one in the morning. When I have to work that late, I always take a cab home, and when the driver dropped me off, I noticed that a light was on in my window. I knew right away something was off because I am very careful never to leave the lights on when I'm out." She moved away from the window and back to the couch.

"You're sure you didn't leave it on by mistake?"

"I'm a widow; I make it a habit not to waste what little money I have by lighting a room I'm not occupying."

I nodded. All this fit with her appearance. If I'd had to guess, I would have said she was a widow living on a small income. While it was good for my professional ego to guess so close to the truth, it was bad for my professional income to be right, because there was no way this woman could afford to hire me. I resigned myself to listening to her story and giving her some free advice. I also resigned myself to no further sleep that night.

"Against my better judgment I went upstairs and entered my apartment anyway. It was a mess. Furniture thrown backwards and tipped over at crazy angles, drawers open, linens on the floor. I just stood there in shock for a moment, but then I

17

heard the voices coming from my bedroom. I didn't wait to find out if it was overcoat and lamp-post; I just ran out of there as fast as I could. There was the sound of a gun firing as I ran down the stairs. I ran as fast as I could and just kept going. I've been walking all night, checking to see if I was being followed, looking over my shoulder. I was beginning to think I was safe when I noticed someone standing in the shadows about half a block behind me. I panicked. I saw your office with the light on and ran inside just to get away." Mary's story left her breathless, and she turned her big eyes to me, looking for an answer.

"Do you need a place to stay until you're sure you've lost them?"

Mary started, and her eyes narrowed for a second. "I suppose that's the best plan."

"You're welcome to wait out the night here, but when the office opens in the morning I'm going to have to ask you to move along. I've got an appointment first thing." I felt bad being so harsh, but one thing I'd learned is that you can't solve everybody's problems for them.

"I don't think I'm making myself clear, Miss Fortune."

Again, the instinctive cringe at being called Miss Fortune. I wasn't superstitious, but being called *misfortune* over and over again could make a person feel unlucky. Like naming your kid Jinx.

"Please, call me Allie."

"Allie. You don't understand. I want to hire you."

I sighed. It was an unexpected and unwelcome development. There was no way to avoid feeling like a mercenary lowlife when I gave her the speech. The one I'd recited a hundred times at least. Usually reserved for distant relatives or the friend of a friend who wanted me to do some work for them for free. I always felt like a heel when I gave the speech, but I was used to that feeling. "Mrs. Gordon, I am a professional private investigator. My rate is thirty-five dollars a day plus expenses. I don't accept checks, and I don't do investigations on the payment plan. I get my money up front and in cash. I'm sorry." I felt like low-life scum, but it had to be done. I wasn't running a charity. It was way too easy to get suckered by a sob story and then get stiffed when it was time to deliver the bill.

Mrs. Gordon blinked and leaned back. "I didn't expect you to work for free."

She sounded offended, but I tried not to let it affect me. I watched as she looked down and started fiddling with the belt on her dress. She undid it, and I wondered what she was up to. After a moment of inspection she found a seam on the belt that apparently wasn't stitched properly and pulled out a small wad of bills. I could have predicted that she'd have an emergency stash of money—she seemed like that kind of person—but what I wouldn't have predicted was that the stash would be made up entirely of hundred-dollar bills. My rough estimate was that she had five or six hundred dollars in there.

A flashing red warning light was going off in my brain. Where did she get five hundred dollars? That was a fortune to someone like her. Something wasn't right.

She peeled out a bill and handed it over to me. "I can pay you in advance for three days' work. If you haven't discovered why these men are following me by then, perhaps I'll ask you for a referral to a colleague."

Chapter 3

THAT WAS A surprising development.

I walked to the window and looked out at the deserted street to give myself a minute to think. I was pretty good at reading people, and I thought Mary Gordon was genuinely afraid of something, but I also had the feeling that she was playing fast and loose with the truth. Nevertheless, I was curious—about her, about the money in her belt, and about the people chasing her.

"All right, Mrs. Gordon. I'd be willing to take your case—"

She tried to say something, but I stopped her by lifting my hand. "As I was saying, I'm willing to take your case under three conditions." I took a deep breath. "I've been around the block a time or twelve, and experience has prompted me to come up with a set of rules. If you're not willing to agree to them, we can both walk away from this right now." I paused.

Mary's face went from apprehensive to annoyed in the blink of an eye. "Well, what are your rules then?"

"Rule one is that you tell me the truth. If I find out that you've lied to me, our business arrangement is terminated immediately."

"Of course I'm telling the truth. Are you saying you don't believe me?"

"Rule number two, I want the whole truth. You omit nothing to do with the investigation. Again, if I find out you had information that you didn't share with me, I will consider our business arrangement null and void as of that moment."

"And rule three?" Mary's cheeks were flushed, and she no longer tried to hide the irritation in her voice.

"Rule number three is that if you're involved with anything illegal, I will go to the police myself. I won't even feel bad about it. I don't help anyone break the law." I crossed my arms and stared her down. "Those are my rules."

"And you seriously think they apply to me? That I'm going to break any of your precious rules?"

"Mrs. Gordon, those rules apply to everyone." I

let that sink in. "Clients hear my rules before any money or promises are exchanged. It's how I do business."

Mary stared at me in silence for a long moment with her back to the window. I noticed that the first rays of morning light were beginning to edge out the darkness.

"All right. I have no problem with those terms." Mary stuck out her hand, and we shook on the agreement.

I had a new case.

By the time the sun was high in the sky, Mary Gordon was on her way back to her apartment. She wasn't eager to go, but I arranged to have policemen meet her there. It gave her a chance to make an official police report, and it got her out of my hair for a little while. I was going to meet her back at the office later that night, after my regular Wednesday night trip to purgatory.

The day was pretty full—meetings with clients and all that—but I was hoarding most of my energy for the evening. If I wasn't fully alert and in control of all my faculties, who knows what could happen.

I stretched in my chair, unkinking my tense muscles before smoothing down my grey suit jacket again. I tried to move past the lethargy I was feeling. Sleepless nights were nothing new, but my body could only handle so many of them in a row, and I hoped against hope for five straight hours of unconsciousness that night.

As I read over case files I ended up eating lunch at my desk, corned beef on rye from the little deli around the corner.

Two more meetings and an hour of phone calls later, I looked at the clock on the wall and was shocked to see that it was already ten to five. Instantly I slammed shut the file I was reading and grabbed my hat from the rack in the corner. By the time I got home I'd have less than an hour to clean myself up and get to the subway. Dinner was always served at precisely six thirty, so I'd be cutting it desperately close.

Within ten minutes I was back at my apartment. I ran the entire way, high heels clattering across pavement, and by the time I arrived I was hot and sweaty. The lukewarm shower felt fantastic, but I didn't tarry.

Once I was out and dry my first thought was, how could I possibly be ready in time?

I grabbed a forest-green suit out of my closet and started the search for stockings. It was such a luxury to be able to wear silk stockings again. During the war, scratchy nylon was the only thing available, and even that was sporadic. I slid the soft, smooth ones up and did my best to make sure the seam running up the back of my leg was straight. I knew that if it wasn't, the oversight would be noticed and commented on. I pulled on the skirt and blouse and buttoned myself into the lovely flattering jacket, my fingers lingering only a moment to rub against the black velvet lapels.

Jewelry, shoes, and makeup were last on my list. I shoved the triple-strand pearls into my purse, because wearing real jewelry on the subway was never a good idea, and then I was ready. For a second I looked at my bed and gave in to one wistful thought of how good it would be to sink in to it and close my eyes. I could probably have slept. On Wednesday nights it always felt as though I could sleep. Unfortunately, I knew that it was only a combination of wishful thinking and avoidance tactics.

Wednesday nights, for as long as I'd been living on my own, had belonged to my mother. I hadn't missed more than a few times in those seven years, mostly because I didn't want to disturb the relative peace we'd achieved. Wednesdays belonged to her, but the good thing about that was that they only came around once every seven days.

Shoving a little emergency money into my purse, I grabbed my keys and stopped at the door. Taking a deep breath, I shored up my defenses and got myself ready for the evening ahead. Funny how dinner with my mother intimidated me more than a three-hundred-pound thug in a dark alley ever could.

Chapter 4

THE COLUMNS on either side of the front door were perfect for leaning against as I put on my earrings. I checked my watch one last time and slumped against the column in relief. Six twenty-seven. I'd made it with three minutes to spare. It was perfect this way; supper would be served momentarily, and I'd completely missed the pre-dinner cocktail hour.

I peered out at the driveway and picked out the unfamiliar car. A grey Buick, fairly new, washed and waxed to blinding, showroom perfection. I moved to the door and pressed the bell, all the while playing my little detective game in my head about the owner.

My guess was an accountant or a banker, based on the car's color and the fact that it looked as though the owner had it cleaned and polished weekly with resale value in mind. My guesses at the occupations of my dinner companions for these Wednesday evenings were running at about a 75 percent accuracy rate. The notion that I was going to be bored stiff or annoyed by the stranger my mother had invited to dinner in an attempt to get me married off, unfortunately, was running at 100 percent accuracy. Over the course of seven years those were pretty amazing odds, in my opinion.

The door swung open, and I was greeted by an unfamiliar face.

"Good evening," she said. Her black-and-white uniform was starched and pressed to within an inch of its life, and I guessed that she'd only been on staff for a day or two at the most.

"Hello." I reached my hand out to her, and she looked surprised, but shook it nonetheless. "I'm Allie."

She was silent for a second until she realized I was waiting for her to introduce herself. "Kate O'Shaughnessy, ma'am."

"Nice to meet you, Kate. I suppose that my mother is entertaining tonight's bachelor in the drawing room?"

"Yes, ma'am—I mean, yes, that's where she, your father, and Mr. Vanderlaan are having their aperitifs."

"Well, Kate, I'll head in there and find them, but first, could you do me a little favor?"

"Certainly."

"Do you happen to know what Mr. Vanderlaan does for a living?"

"Ma'am?" Kate looked startled.

"It's just a little game I play. I try to guess what a man does by the car he drives."

"Well, I'm not sure, but I thought I overheard your mother tell your father that their guest for the evening was an investment banker."

I couldn't help the grin that broke across my face. "Right again."

Kate looked at me like I was speaking in Latin. I sighed. "Never mind—I'll just see myself to the drawing room. It was good to meet you, Kate."

"And you, Miss."

With one final deep breath for courage, I walked down the hall and through the open doors of the drawing room.

"Well, hello." My mother rose the second I walked through the doors. She glided toward me and kissed me on the cheek before turning to my father. "William, look who finally arrived." She made a big point of looking at her watch. "And with less than a minute to spare." She arched her eyebrow at me as I crossed the room and lowered myself gingerly onto the Queen Anne settee.

My father grunted from behind his newspaper, acknowledging my mother's comment.

I snuck a peek in his direction. He flipped down the corner of his paper and winked at me before pulling his shield up again with a snap.

My mother saw the exchange and sent my father a glare before clearing her throat to take control of the situation. "Allan, I'd like to introduce you to my daughter, Alexandra Fortune."

I winced. Oh, how I hate my name. Alexandra Beatrice Victoria Fortune. Somehow I doubt my mother was hoping her only daughter would grow up to be a private investigator. More likely, she wished I would grow up and marry into royalty. At this point even she realized that was never going to happen, so she'd set her sights a little lower, trying to marry me off to any eligible bachelor, from a socially acceptable family, who would have me. She was looking for someone to sweep me away, out of the world of investigation and into a more acceptable life.

A life, I feared, that looked a whole lot like hers.

I loved my mother, but I couldn't think of anything I'd enjoy less than entertaining, performing socially acceptable charity work, and keeping up with the latest society gossip.

Still, for her sake, I tried to make conversation with Allan. "It's nice to meet you." Okay, that was about all I could come up with. Luckily I knew a tried and true way to get a man to carry the conversational ball all by himself. "That's a nice car you've got out there."

Allan's face lit up. "She's a real beauty, isn't she? It's a brand-new '47 Buick. I was on the waiting list for six months. For everyone else, the waiting list is over two years, but I'm connected. I had an in that pushed me to the top of the list. She's got all the latest . . ."

Blah, blah, blah. I tuned him out, knowing that car conversations, one-sided as they might be, were never short-winded. My father pulled down his newspaper again to glare at Allan, who remained thankfully oblivious, before snapping his paper up once more.

I saw my mother's narrowed eyes, but I refused to meet her gaze. Instead I pretended to be listening to Allan talk about horsepower.

We were interrupted from the scintillating conversation by Kate clearing her throat in the doorway. "Dinner is served." My mother nodded, and we all rose and made our way to the dining room, my father in the lead. It was next to impossible to hold Dad's interest in a conversation, but he didn't miss much, and he certainly didn't miss any mention of food. Allan continued with his chatter, walking behind my father, now directing the monologue at him.

Unfortunately, this left me and my mother bringing up the rear. She made the most of the opportunity and stopped me midstride with a hand on my arm. "Do not think I am unaware of what you're doing."

"What am I doing, Mother?"

"You've distracted Allan so that you don't have to get to know him."

"What are you talking about? I only mentioned that he has a nice car."

The look she sent me was one I recognized from childhood. It said clearly that she was on to me. It was the same look she used on me when she found out I'd cut off Margaret Neidermeyer's braid back in grade school. Still, I'd learned with this woman to show no quarter.

"What would you like me to talk to him about?

Would you like me to tell him about my day?"

Horrified didn't describe her expression. "Alexandra, you wouldn't dare. If you mention anything about one of your . . ." She couldn't even make herself say the word. "I'd make sure Cook is serving bouillabaisse for supper next Wednesday night."

My stomach heaved at the thought. Fish soup was heavy ammunition indeed.

"Why couldn't you do something to show him what a good wife you'd make?"

"And that would be what? Would you like me to ask him if his socks need darning?"

"There is no need for sarcasm, Alexandra." She was amazing with the icy disdain. I hoped that one day I could emulate that exact tone. It would prove useful in my line of work.

"You could try engaging the man in a real conversation."

She was right. It was the least I could do. A sigh worked its way out.

"I will do my best at supper to get to know him." My mother's eyebrow winged up, and I continued. "And I will not mention my investigative work."

She nodded, smiled, and laid her hand on my arm to keep me from entering the dining room for a second. "You look lovely tonight, Alexandra." She gave my arm a quick squeeze before guiding me into the dining room and my waiting blind date.

Chapter 5

DINNER WAS pretty much what I'd expected, but I had made an attempt to get to know Allan. He was probably a nice man, though perhaps a little boring. But it was a moot point. I wasn't interested in him, or anyone.

My mother knew why, I'd told her years before, but she kept trying to find me a husband anyway. She thought it was past time for me to move on. And to be honest, I agreed with her. It wasn't that I hadn't tried. I would've if I'd had a choice, because the last thing I wanted was to be hung up on a ghost.

All I knew is that I had loved David Rubeneski since I was sixteen years old, and I couldn't seem to let him go.

The last time I'd seen him he'd told me that he was leaving for France, for the war that waited there. He left me in January. I found out that he was declared missing and presumed dead eighteen months later.

When the war ended and the boys started coming home, the trains, the subways, and the streets were full of men in uniform, some broken and some whole. I searched every face, hoping against hope I'd find him. And I'd never stopped looking.

I used every connection I had to find out what happened to him, thinking that maybe if I knew for sure that he was dead, I'd be able to move on, but I'd reached the end of my resources and contacts, and still nothing.

And I just didn't know what to do next.

Mary Gordon was waiting when I got back to the office. I didn't bother to stop off at home after dinner because I knew I'd be tempted to curl up in bed and take a catnap. I was dead tired, exhausted, in fact—that's the only possible way my mother could have talked me into going for supper again on Friday. Twice in one week was unprecedented. She had some sort of special event that she absolutely needed me to attend. I didn't listen to the details; I was so tired that I acquiesced out of a screaming desire to make the nagging stop. I couldn't imagine what happened to my willpower, but it looked like I was going to break my once-per-week rule. Heaven help me.

Mary stood in front of my door, tapping her foot with impatience, and I barely contained a sigh. Without a word I pulled out my keys, unlocked the door, and let her in.

She moved to the couch. I took off my hat, hung it on the rack, and tried to stretch my tired back as unobtrusively as possible.

"How did it go with the police?"

Mary glared at me.

Oh. That well.

"I spent the entire afternoon and evening talking

to two blundering fools. They kept patting my hand and asking me if I was overwrought. I'm not overwrought, I'm furious. Those men ransacked my home, broke my dishes, and tore apart everything that wasn't nailed down—and here these two policemen are waiting for me to sit down and cry. Tears don't even *begin* to cover it." Despite her claims to the contrary, Mary's eyes filled.

I felt a surprising swell of sympathy. "Was anything stolen?"

Mary shoved herself up off the couch and crossed the room, stopping in front of the window. She looked down at the street below. "Not that I could tell. The place was such a mess, and I really don't have much of value. I have no idea what these men could possibly want." Her tone was just a shade away from pleading, like she wanted me to tell her this was all a bad dream. Like if I just tried hard enough I could make it all go away.

"Well, keep thinking about who could be doing this and why. Meanwhile you and I are going to have to come up with a plan."

Mary turned to face me again. "You're the professional; what do you think we should do?"

"At this point, all we know is that unknown parties have followed you, kept you under surveillance, and ransacked your apartment. Somebody wants something from you, and we've got to figure out what it is."

"How are we going to do that?"

"Given the fact that you don't think they took anything from your apartment, my guess is that they haven't found what they're looking for. So, I'm going to follow you and see if I can't spot them. I think this would be the wisest course of action."

"Follow me where?"

"Don't you work tonight?"

"Yes, I should be there now as a matter of fact."

I reached for my hat. "Well, what are we waiting for? I'll be right behind you."

Chapter 6

AFTER TWO DAYS of surveillance I was starting to wonder if Mary Gordon wasn't a bit of a nut. As far as I could tell, no one was following her. She got up in the morning, cleaned her apartment, got ready for the day, and then went to work. Work consisted of cleaning. It looked like she had a rotating schedule of apartment buildings and office buildings around the city. One thing I could say for the woman—she wasn't lazy. It seemed she worked from sunup until long past sundown, and for the life of me I couldn't figure out why anyone would take an interest in her at all, never mind watch her every move.

Way behind on cases for my other clients, I truly couldn't wait for this one to be closed. At the start Mary and I agreed that I'd spend three days looking into her problem, and so far I'd come up with nothing. I'd be glad to shake her hand and show her to the door. Probably should've said no in the first place, or at least referred her to another P.I. I'd known I didn't have time for another client, but I let tiredness and sympathy override my better judgment. That's the same way my mother talked me into going over again tonight for some sort of event my parents were hosting. For my own self-preservation I had to start getting more than an hour of sleep a night. Exhaustion and emotions couldn't continue to rule me like this.

I shook my head to clear the unproductive thoughts. I didn't have time for sleep or wishes right now. I was standing in the doorway of a little tobacco shop across the street from where Mary should've been finishing up for the day.

My eyes had been open, but there'd been no one watching Mary but me. I glanced across the street in time to see her come out the front doors of the office tower. She looked over, trying to spot me. It was funny, but the sheer fact that I was a woman made me all but invisible in this city. All I needed was a shopping bag on my arm and I could disappear. I thought it would get better when the war ended, that New York wouldn't look so much like a metropolis made up solely of women, children, and old men. It had changed some, but there were still ten women for every man on the streets.

Even Mary, who was looking for me, couldn't

pick me out until I raised my hand in a little half wave and motioned for her to start walking home.

By the time she'd gone a few blocks in the direction of her apartment I crossed over and came up behind her.

"I've got plans for tonight, so I'm going to leave you once we make it safely to your apartment." I was expecting anger at the announcement, but instead some of the tension seemed to ease out of her posture. "I'll be back in the morning, and then we're going to have to discuss where to go from here."

Mary nodded. "I'll come to your office after lunch tomorrow then."

She surprised me. I'd been expecting more . . . drama. Maybe she was starting to see that this could be an odd set of coincidences and a little bit of paranoia on her part.

With that I slowed until I was a good twenty paces behind her again. I followed her all the way to her apartment without incident, and as soon as I saw her apartment light go on, I took my leave.

It was to be no simple supper at my parents' house. It was some sort of elaborate event. I couldn't remember the cause, but I knew that I was supposed to dress up. Way up. I was expected to arrive looking every inch the wealthy heiress that I was. Luckily, I had the perfect dress. I also had plenty of time to get myself ready.

I wasn't sure why I'd bought the dress; all I knew

is that when I saw it in the window of a beautiful little boutique, I had to have it. For once, I didn't even try to justify the expense. It'd been decorating the back of my closet for months, and the prospect of finally wearing it thrilled me. A full-length evening gown made of the palest pink silk, it had a full skirt that glided down past my ankles. There was a long column of silk-covered buttons all the way up the back, and the bodice was fitted. I took a final look at myself in the mirror perched above the fireplace mantel. Hair—done, dress—lovely, shoes—good. All that was left was the hat. I reached over and plucked it off the hat rack in the corner without taking my eyes off the mirror. I have so few hairdo successes that it seemed almost a waste to cover this one. Nevertheless, I placed the pale pink silk hat down gently and adjusted it until I was happy before sticking the hatpin through, anchoring the whole arrangement in place.

All I had to do now was make it through the rest of the evening.

A Democrat-party fund-raiser. That's what I'd agreed to attend.

I liked Harry Truman as much as the next girl, but I'd rather spend my evening at the dentist than at a political fund-raiser. My parents had always been politically involved, and so I knew without a shadow of a doubt that politicians are the most boring dinner companions imaginable. Apparently Harry himself would show up sometime, and that could be interesting, if only to watch my mother fret about the tablecloths being straight and whether all the flower arrangements were symmetrical. She was known all over the state of New York for her perfectly coordinated parties, and her attention to detail was what her reputation was built on.

Her attention to detail was also the reason for the constantly changing household staff. Being a perfectionist, she was rather hard to work for. The only member of the staff who'd been with us long enough to not be intimidated by her was Mrs. Schmidt. A fixture in the kitchen since I was five, Mrs. Schmidt must've been over sixty now. She emigrated from Austria and made the most glorious pastries, but I was sure the only reason she lasted under my mother's constant nattering was that for the first ten years she worked for us, she refused to learn English.

Dinner was going to be served at eight o'clock. From the swarm of people milling around by quarter to eight, I would have said that this party was a success. The living room, dining room, and study were all located at the back of the house, and they all had access to the backyard through sliding glass doors. The tables for dinner were set up outside on the flagstaff courtyard next to the rose gardens. I guessed from the tables lined up that my mother expected a little over a hundred guests tonight. Most of them appeared to be here already, and unfortunately I didn't see a soul I recognized.

Rather than stand and make awkward conversation with a stranger, I walked over to the tables and scanned the seating arrangements, looking for my name. I found it at one of the outer tables, nowhere near Harry Truman. My eyebrow rose when I saw that J. Edgar Hoover would also be attending tonight. The head of the FBI was rumored to be a little strange and also to have had an on-again off-again friendship with the president. Must have been one of the on-times.

I was scanning the rest of the place cards just to kill time when I felt someone's hand touch my shoulder.

"Good evening, Alexandra. You look lovely tonight." My mother looked rather fabulous herself. Her hair was swept up, and she wore a glittery midnight blue evening gown. Fifty-two in April, she could've passed for early forties. She pulled me close and kissed me on the cheek.

"Thanks. I've had this dress for a while and I've been waiting for a reason to wear it, although I didn't think it would make its debut at a political fund-raiser. Did you mention that's what this party was for when I agreed to attend?"

She smiled and widened her eyes. "I don't suppose I did. It must have slipped my mind."

The mock-innocent look made me laugh.

Nothing slipped her mind, ever. She had the memory of a loan officer.

"Is there a reason then for my invitation tonight? I'm sure you could have found someone else to fill my seat that would be willing to make an actual contribution to Mr. Truman's campaign funds."

"I'm sure I could have, but I have a special surprise planned for you."

Dread thumped in my chest. My mother had a surprise for me? That couldn't be good. "What did you do?"

"I said I've got a surprise for you. There's nothing to be worried about. Just a nice little surprise."

She had to have been practicing her innocent looks in the mirror for a while to pull off one that convincing.

She laid her hand on my arm again. "It's almost time for dinner and I need to go attend to the last-minute details, but why don't you relax and mingle for a moment? I promise, there's nothing for you to be worried about."

She released me, gave me a smile, and then made her way back into the house. Heads turned to watch her as she made her way through the crowd. She really was a stunning woman. She had a mixture of elegance and confidence.

I looked around at the faces of the people that surrounded me, and I couldn't help but wonder what I was in for.

Chapter 7

MY SURPRISE was a man. Moments after we were asked to take our seats for dinner, a man about thirty-five, in a navy blue pin-striped suit, pulled out the chair next to me and introduced himself.

"Ma'am." He looked at my place card. "Miss Fortune, I'm Jack O'Connor. It looks like we'll be sitting next to each other for dinner."

I sent him a wan smile, knowing instantly I'd been set up. Pushing the thought aside, I nodded and sent him a real smile this time. "Please call me Allie. I'm delighted to meet you, Jack."

He smiled back as he sat down. I faced front but watched him from the corner of my eye. I didn't get to see his car, so it was going to be harder than usual, but it was time for testing out my deductive reasoning skills on someone a little tougher than my mother's usual and predictable blind dates.

His suit was finely cut, but unremarkable; he had a bit of a dent in his hair from where his hat had rested, and his shoes were well polished and clean, but he didn't strike me as a banker or an accountant.

He caught me looking at him and grinned. He had mischief in his eyes as well as a twinkle of good humor. He wasn't the stodgy sort I was used to, and so far he'd stumped me. "What kind of car do you drive?"

41

He looked surprised for a second, but it didn't appear to throw him. "A 1945 Chevrolet Venture."

Hmm. Not much help. I could narrow it down with what I would say he wasn't, but I wasn't coming up with what he was. I took one last look. It was the line of his jacket that did it. I didn't have it nailed precisely, but I thought I was looking in the right direction.

All that time Jack sat there under my unexplained scrutiny with a smile and waited for me to tell him what I was up to. I liked that. "Jack, I play a little game sometimes. Judging a man by his appearance and his car, I try to guess what he does for a living."

"And you think you've got me all figured out?"

"Why don't you tell me how I've done?"

Jack nodded and turned more fully toward me. "Shoot."

"I'd say that you work in some sort of law enforcement, had a busy day, rushed to get here on time, and come from a well-to-do family."

Jack blinked. "Before I tell you how close you are, I'd like to hear the reasoning behind all that."

I nodded, liking that he wasn't offended, just curious. "I know you rushed to get here because your hair was still wet when you put on your hat. I think you're in law enforcement because I can't imagine any other reason for you to be packing a gun at a political fund-raising party. Clearly your suit jacket has been tailored to conceal it, but your shoulder holster is visible if a person knows what to look for."

Jack's expression remained neutral. "And being from a well-to-do family?"

"That's easy. You wouldn't have been invited to this party if you weren't." I made no apologies for the assumption and waited to see what he'd do.

"Very good, Miss Fortune. I can see that your reputation as one of the better P.I.s in the city hasn't been exaggerated."

It was my turn not to betray my surprise.

"I guess they don't call you the P.I. Princess for nothing." Again he waited for a reaction, but I betrayed none. "It took me a few seconds to put the facts together, but once I saw your investigative skills in action, it wasn't much of a leap to super-impose the face of the lovely Alexandra Fortune onto the reputation, nay, legend—" his eyes softened the mocking tone—"of Allie Fortune, P.I."

We looked at each other in silence for a moment. I needed a minute to determine if he was friend or foe. It took me a few seconds to decide that I didn't like being bested at my own game, but that he was no threat to me. I smiled at Jack. "Touché, Mr. O'Connor."

A waiter reached between us and placed down the first course of what would surely be a three-hour, seven-course meal. Suddenly I wasn't as impatient for dinner to be over as I had been.

For once my mother set me up with someone I actually liked. Jack O'Connor was a special agent with the FBI, and we had plenty to talk about through dinner. In fact, it was with some regret that I made my excuses and pulled myself away. Sometime about halfway through dinner, I got the feeling that I needed to check in on Mary Gordon one last time. Once the dessert plates were whisked away I couldn't ignore the feeling any longer. I told Jack that I'd enjoyed his company, we exchanged business cards, and he told me to call him if I ever needed anything. He looked a bit disappointed that I was leaving, and right then I decided it was a good thing I had to go. I liked Jack, but I would never want him to get the wrong idea about us. I didn't want to have to explain to anyone that there was no room in my heart for anyone but David. It was better this way. I'd had a nice time, but I'd probably never see the man again.

I looked down at his business card and tucked it into my purse for safekeeping anyway. Just in case.

I made my way back to Mary's apartment after a quick stop at home to change. Somehow I didn't think a pink silk evening gown would be inconspicuous enough for surveillance at eleven o'clock at night. I changed into a dark suit and hat that would blend well with the shadows and headed for Mary's.

I didn't know why I felt so unsettled, but something wasn't right. Nothing I could explain, just a feeling, but experience had taught me to listen to my feelings. All my instincts told me not to give up on Mary's investigation just yet.

I picked up my pace and within ten minutes stood on the street across from her apartment building looking up at her lighted window. It was after eleven, but I'd already learned that Mary kept strange hours. I settled in for a long wait, leaning my back against the harsh brick of another unremarkable building. I wasn't directly across from Mary's apartment; instead I'd picked a spot diagonal to her window, in the recessed doorway of another apartment building, away from the backwashed light of the lamppost and slightly harder to distinguish from the shadows.

Mary's light may have been on, but there didn't seem to be anything going on inside her apartment. Her window was framed by a shade that was only pulled down a third of the way over the window, leaving the other two-thirds open and giving me a mostly unobstructed view. With all that had gone on, I thought she'd be smarter than that. I shook my head. It was amazing how oblivious people could be. I stretched, trying to work a kink out of my back and shoulders.

The next time I looked at my watch it was past midnight. All was still quiet from what I could see through the window, and there was really no reason for me to continue hanging around, but I couldn't convince myself to leave just yet. Another half hour. That was all I would give this investigation; then I was going to call it a night and try to get a little sleep, or at least try to rest my eyes.

As I stood watch I let my mind drift. My thoughts found their way back to dinner and my very interesting dinner mate. I found it hard to believe that Allie Fortune P.I. was known in FBI circles, yet Jack had said as much. I'd been in this business a while, and although I wasn't getting rich at it, I was building a reputation for being thorough and getting the job done. Even ten years ago, most people couldn't have imagined a woman making it as a private investigator. I mentally corrected myself— there were plenty of people still who just wouldn't believe that I could be good at what I do. They thought I would get tired of playing at a career and find a husband, have children, teach Sunday school, and basically do what was expected of me. I didn't know if that's what my life would have been like if David had never gone away, but as things stood, I couldn't imagine ever living a traditional life. His disappearance had made me question everything about my life, my future, and my beliefs.

Jolted from my thoughts, I stood straighter as a shadow crossed in front of the window. Movement, at last. I'd been almost convinced that Mary had fallen asleep with the lights on, despite her claims. I straightened and moved a step away from the building at my back. I still was not sure why I'd had to come tonight, or why it had felt so urgent, but the feeling hadn't let up in the least; in fact, it weighed heavier than ever.

Again, the flutter of a silhouette against the window caught my attention. I waited a second, and then Mary moved directly in front of the window, followed immediately by a larger silhouette. This one was definitely male, his frame clearly outlined by the light from behind them. I watched in disbelief as she turned and slid her arms around the silhouetted man before backing out of the light of the window.

What was this? There'd never been any indication that there was a man in her life. I knew she was a war widow, like half the city, and I guess it wasn't totally improbable that she'd found someone else, but something just didn't feel right. Why had I seen no indication of a man in her life in days of watching her? She'd thought I wouldn't be watching tonight—was that why he was here? I let my mind wander, figuring possibilities. When I looked back up, all was still. I continued to stare into the glow from the window, letting it mesmerize me, letting my thoughts percolate.

"What are you doing here?" The voice was sharp, as was the barrel of the gun that suddenly pressed against my spine. I never felt the approach, but now a large figure loomed from behind me and I wondered how I could have missed it.

A hand at my shoulder pulled me back and pressed me tighter into the pistol. I felt heat radiating from the body behind me. A prickle of cold sweat around my hairline provoked a shiver, but I held myself completely still.

"I said, what are you doing here?"

I raised my hands to show that I was no threat, but it did nothing to ease the pressure on my shoulder or back. "I'm just standing, getting some air."

"Try again. You've been standing there, staring up at that window, for at least forty minutes."

Prickles shimmied up the back of my neck. Someone had been watching me, and I hadn't felt it. I forced myself to concentrate on what was important.

"What are *you* doing here? Why have you been watching me?"

"I'm asking the questions. And you still haven't answered. What are you doing here?"

"I'm working." That was all I was willing to say.

"Working?" He let out a harsh laugh. "You're in the wrong section of town, lady, and I hate to tell you, but you're not going to get a lot of business dressed like that."

The implication and the laughter in his voice made my cheeks flame and straightened my spine despite the steel prodding just to the left of my spinal cord.

Checking myself, I worked on consciously

relaxing my body, muscle by muscle, radiating that I wasn't a threat, that I posed no danger.

It took only a second to feel the corresponding relaxation in his body as well. "Okay, I'm going to put this gun away and we're going to talk, but you're not going to do anything stupid. Got it?"

The words had barely left his mouth before I felt the pressure of the gun ease. His shoe scraped against the pavement as he took a step back to re-holster it. That was all the room I needed. I lashed out, kicking straight back, connecting solidly with his knee. He was knocked off balance as I pivoted outward. He lunged blindly in the direction I was standing but hit only air. He hadn't had a chance to regain his balance yet, so I took advantage, grabbed him by the wrist, and yanked forward. Already overbalanced, it took very little force to send him sprawling to the pavement. I dropped onto him, using the point of my knee at the center of his back to pin him and to force out his breath.

I took a quick breath, but didn't relax. I'd only temporarily stunned him. Advantage went to me, but now came the hard part of keeping him restrained. "Who are you, and why were you watching me?"

He said nothing, but I felt his muscles tense. Using the hand I had at the back of his head I pressed his face into the pavement. Some part of me winced at the thud of contact, but I forced the reaction back. With one hand still locked in his hair I used the other to reach into his jacket and feel for his holster. Running my hand along his side, I reached in and pulled out the gun he hadn't had time to secure. Once my hands were on it, I shifted the balance of my weight to the hand on the back of his head, pressing his face harder into the pavement, long enough for me to get a firm hold of the gun and stand up in one quick motion.

I took three quick steps back, out of his striking range, all the while aiming at him with his own pistol. "Okay, get up. I need a few answers."

He lifted his head and pushed himself up with his arms with his back to me. I saw him wipe at his face with the sleeve of his jacket. He leaned down to pick up his hat that had been dislodged in the struggle. After several seconds he turned to face me and I got my first good look.

"Jack!" My heart skipped a beat. "What are you doing here?"

He swiped his hand across his jaw and smeared blood across his cheek. He looked up. "Miss Fortune. I shouldn't be surprised, I suppose."

"You shouldn't be surprised?" I spluttered for a second. "You're the one who pointed a gun at me. What was that all about?" My voice cracked on my last words, and I sucked in a deep breath. I sounded slightly hysterical and needed a second to process what was going on.

"I didn't know it was you. All I knew was that someone was standing in the shadows surveilling my suspect. I needed to find out who you were and who you were working for."

"You're telling me that sitting next to me at supper and accosting me at gunpoint in the same night are a total coincidence? That this is just random happenstance? And what do you mean I'm surveilling your suspect? Who's your suspect?" I kept the gun aimed at him, but my heart wasn't in it anymore.

He looked at me and his eyes narrowed. "Who are you watching?" He threw the question back at me.

I pressed my lips together.

"I'm going to guess that you're here because of a client. I'm here on business too, and I think our work lives are about to intersect. Why don't you put the gun down and we can talk about this. We need to sort out the facts. I promise, I'm no threat to you. In fact, why don't you keep the gun if it makes you feel safer. I just want to talk." He ran his fingers along the brim of his hat before replacing it.

"Your gun doesn't make me feel safer; it makes me feel like I'm in danger of putting a hole in you. As I've already proven, I can take care of myself without one."

He looked at me and nodded, then rubbed the heel of his hand along his jaw and sent me a grin.

It knocked me a little off balance. I expected him to be embarrassed and hostile that I managed to pin him, not to concede and send me a killer grin. I couldn't help but be charmed. I lowered the gun, but still held it by my side.

"Look, there's an all-night diner a few blocks from here. Why don't we go there and talk. If you're working the case I think you are, I can fill you in on some of the more pertinent details. Either way, you get a free breakfast. How does that sound?"

It sounded like he was trying to con me, but I was intrigued. I took one last glance up at Mary's now-dark window. I had a lot of questions, and there was a glimmer of hope that Jack had some of the answers.

Chapter 8

"WHAT DO YOU know about Helen of Troy?"

We were in the diner, sipping coffee that had probably been brewed eight hours ago for the supper crowd. Sitting across from Jack, I had to check his expression to make sure this wasn't a joke.

"What do you mean? The Greek legend?"

"Exactly. Most beautiful woman in the known world, the face that launched a thousand ships, and all that."

"I think you just summed up everything I know about Helen of Troy. And what, exactly, does this have to do with Mary Gordon?" I winced as soon as the words came out of my mouth.

"That your client? Mary Gordon? I thought maybe you'd been hired by someone else to follow her or Clive—"

"Who's Clive?" This was a bit tricky. Technically, Mary was still my client and I really couldn't discuss what I was doing on her behalf with anyone.

"Clive Gordon. Mary's husband."

"Isn't he dead?"

Jack looked at me as though I was insane. "Who do you think was up there with her tonight?"

"I don't know, but Mary Gordon told me she was a war widow. That her husband died overseas."

"Clive Gordon is alive and well." Jack hesitated for a moment. "For now anyways."

My shoulders relaxed. "Well, that's it then."

"What's it?"

"I am no longer in the employ of Mrs. Gordon. She broke rule number one."

"And rule number one is?"

"No lying to the P.I. I explained the rules very carefully to her when she hired me, and I also warned her that our business arrangement would be null and void if she broke any of them."

Jack just looked at me.

"As of now, I am unemployed. On this case anyway."

He nodded.

"So, why don't you tell me what's going on?"

His jaw was starting to bruise, and a crust of

blood covered the scrape on his face. Still he looked handsome in the harsh lights of the diner. "Clive and his lovely wife, Mary, are confidence artists. Before the war, they had amassed quite a record with the Bureau—nothing huge, but lots of little cons. They were quite good, I'm told."

"Good enough," I said with distaste.

Jack grinned at my annoyance. "Clive did go overseas. Mary told the truth about that, but he didn't die over there. War affects everyone differently, but it doesn't change the core of a person. And at the core, Clive Gordon is little more than a petty thief and con man."

"And he got into something over there that's followed him all the way back here?" I guessed.

"Like I said, Clive and Mary are small time. Clive stole something, and he is in *way* over his head."

"So that's why there were men following Mary. She has something she shouldn't."

Jack leaned across the table. "What did they look like? The men that were following Mary." Gone was the easy-going grin. Jack was all business now.

"I never saw them. Mary hired me to find out why these men were following her, but I never found any signs of them. I was starting to think she was a little nuts."

"Did she describe them to you at all?"

"All she said was that there were two men following her. Actually, one following her and the other watching her apartment. The one that followed her was a big guy. Very large, she said, wearing an overcoat that would be better suited to fall or winter than steaming summer temperatures of New York."

Jack shook his head. "It's probably the Soviets. I can't be sure; that's not much to go on . . ." He broke off and stared into space.

I needed to know what was going on here. "What do Mary and Clive have that a couple of Soviets want?"

Jack leaned back and signaled the waitress. He motioned for her to fill our coffee cups. "This is a long story, so I hope you don't have anywhere else that you need to be."

I pulled the refilled mug toward me and slouched back in the red vinyl booth seat. "I have nowhere to be other than right here. So, Helen of Troy . . ."

Jack smiled, but looked tired. "*The Iliad* by Homer is one of the most famous pieces of classic literature in the world. Men have been captivated by it for thousands of years. Especially the story of Helen and the Trojan wars. I think it's the mystique of a woman beautiful enough to provoke nations to war."

"You're telling me that Clive and Mary are involved somehow in a myth that may or may not have taken place millennia ago?"

"It's more complicated than that. And more

recent." Jack laid his hand over mine on the table for a moment. "This is a complex story. It would be easier if you just let me tell it all at once."

"Fair enough." I slid my hand out from under his.

"Homer wrote a fascinating tale, but as you say, no one has ever known if it was myth, legend, or truth. There was one man, however, who was so convinced that the story was true that, using only *The Iliad* as his guide, he searched for the place where he believed the ruins of Troy lay.

"Heinrich Schliemann was obsessed with the story of Helen of Troy. In 1870 he made his way to the northwest tip of Turkey, where *The Iliad* indicated that the city of Troy should lay, and set up an archaeological dig, desperate to prove the stories of Troy and her queen were true. Legend had it that King Priam of Troy buried the jewels of Helen somewhere in the city to protect them during the war with the Greeks. Schliemann believed that if he was able to find Helen's treasure, he could convince the world that Troy existed."

"He put a lot of faith in an old book."

"To him, Homer's words were gospel. Three years he worked, with as many as 120 workers, for twelve hours a day. Then one morning, just before the workers' morning break, he saw something glimmer at him in the dirt. He bent down to pull it out, and within minutes he was unearthing one of the greatest archaeological finds of all time.

"Schliemann found his dream. The gold of Troy. As was typical of the time, Schliemann didn't believe that the treasure could be entrusted to the hands of the Turks on whose land the treasure was found, but he thought it should be in European hands. So over the course of six months he smuggled the vast treasure out of Turkey. He eventually, and with great ceremony, donated it to the Berlin museum."

Jack pulled his coffee cup toward him, but didn't take a sip. "There were hundreds of pieces: copper, silver, and gold; jewelry, ornamental tools, and bowls. Some pieces that would be of interest only to archaeologists, but the most famous pieces were part of a set of gold jewelry that Schliemann believed was once worn by Helen herself. There was a diadem, like a cross between a headdress and a crown, made of intricately woven gold with matching earrings, bracelets, necklaces—all of pure gold and of craftsmanship that modern experts can only marvel at. That's the true centerpiece of the collection. It's like a legend come to life."

"That sounds amazing."

"When Schliemann donated the entire collection to the Berlin museum, he was convinced that it would be on display there forever. But he didn't count on a war that in its final days would bring the entire city of Berlin to its knees."

"The fall of Berlin." My tone was flat. I remembered the stories.

"The British came in from one direction and the Soviets from the other. The war was essentially over, and despite the claims of the Allies, the city itself was sacked and looted. Everything from art and gold stolen by the Nazis to national treasures from the museums, they took it all."

I leaned forward, making the vinyl seat squeak. "That definitely goes against the official position of the governments."

"I work at the FBI. I've seen the files. The words 'spoils of war' come to mind. From here on out, most of what I'm telling you is speculation. No one knows exactly what happened next. According to stories, the curator of the Berlin museum was an old man, and he knew that the end of the war was coming, so he tried to hide and protect as much as he could of the museum's inventory. That included what had come to be called Schliemann's Gold—including Helen's Gold. According to gossip, he hid three wooden crates marked simply 'Troy' in a bomb shelter underneath the Berlin Zoo."

"But someone found it anyway?"

"The Soviets. They deny that they stole anything from Berlin, but that's a ridiculous lie. Anyway, the Soviets found it and soldiers loaded it onto trucks along with everything else of value they could find and flew it directly to Moscow. Schliemann's Gold hasn't been seen since. Mostly."

"Mostly?"

"This is where your friends Clive and Mary come in. Clive was one of the Allied troops in Berlin during the fall. I'm guessing that he did there what came naturally to him. He stole. He was an excellent pickpocket, and during the chaos I'm sure he couldn't help himself. Or more succinctly, he did help himself. He probably happened to run across a few Soviet soldiers carrying boxes and bags out of the Berlin Zoo. All it would take is a bump on the shoulder, or some sort of random contact, and then . . ."

My eyes widened. "He stole pieces of the treasure."

"That's our guess. Somehow he smuggled them home from the war, and he and Mary have been sitting on them for over three years. I don't know what prompted it, but suddenly they take out these bits of gold jewelry and decide it's time to try and fence them."

"Fence them?" It came to me all at once. "They don't know what they have." My breath huffed out at the new revelation.

Jack shook his head. "It's essentially like trying to hock the *Mona Lisa* for rent money."

I rubbed my forehead trying to digest the enormity of what Clive and Mary were into. "It seems so unbelievable. They don't know the value of what they've got."

"They also don't know that the Soviets now

know who has it, and that they've activated a couple of their agents to retrieve it." Jack ran his hand through his hair.

"How would the Soviets find out?"

"Same way the FBI did. The fence they went to see moonlights as a respectable museum undercurator. He knew exactly what the gold was as soon as he saw it. According to him, he may have gotten too excited, tried to buy it from them right then and there, offering them far more than they were expecting. It made them both nervous, and they sold him only the two small pieces that they'd brought with them. They said that they'd return with the rest of the pieces, but they never did. Anyway, the fence started bragging a little too loudly about what he'd just acquired and mentioned that there was more where that came from." Jack rolled his eyes at the man's stupidity.

"So, he yapped too loudly and brought both the FBI and the KGB down on top of Clive and Mary?"

"That's the gist of it, yes."

"So, why don't you just go and tell Clive and Mary what's going on, and get the gold back from them?"

"Two reasons. Number one, Clive and Mary have a pathological hatred of the FBI and the local police."

I could imagine that. Mary hadn't liked the police coming to her house after the break-in one bit. She'd been very hostile. I'd blamed it on the stress, but maybe it went deeper than that. "Surely you could find a way to get at it."

"Well, our biggest fear at this point is that when they realize how over their heads they are, they might just hand the treasure over to the Soviets to spite us. They hate our government that much."

"And this would be so terrible because?"

"Because relations between the US and the USSR are at an all-time low. In fact, there are rumblings of an official declaration of hostile relations, one step away from a declaration of war. The Soviets are desperate to get these pieces back. Not only could it implicate them in the looting of Berlin, but the treasure has lost a huge amount of its symbolic and financial value if it's not complete."

"Not to mention that Clive and Mary could conceivably have the gold melted down in order to get rid of it."

Jack winced. "That's another worst-case scenario. The FBI has orders from high up that we are to be the ones to retrieve the pieces from the Gordons and to cut the Soviets out at all costs. If we end up in possession of it, it could be a very valuable bargaining chip for the future."

I let my shoulders slump and tried to take it all in. Images of Troy and treasure floated through my mind along with the pictures of Berlin during the fall, which I'd never been able to forget. I took a sip of the now-cold coffee to buy myself a little time, but the bitter taste made me wince. I put the cup back down on the Formica table. "So, what exactly is my place in all of this?"

Chapter 9

"YOUR PLACE in all this." Jack drew the words out as if buying time to think up an answer. "Until two hours ago, you didn't have one, but it seems like too much of an opportunity to pass up."

"I present some type of opportunity for you?" I arched my eyebrow and fixed him with an icy stare that came directly from my mother.

"You're an insider. She thinks you're on her side. You could probably apply a little pressure and get her to hand the gold right over." He wasn't looking at me as he spoke. If he had been, he would have seen that I was not about to jump on board this suggestion.

I pushed my coffee cup forward and leaned toward him. "Let me get this straight, Jack. You think that I'd betray my former client, my ethics, and my profession as a whole to help the FBI recover a couple of pieces of gold?"

His gaze snapped back to mine. I could almost see him backtracking, searching for firm footing. "You're right. I wasn't thinking."

"You were thinking, all right, but not about me. You were thinking about you and how good it would look on your permanent record if you were the one who arranged the recovery of something the government wants very badly. Well, good luck. I wish you well, but I'm not about to pitch everything that's important to me so that I can give you a hand."

"Wait. Wait." He held up his hands in surrender. "You're right. I was already trying on my new promotion. But don't walk away just yet. You need to think this whole situation through."

Arms folded, I gave him another second to explain.

"To begin with, Mary and Clive Gordon are in danger. They won't accept help from the FBI, even if we were to offer it, and they certainly wouldn't believe anything we said to them. If the Soviets are already after them—and you've given me reason to believe they are—then they're in big trouble."

"What would the Soviets be willing to do to get the gold back?"

"Easier question to answer; what wouldn't they do to get it back? That's a much shorter list."

I paused to consider.

"The fact that the Soviets have activated agents here on American soil means that they're very committed to recovering the gold. I'm sure they've been instructed to do whatever is needed to succeed. That doesn't leave Clive or Mary in a very good spot. Especially when they don't have any idea what's coming for them."

The waitress made another pass by our table with the pot of coffee. There was only an inch or so of sludge in the bottom. Shaking my head when she asked if I wanted a refill, I decided it was time to go.

"I need to talk to my former client, so I'm going to have to get back to you." I rose, and Jack rose too.

"You have my card. My number is on there."

"I'll let you know what I decide."

My shoes squeaked on the greasy linoleum as I crossed to the door. My hand was on the knob when he called out my name.

"Allie, one more thing."

I was waiting for it. The hook. I looked over my shoulder at him. He stood back at the table with a small smile on his face. He picked his hat up off the table and dusted the brim before replacing it and pulling it low.

He was dragging this out. I watched as he came toward me. He moved close enough that he could whisper.

"The FBI is serious about getting these items. They're offering a ten-thousand-dollar reward to whoever finds them and hands them over to our government."

I did my best to show no reaction. Clearly they really wanted this gold.

I took a breath and sent him a cool smile. "Like I said, I'll let you know." I turned and walked out of the diner.

Chapter 10

ANOTHER SLEEPLESS night, this time punctuated by thoughts of Clive and Mary's precarious situation and the possibility of finally knowing what had happened to David.

My morning was full of telephone inquiries and paperwork. Saturdays were always catch-up days. Still, those jobs had only half my concentration, as the other half kept running back and replaying the conversation with Jack. I didn't know what to do. If what he said was true, Mary had broken all three of my rules, including being involved in illegal activities, but I couldn't help but feel that I still owed her something, my protection at least. It was only ten o'clock, so I was still a few hours away from our scheduled meeting. That meant I had time to think the whole situation over.

By ten after eleven I was starving and still no clearer on what to do. I slipped out of my chair and pulled my purse from beneath the desk. I planned to run to the deli down the street for a quick lunch and make it back in time for my meeting with Mary.

It was quarter to twelve by the time I got back, and I clattered up the stairs to my office in a rush. When I reached the door my heart sank. There was a folded piece of paper shoved between the door and the door frame. I plucked it out and unfolded it. Skipping the text, I moved down to the last line.

Just what I'd been worried about—signed by Mary.

Frustrated, I plucked my keys out of my purse and moved to unlock the door. With the note and key in one hand and my purse in the other, it was rather awkward to maneuver. I found myself off balance when I grasped the doorknob and the door swung open. Apparently I'd left it unlocked.

I stumbled through feeling like a fool, but managed to keep hold of everything in my arms and to recover without going all the way down.

Dropping everything but the note onto my desk, I waited for my heart to stop pounding so hard. When I'd recovered my breath and poise, I opened the note and read.

Miss Fortune,

I came by, as suggested, but you weren't present, hence the need to conduct business by note. I only came by to let you know that I have decided to terminate our professional relationship. I have not been satisfied with your performance in this matter, and I will speak to other private investigators should I have any further reason to continue with this investigation. I will be out of the city for the next few days, so please consider this our final communication in this matter.

Mrs. Mary Gordon

Was it hypocritical for my feelings to be hurt when I intended to fire her as a client that afternoon?

I slid into my chair and stared at the slip of paper for a long moment.

All morning I'd spent wondering what I should do, and I was no clearer yet. I'd had a bit of a plan worked out in my mind. I would fire Mary as my client, but I would also tell her most of what Jack told me. I'd offer to help her out of this mess, she would accept my help, and we would deliver the goods to Jack and the FBI and then get Clive and Mary out of sight. I would get them out of New York and wish them well. Okay, maybe the entire thing had been scripted out, but it was a good plan. Mary and Clive leaving town, without knowing who was after them or why—that was not a good plan.

I cradled my head in my hands and tried to think. What now?

The only option I could think of was to go by their apartment and see if I could catch them before they left for wherever. They didn't have all the information, and that lack could put them at further risk. It was my responsibility to at least let them know. But just as I feared, their apartment was deserted. Lights off, blinds closed, and no sign of habitation at all. I watched their window from my spot across the street for more than an hour, but I knew in my gut that it was futile. They were long gone.

I pushed myself away from the building at my back and decided it was time to take a walk. Meandering through the streets was my tried and true way of thinking a problem out. The problems of Jack, Clive and Mary, Helen of Troy, and even David were all jumbled up into a complicated web that I couldn't even begin to untangle. The biggest problem was that each possible solution I came up with had implications that veered into and affected all of the other issues. So, I did my best to put it all out of my mind and just walked.

The streets of New York were busy but relaxed this Saturday afternoon, with lots of fellow wanderers out. People barreled along who clearly had somewhere to be, but at least as many were out enjoying the air and the sunshine.

I walked for hours thinking about clients, plans, and things I needed to do. Anything but the problems at hand—I just let them rest, simmering at the back of my mind.

What I wanted to do, the opportunity that had just opened up, was at war with my sense of ethics. How could I get what I needed from the FBI without compromising the trust Mary Gordon placed in me? Or at least the trust she should have placed in me.

I had no answers, and that night I lay in bed, awake and staring at the ceiling. When my eyes finally drifted shut around four, I dreamed of the day I met David Rubeneski.

Chapter 11

September 1937

I PICKED UP a smooth grey stone, rubbed it between my fingers for a moment, and then heaved it into the water. It sank below the surface with barely a sound but sent out ripples across the still waters of the reservoir. My stomach knotted with worry and frustration. The school year had only started seven days ago, and yet here I was, already walking home two hours late. I'd thought I was finally able to control my temper, no matter how I was provoked, but today's detention had proved otherwise.

Almost dusk, the sun had already sunk below the trees and buildings of the city, and darkness was falling quickly. The light of the moon reflected off the clear glassy surface of the water and reminded me that Central Park at night was not a safe place for a sixteen-year-old girl. Or anyone, for that matter.

I lifted one last stone and whipped it into the reservoir, watching the motion of the water until it was utterly still again. Breathing a sigh, I turned to grab my satchel. Leaves rustled behind me, making me close my eyes and hold my breath. The rustling stopped, and I glanced around. I didn't see anyone, but it was warning enough. Time to get moving.

I walked this route every morning and every night, but it felt completely different now, with the light almost gone. My school, the Marymount Academy, was an all-girls private school located on the east side of Central Park, and the Fortune House, my house, was located on the west side of Central Park. So, five days a week for the past ten years, I'd made the walk across the park, past the reservoir, to and from school. But I'd always been smart enough to make that trek during the daylight hours.

Bag in hand, I took another quick look around before heading back onto the path and toward home.

I'd only gone a few steps when I heard the rustling again. My lungs tightened and my palms started to sweat. My mind screamed at me to get moving, and I picked up my pace. Head down, satchel clasped to my chest, I strode up the embankment. When I reached the top I looked up.

My heart stumbled. Directly in front of me, high-lighted by the light of the moon, stood two men. They weren't walking or moving; they just stood there. They watched as I stood frozen in fear. I wanted to run, but all I could manage was an unsteady walk as I tried to circle around them both.

"Hey, lady, can you spare some change?"

I ignored them and continued walking, but my heart slowed its staccato drumming when I heard the question. During the height of the Depression there had been men like this all over New York. Honest men who were out of work and reduced to asking for spare change. According to my mother, the appro-priate response was to ignore them and keep walking. I may have disagreed with almost anything she said, but I was nervous enough to take her advice in this instance.

I made my way past them, crossing the grass until I was on the path to home. For some reason I felt safer on the path. There was silence for a moment, then the sound of two sets of footsteps echoing on the path behind me. Terror circled in my brain.

"Hey, lady, I'm talking to you." I heard them pick up their pace, closing in on me, and I wished I'd never turned my back on them. But it was too late, so I continued to stride, going as fast as I could without breaking into a run.

I felt them behind me, close enough that one of them reached out and ran the tip of his finger down my neck. I suppressed a shudder. They kept pace just a foot or two behind me, threatening me with their presence.

Without warning, one of them broke stride and circled to the front of me. The other stayed behind, hemming me in.

"That's not very nice. It's rude to ignore someone when they're talking to you." This came from the man in front. He moved closer, and I took a step back. I closed my eyes for a second. How could I have been stupid enough to get caught out in the middle of the park, alone, in the rapidly descending darkness?

"I don't have any money."

The man in front looked me up and down, probably

taking in my uniform for the first time. Surely he hadn't realized that I was just a schoolgirl, and now that he had, he'd apologize and let me past. I tried desperately to convince myself that this was all just a big mistake.

"It's not a good idea to linger in the park after school, princess. Especially after dark." He laughed, and a chill skated up the length of my spine.

I forced myself to think. The pounding I could hear in my brain made it hard to come up with a plan, but passivity wasn't working. I moved on to a tactic that had worked on bigger men than this. I closed my eyes for a second, making sure I got the tone right. "You will move aside and let me pass. Now." I heard my mother's voice come out of my own mouth and found it momentarily disconcerting. I'd never seen any man defy my mother, so I hoped that this would resolve the situation.

It took less than the blink of an eye to see that this tack didn't have the intended effect on him. Instead I saw his face, lit by moonlight, curve into a snarl that could only be interpreted as a direct threat.

I'd never seen it have that effect before. I took another step back. My pulse pounded in my ears. My breathing quickened. The man took another step closer. I moved half a step back. The man standing behind me was close enough that I could feel his body heat. I thought I might be sick.

The man in front of me reached out his hand and ran his finger along the side of my face. I turned my head away but couldn't pull out of his reach because of the man behind me.

I felt tears welling in my eyes. I took a deep breath, trying to force the panic down.

Suddenly a new voice cut through the darkness. "Back away and let the lady pass." The voice was strong but calm, almost lazy. I couldn't see anyone, and neither could the man in front of me, from the way he scanned the darkness. Unfortunately the voice in the darkness hadn't made either man move away.

For a long moment no one moved. I didn't realize until my lungs were burning that I'd been holding my breath.

"Let the lady go, and find somewhere else to be." The voice was so sure, so calm and steady, that the man in front of me shifted back and glanced around.

"Why would I?"

There was another few seconds of silence before the man spoke again. "Because you'll regret it if you don't." I looked around, but I couldn't see anything.

The man in front of me shifted from foot to foot and took a step back. "Come on," he addressed the man behind me, "let's get out of here. Teaching some snotty rich girl a lesson isn't worth the trouble."

In the space of a few seconds both men melted into the darkness. I looked around, not entirely able to believe the sudden change in my circumstances. When the man attached to the voice failed to materialize, I called out, "Are you going to show yourself?"

The silence stretched, and it took several seconds before I caught a glimpse of movement from the corner of my eye.

A man materialized out of the darkness. Tall and broad, he moved into the moonlight with his arms outstretched in a nonthreatening gesture. "At your service, princess." He had a small smile on his face, and his comment made me blush. My command to show himself may have come across a bit more imperious than intended.

"Thank you for your help. I don't know what I would have done if you hadn't come along." The nausea came back as I let myself think about it. I felt a bit wobbly in the knees as the realization of what could have happened kicked in.

He came along beside me, took me by the elbow, and led me to the closest park bench. "Take a moment to calm down. Everything's all right. They're gone now."

I took several deep breaths to steady myself, then pushed off the bench. "I need to go. I'm already two hours late."

"Won't your parents be worried?"

"My parents are in Europe. Servants aren't paid enough to worry. Notice I'm not home when I should be, yes; worry about me, no." I let a little bit of bitterness spill into that statement. Clearly I was still off balance.

"Where do you live?" The man turned and looked down at me. My breath caught as he held my gaze.

"On the other side of the park." I pointed in the general direction.

"Let's go then. We shouldn't hang around here any longer than we have to."

"We?" I still hadn't looked away yet and was having a difficult time following the conversation.

"It's not a good idea for you to walk all the way across the park by yourself, so I'll take you home and make sure that you're delivered safely to your door."

I wanted to protest, to say that I'd make it fine on my own, but I couldn't push the words out. The truth was, I was terrified at the thought of walking the rest of the way home in the dark. So I nodded. "Thank you. Again."

He motioned for me to lead the way, and I headed back to the path. We walked side by side in silence for a while, and I used the time to sneak looks at him.

He was very tall, probably a bit over six feet, with dark hair and I'd guess brown eyes. He was probably considered very handsome in a romantic Heathcliff kind of way, and he was also much younger than I'd first assumed. I'd guess that he was no more than twenty-four or -five. When he caught me looking up at him out of the corner of my eye, he sent me a grin, and that was all it took for my romantic teenage heart to pound harder.

I looked away and felt a blush heat my cheeks, but still we walked in silence. As we got closer to home, I found myself slowing the pace a little. I wasn't eager for this time to end.

I racked my brain for something intelligent to say, but came up dry. By the time we reached the front door of Fortune House I was mentally castigating myself for being completely unable to carry on a semi-intelligent conversation.

For his part, my rescuer didn't seem to feel the need for chitchat. When I reached out to open my front door, he shoved his hands in his pockets and took a step back. "I guess you're home then. Do me a favor and don't hang around the reservoir at night anymore. It's not a safe place for pretty young girls to spend their time."

He turned and walked away, and I had to force myself to keep breathing. I was nearly giddy at the words of my mysterious rescuer. Suddenly the events of the evening seemed less terrifying and more like something out of a romantic movie.

I went up to my room and shut the door, replaying the evening in my mind.

When I woke up, I felt rested and at peace, and I'd figured out how to proceed with Clive and Mary.

I made my way outside just in time to see the very first hints of dawn light the sky. It was only a short hike back to my office. Being Sunday, I had no clients I needed to see; I just needed to work out the details on how I would enlist Jack's help with my plan.

Since moving out of my parents' house, Sundays

had always been a bit of a twilight day. They weren't officially work days, but I usually used them to catch up on reports and to get ahead for Monday morning. Sunday mornings hadn't been about church since I'd been living on my own, but this morning there was something inviting about the Methodist church I passed on the way to the office. There was no one there yet, as it was still far too early for services, but I felt almost a beckoning—a strong, unreasonable desire to flit up the steps and in through the heavy wooden doors. Seeking something. Wisdom maybe. Solace. Instead I turned my eyes away and walked faster. Why waste an entire morning mouthing the words to songs I didn't believe and bowing my head to prayers that were no more than spent breath aimed at the sky? And all because I was looking for guidance. Whatever I needed, it wasn't going to come from that direction.

I'd grown up in Catholic school and I'd heard all the Bible stories and sermons. But I couldn't reconcile a God who was all-powerful and who loved me with a God who would let me go through the anguish of not knowing, of losing David. If He'd really loved me, if He was someone I could trust, He wouldn't have let that happen. I'd spent my breath praying to Him for a while, but He'd never cared enough to respond. And it had taught me that I was on my own.

I unlocked the door and let myself into the office. I pushed my philosophical thoughts aside and focused on my plans. I'd clarified my position in my mind, and I was pretty sure I could convince Jack and the FBI to accept my proposal. Of course I was going to need to get a huge amount of work finished, and I had to close a bunch of lingering cases to take off the time I needed to pursue Clive and Mary. I pulled Jack's card, safely tucked into the silk lining of my purse, and laid it on the desk. As soon as I had all the details worked out and on paper I decided that I would give him a call and see if he'd accept my terms.

Chapter 12

I HAD AN APPOINTMENT to meet Jack in ten minutes.

We were going back to the same all-night diner where hopefully we could talk and I could get Jack to see the wisdom of my plan.

I had spent Sunday thinking through the situation from all angles and getting my life in order. If I planned to immerse myself in the search for Clive, Mary, and the gold, then everything else in my life was going to have to be put on hold for a while.

When I entered the diner I noticed there were more people than last time filling the booths, but it still wasn't crowded. I found a table at the very back of the restaurant and sat so that I was facing the door. I'd gotten there a few minutes early on purpose, determined to use every possible advantage. It had to seem as though I were the one holding all the cards if there was any chance of the FBI agreeing to give me what I wanted. *If* I could deliver Helen's Gold.

The waitress came along and filled my coffee cup to within a hairsbreadth of the rim, and I brought it up for the first burning sip. It scorched all the way down, and that did as much to wake me up as the caffeine did when it hit my bloodstream.

Jack finally arrived, ten minutes late and out of breath. I was on my second cup, and my stomach growled at the scent of bacon, eggs, and toast all around me.

Jack rushed toward the table, in a rumpled charcoal pin-striped suit. As he approached he pulled off his hat and hung it on a hook at the back of the booth. I didn't say anything as he folded himself into the red vinyl seat and got settled.

"Sorry I'm late. I got caught up in some work and had to race all the way here."

I nodded. "I called because I think I can help the FBI get the gold back, but I need to know how badly the FBI wants it."

Jack's eyes narrowed, and he leaned back in the booth. "They want it badly." He slid into professional mode, and I was glad. "I think the ten-thousand-dollar reward they've offered shows just how badly they want it."

"That doesn't interest me; I'm after something bigger."

Jack's eyes widened and went cold. "How much are you after?"

"I'm not interested in the money. I need a reward of a different currency."

His face was blank. "And that would be?"

"Information." I let the word hang.

Jack lifted his hand and signaled the waitress. I held my breath, but he didn't say anything more until the waitress had filled his cup and wandered away again. He maintained eye contact as he took the first sip. "What kind of information are you looking for?"

I took a deep breath and tried to remember what I'd rehearsed in my head. "I'm looking for someone. I've exhausted every lead and every resource. All I've hit are dead ends. I want the FBI to find this information for me. That's my price."

Jack placed his coffee cup back on the table. "It doesn't seem like such a high price, but getting information is always tricky. I don't know that I can promise something like that without knowing the details. Maybe you should consider taking the money and using it to fund your own investigation."

I leaned forward and looked straight into his eyes. I worked to keep the shaking out of my voice, to sound strong. "This is not negotiable. I will not bargain or dicker; the FBI either promises me this favor or they can look for the gold on their own."

He held up his hand. "Hey, I didn't say it couldn't be done, I said that I didn't know. I can't make a promise like that blind. I'll need the exact details of what you're asking for, and then I'll have to run it by my superiors."

"That's fine. I have a proposal and a contract written up. The contract will need to be signed before I begin looking for the gold, and the proposal outlines exactly what information I'm looking for, with all of the pertinent details." I finished the sentence in a rush, terrified that the FBI or Jack would decide my terms were too much of a hassle, that it would be easier for them to just search by themselves.

Jack's eyes revealed nothing. I pulled the proposal and the contract out of my bag and handed it over. He skimmed the pages one at a time, his face still impassive and blank. Finally he folded the papers and shoved them into his inside jacket pocket.

On those papers lay my last hope, and I winced at the callous treatment.

"I'll take these back to the office and talk to my superiors about your proposal. I can't make any guarantees." Jack grabbed his hat off the hook and placed it on his head as he stood. He was very much the government man now, impersonal and cold, and I was surprised that it bothered me. Still, I stood when he did, and I reached across the table to shake his hand.

"Good day, Miss Fortune. I'll let you know as soon as I have an answer." With that he was gone, stopping only to pay the bill on his way out.

I let out my breath. I'd done all I could do. Now I could only wait. Taking one last sip of my coffee, I pushed myself out of the booth. It was time to get back to the office. There was plenty of work waiting for me, and I'd much rather be accomplishing something while I was waiting to hear. It made the waiting almost bearable.

But what if the answer was no?

It was another day before I heard back from Jack. I'd been making excuses to stick close to the office so that I didn't miss his call, but I needn't have bothered. Jack decided to forego the telephone and instead showed up at my office door bright and early Tuesday morning.

I sat at my desk, phone balanced on my shoulder, pencil held between my teeth, pounding furiously on my typewriter. I was waiting for a detective at the 33rd precinct to pick up the phone and answer a few questions, but I wasn't one to sit and idly wait. So, I also typed up a report for another client. My day was only beginning, but I was already running behind.

Just as a gruff voice boomed out "McGilvery here" across the phone lines, there was a knock at the door.

Sighing, I turned to wave in the person at the door and tried to remember why I'd called Detective McGilvery in the first place. I had to spit the pencil out before I could speak.

"Yes, Detective, this is Allie Fortune calling. I'm a private investigator, and I have a few questions I'd like to ask you about the Linden case." There was some vicious muttering on the other side of the line and a few unflattering comments about P.I.s, but I'd heard it all before, so I just ignored it. Instead I looked to see who'd just walked into my office.

Jack stood a few feet inside the door and looked around with unabashed curiosity. I cleared my throat, and his gaze whipped to mine. I held up two fingers, telling him that I'd just be two minutes before I could get to him, and he nodded. I turned my attention back to the still grumbling detective and threw my questions out to him. His answers were clipped and to the point, and they were also pretty much expected. I didn't learn anything new, but I did get my own information confirmed from one more source, and that counted for something. When I got the information I needed, I hung up and turned back to Jack.

He still stood there, but he'd moved farther into the room and was inspecting my bookcase.

I waited, and finally he met my eyes, yet he stayed silent.

"Well, what's the verdict?"

He smiled at my directness. "The FBI is willing to give you what you want, in principle, if you can recover the gold, but they have a few conditions of their own."

My heart thumped, then stumbled in my chest. They'd agreed. I couldn't believe it. I didn't know whether to be thrilled or terrified. Probably a little of both. If I was able to hold up my end of the bargain, the FBI would find out what happened to David. It was most likely an answer that would remove all doubt and kill another piece of my heart, but at least I'd know for sure. For more than four years I'd been stuck in the same place because I didn't know what had really happened. That could end. I was pretty sure relief would win out over the desire to continue to hold out hope. Still I tried not to show Jack how much the news meant to me. "What conditions?"

"There are really only two. One is that you keep the details of this investigation a secret, and two is that you work with an FBI liaison for the duration of your investigation." He grinned. "That would be me."

I ignored the last statement. "They want me to keep the investigation secret, or they want me to keep our agreement secret?"

"Both."

I thought about it for a second. "Okay." It really didn't make a difference to me either way. "And I get a partner. Or is it a babysitter?"

"Think of it any way you want. You get me for the duration of the investigation. If you're smart, though, you'll see that we have a better chance of getting that gold if we pool our resources and our time. We can help each other."

I didn't love the thought, but this whole thing wasn't about what made me comfortable. It was about getting the information I needed to move on with my life. That was worth the inconvenience of a partner.

"Okay, I agree to those terms."

Jack nodded and moved to sit in the chair beside my desk. He pulled papers out of his inside pocket, unfolded them, and laid them on the desk before sliding them across to me. I brought them toward me and started reading. It was a contract, much more complicated and lawyerly than the one I'd drafted, but it appeared to say almost the same thing. I leaned back in my chair and read the entire five-page document word for word. I didn't let Jack's presence rush me, and I only placed pen to paper when I was satisfied that I understood what I was signing. I looked up at Jack.

"You ready to make it official?" he asked.

I didn't answer, just signed and dated the document before passing it back over to him to do the same. When he scrawled his name across the bottom I breathed a sigh of relief. This was my ticket to getting what I needed more than anything else in the world.

Now all I had to do was find the gold.

Chapter 13

I LEANED BACK in my chair and studied Jack O'Connor for a moment. He was a good-looking, open kind of guy, or at least that's how he seemed, but I also knew that the FBI didn't hire cream puffs. Apparently there was more than one side to Jack, and it would be a good thing for me to keep that in mind over the course of our involvement.

"Now that we're partners you'd better bring me up to speed on your investigation."

Jack removed his hat, set it on my desk, and looked around at my office. "If we're partners, the first thing I'm going to do is tell you that you need to do something about this office. Peeling paint isn't what I'd call décor."

"My clients usually aren't big into ambiance, and it's never bothered anyone other than you."

"Still, it makes the place look unsuccessful."

"Speaking of unsuccessful, Jack, let's get back to your investigation."

He winced, and I bit my tongue. I was irritated at his assessment of my office, and it came out in sarcasm. Probably not the best way to start a partnership. I tried again. "Why don't you tell me what you've come up with."

He picked his hat back up and brushed a bit of dust off the crown. "The whole matter came to our attention a little over two weeks ago when Clive and Mary sold the first pieces of Helen's Gold. I was given the case and told to look into what it would take to recover the gold. When I realized that Soviet agents had been activated to retrieve it as well, I knew that we had to move fast. I kept Mary and Clive's apartment under surveillance for a few days, but it was sporadic and I didn't glean any new information. I was authorized to do a discreet search of their apartment but didn't find any evidence of the gold."

I bit back a smile. No wonder Mary came running to my door; she had more people watching her than Veronica Lake. "Then what?"

"Then I wrote up a report, saying that the likelihood of retrieving the gold through negotiation was negligible, and that if we wanted to get to it before the Soviets did, we needed to take more direct action."

"What kind of direct action?"

"The night of your parents' party, the night we met, I was waiting to get the okay on bringing Clive and Mary in for questioning. Unfortunately, I didn't get authorization until midmorning on Saturday—"

"And they were already gone by then."

"Right. I still had hopes that they'd be back, but when you called I felt like my only real shot of getting back on their trail again would be with your help."

"Okay, that helps. It gives me a bit of a timeline to work with." I stood up and began to pace behind my desk. Jack remained seated and just looked at me. "What started all of this? Why now? They've had the gold for years at this point. Why try to sell it now?" I didn't expect an answer and didn't get one, but Jack picked up a blank pad of paper and a pen from my desk and jotted something down.

"The next question is, why did they go to the fence they did to sell their stuff? Did they know him from before?" I picked up a pen and fiddled with it. "One of the most important things we need answered is, do they know they're in danger? Is it possible that they don't have a clue how much trouble they're in?"

Jack, head bent to the pad, kept writing. "Another pertinent fact we need to discover is, where are they right now?"

"So, those are the questions we need to answer. What do we know about them?"

Jack pulled out a little notebook but didn't even look at it. "Clive Gordon: age 35, married, no children. Arrested twice and convicted of confidence games once. He served six months in a penitentiary and has had no arrest warrants issued for him since—"

I interrupted the recitation of facts. "Because he's stopped committing crimes?"

"Because he's gotten better at committing them."

I nodded, and he went on. "He served with the army overseas for two years. He was in Berlin at the fall. The rest of the information we've got is more supposition than fact."

"And Mary?"

"Mary Gordon was born Mary Black. She married Clive at age twenty-two. She has no criminal record, but she is believed to have been involved with the cons that Clive has run in the past."

"Okay, I'd say that we've got a basic picture of our targets. Now we've just got to find them."

We spent the rest of the afternoon forming an investigation strategy. Jack, after the first hour of our collaboration, made himself more comfortable. He took off his jacket and loosened his tie, a concession to the overpowering heat of New York City in August. He also commandeered the far side of my desk to use as his workspace, although I think he spent as much time pacing the confines of the office as he did seated at the desk. He seemed to be in constant motion—thinking out loud, muttering, and wandering. He needed to touch everything. He picked up and set back down all the knickknacks in the room, even pulling books out of the bookcase to flip through them for a moment before replacing them.

I took the job of making phone calls while he

compiled the information into a file. He was unable to bring the official FBI file to my office, so he wrote down the contents of it, from memory. I thought to myself that he must be one of those people who can remember everything they see. From what I could tell he only needed to hear or read something once and it would be imprinted on his brain.

"Allie, I need to get out of here for a while."

His voice interrupted my train of thought. "Um, yeah, go ahead. I can take care of the rest of this."

"No, Allie. You need to get out of here too."

I looked at him, not following. "And go where?"

"Anywhere that isn't a stuffy, ninety-five-degree office, for starters."

"Oh, okay. I guess I could do the rest of this at home."

He shook his head at me before pulling his suit jacket off the coatrack and draping it over his arm. "Allie, let me make this simple. I'm starving, you should eat, and we both need to clear our heads. Let's go out for supper. I know an Italian place not too far from here."

My heart sank. I couldn't let this happen. I needed to explain.

Jack saw the look on my face, and he held up a hand to stop whatever I was about to say. "I read your file, and I'm pretty good at reading between the lines. This isn't me suggesting a date; this is me suggesting that we share a meal and get to know each other as investigative partners."

The nervous kink in my stomach immediately eased. "Okay, that sounds good." Jack grabbed his hat from the coatrack and made me laugh by flipping it by the brim, up his arms, and onto his head. Just a silly trick, but combined with his grin, it's just what I needed to make me relax.

I grabbed my own hat and purse from the rack, pausing only long enough to lock the door behind us as we left. Once out on the open street I couldn't believe how good it felt to have the slight breeze cool my skin. Jack seemed to know exactly where he was going, so I just followed along.

The little Italian place was owned by Jack's family. I could hardly imagine an Italian restaurant being owned by a family named O'Connor, but one look at Jack's mother told me that Jack was a unique combination of Irish-Italian.

Jack smiled at my reaction to the restaurant. *Little* was an apt description. There was only room for six small tables in the seating area, and the pungent aromas coming from the kitchen inundated the small space. The smell of baked bread, garlic, and tomatoes made my stomach growl. I followed Jack to the back of the restaurant, to the farthest table from the door. We sat, and within a few seconds a young girl, maybe seventeen, brought us glasses of water and a basketful of hot bread.

"Nancy, this is Allie, friend of mine. Allie, my sister Nancy." He took a drink from his water and smiled at the girl. "Make sure that you repeat that correctly to everyone." He turned back to me, and at my look of confusion he explained.

"I imagine that every female member of my family is standing behind that door right now whispering and giggling, waiting to find out who you are and what we're doing."

I raised my eyebrows. "A lot of females in your family?"

"Way too many. Each of them eager to get me married off, so it's best to head off that rumor right now, before they start sending out wedding invitations."

While Jack explained, Nancy stood there, mouth open, clearly committing every word to memory. I had a suspicion that this conversation would be repeated word for word in a few moments. Jack caught my eye and grinned. His good nature was contagious, and I felt a smile cross my own face.

The food was good, and it was wonderful to get out of the office for a while. I didn't often go out for dinner, as I hated eating out alone. In fact, other than eating at my desk and my Wednesday night suppers at my parents', I couldn't remember the last time I had more than a quick sandwich for supper.

"So, tomorrow."

I looked up. "It comes after tonight. What about it?"

"What's on the agenda for tomorrow?"

"I think we should take a little field trip to the museum. Look at a few paintings, absorb a little culture—"

"And question a certain undercurator?"

"That's my plan."

Jack eased back in his chair. "I'm glad we think alike. It's going to make this whole partnership thing easier."

"What's the art fence/undercurator's name?"

Jack didn't even bother with the pretense of the notebook this time. "Robert Follett, age fifty-three, employed at the New York Museum of Antiquities for twenty-two years. He's eager to cooperate with our investigation in exchange for us not charging him with possession of stolen goods. He would lose his job at the museum and never be employed in one again if word leaked out about his extra-curricular activities."

"It's nice to have leverage."

Jack smiled. "That's how I've always seen it too."

"I forgot to ask, but where are the jewels that he bought from the Gordons?"

"They've been entered into evidence at the FBI field office."

"That's another field trip I think I need to take. I need to see the gold for myself."

Jack looked a bit uncomfortable. "I'll see what I can do, but it's not easy to get access for a civilian."

"Do what you need to, because it's important to the investigation that I have all the facts and details clear in my mind."

Jack still looked uncomfortable, but he nodded. I took a sip of my water and pondered for a second.

He was keeping something from me. I didn't know what it was, but I knew it was there. Good thing I was an expert at looking out for my own interests or I might be worried that the FBI was trying to take me for a ride.

Chapter 14

BRIGHT AND EARLY Tuesday morning Jack came by the office to pick me up. We were headed to the museum, trying to get there just as they opened to the public.

Traffic was heavy, and we were a lot later than we'd hoped. The museum wasn't one of the best in the city, but it had a decent reputation. I'd never been inside, so I didn't have an opinion of my own yet.

We ran up the stone steps to the entrance and slowed only when we made our way through the giant wooden doors. When the doors closed behind us it was like entering another world. The noise of cars and people was completely muffled inside the building, which was almost oppressive in its silence. Despite the fact that they had opened almost an hour before, there weren't many visitors. Jack walked over to the admission's desk. After a quiet conversation Jack received dramatized, arm-waving directions, pointing us toward the back of the building. He walked back to me, and we headed for Robert Follett's office together.

Jack knocked on the door but didn't wait for an invitation to enter. It was classic dominant behavior. You had to be in charge going into an interview, and Jack had the aggressive behavior nailed. Even his walk changed as we headed inside. I could see now how people would find him intimidating.

Robert was sitting at his desk, staring up in obvious dread at Jack. He didn't even seem to notice me standing behind him.

"W-What are you doing here?"

"I'm here to talk, Robert."

"Close the door." The curator stood, agitated. "Close the door behind you so we can talk in private." According to Jack, the man was fifty-three, but he looked several years older. He was a heavy man, his face brick-red, a line of sweat starting to trickle past his ear. I would have guessed that the sweating only started when he saw who was standing at his office door.

"Robert, this is my partner, Allie Fortune." Jack motioned to me, then turned back to Follett. "You know why we're here, so let's get to it. I think for your sake, the quicker we get what we want and get out, the more secure your job."

Robert wiped at his forehead and forced a smile. He motioned for us to sit down. I took a quick look around. The office was a complete disaster, books and papers spread all over the desk and spilling into piles on the floor. There were broken bits of pottery and other unidentifiable ancient stuff strewn across every surface. It was the office of a vastly disorganized person, and it was almost enough to make me itch.

The man himself was wearing a home-knit maroon sweater-vest with a stain on the front and looked as unlike a criminal as I could imagine a person looking. He didn't appear to have the wits to pull off any kind of deception. He looked smart enough, just witless.

The only available chairs were stacked with stuff, so I elected to lean against the wall while Jack stood several feet away.

"Clive and Mary Gordon—where do you know them from?" Jack's bluntness was going to set the tone for this interrogation. Clearly we weren't going to try for a friendly discussion; we were going with intimidation. I adjusted my thoughts and slid into the appropriate role.

"I've known them for years. Socially." More sweat beaded at the man's hairline.

"You don't socialize, Robert; you live in your

mother's basement. You've been their fence for years."

"No. That's not true." He stuttered. "I mean, I may have bought a few paintings from them, but it was hardly a regular thing."

"Paintings of questionable origin?"

"I never asked where they came from."

Jack shrugged. "Tell me about the gold, Robert."

He looked defeated. "I got a call from them. Clive said that he had some jewelry that he wanted to sell. Jewelry isn't my field of expertise, but I have handled a sale or two over the years. So, I told them to meet me at my place that night and I'd take a look at it."

"So they knew you well enough to know directions to your house?" I asked the question blandly, but the implication was clear. I'd caught Robert in a lie.

His face went even redder, and he looked down. "I told you. We knew each other socially." He was probably aiming for defiant, but it came out as more of a whine.

"So they came to your house. What did they say to you?" Jack didn't try to mask his impatience.

"They carried the two pins wrapped in a piece of cloth. They weren't even careful with the pieces. Looking back on it, it's clear they had no idea that they were handling something priceless. I'm sure they just thought they had some old gold jewelry.

"When they took out the pieces, I couldn't believe what I was seeing. I went and got my magnifying glass so I could take a closer look. Clive was talking about how he had several more pieces that were from the same collection, but I wasn't really listening. I was too excited at the prospect that these two small pins were a part of Helen of Troy's infamous collection. That collection was one of the most significant archaeological finds of the century. I left Clive and Mary alone in my living room for a minute when I went to get my magnifying glass and stopped quickly to check a reference book. I already knew what they were, but it helped to see a picture of the collection for confirmation. The pins they brought me were some of the smaller pieces, but still worth a fortune in their own right."

I couldn't hold back. I asked the question that had been running through my head for days. "How much are they worth?"

He looked up at me as though I was an idiot for asking. "It's hard to give an accurate estimate, but the collection in its entirety is priceless, and the pieces they brought to me are worth close to fifty thousand dollars, although black market collectors would be willing to pay about double that amount. Each successive piece would add exponentially to the value."

I almost lost my breath. I knew they were significant, but I had no idea. I snuck a look at Jack, and from his flat expression I could see he wasn't surprised at the figure. He already knew this. I wondered how much else he knew and wasn't telling me.

"So, you went to check your book, then what?"

"Then I came back, looked at them under magnification, marveled at the intricacy of the design, and offered them five hundred dollars apiece."

Jack sighed. "It was more than they were expecting."

Robert looked miserable. "Way more. I blew it. The gold, if it had just been ordinary jewelry, wouldn't be worth more than fifty dollars for both. Five hundred was twenty times what they were expecting, and they knew instantly that there was something special about the pieces. I had to work hard to get them to sell them to me after that, really talk them into it, and eventually they acquiesced. I made them promise to bring me the rest of the pieces the next day. We made arrangements and everything, but . . ."

"They didn't show up." Jack finished the sentence for him. "They probably did a little research and found out what they had on their hands."

Robert shook his head. "I don't know where they would have found out. There can't be more than twenty people in this city who could identify Helen's Gold on sight, and I don't mean to be rude, but the Gordons don't exactly run in academic social circles."

"When did all this happen?"

Follett turned to me to answer. "It was just over two weeks ago, and I haven't seen either of them since that night."

"Once you had the gold pieces in your possession, what happened then?"

"I bought them off the Gordons, and it was a bit like carrying a fistful of diamonds in my pocket. I had to tell someone what I had." He shook his head. "Unfortunately, once you tell one person, it's easier to tell the story the next time. And those people feel the need to repeat it and . . ."

"And so on and so forth until the FBI comes crashing down on your head," Jack finished for him.

Robert nodded, making his jowls quiver slightly. He reminded me of an old hound dog a neighbor used to own. Morose was his default expression too.

"Okay, so one last question, Robert. Do you have any idea where the Gordons would go if they were trying to get away, to get out of the city for a while?"

Robert swiped a hand across his bald, sweaty head. Apparently the news that this would be the last question put him at ease. He looked thoughtful for a moment. "I couldn't really say. I mean, I don't know if they have a house in the country or anything like that, but I do know that Clive has a brother who lives upstate somewhere."

"Upstate where?"

"No idea. I never met the man; I just heard Clive say something about a brother once."

Jack looked frustrated as we turned to depart. "Don't leave town, Follett. And if you hear from either Clive or Mary, you call us right away. We can make life very unpleasant for you if we feel that you're not cooperating."

"Yes, sir. I will phone immediately. I'll do just that." He nodded furiously as he talked.

"Good." Jack pulled open the office door, letting me precede him out into the hallway.

We didn't get a whole lot from the interview with Follett, but we had a few more details to work into the overall picture. We were making progress.

Jack and I split up around noon. We both had full caseloads without this investigation, so we had to allocate our time carefully. We were going to meet again in the morning and decide what our next step would be.

I got back to the office and felt the need to take a quick walk. I wanted to replay the interview with Follett in my mind and see if I could glean any more from his story.

When I got back, the details were firmly pressed in my mind and I felt like now I could move onto other cases. As I pulled out my keys to unlock my office, I heard my phone ringing. Hurrying, I threw the door open hard enough to rattle the glass. The phone rang for the fourth time as I reached across my desk and picked up the receiver.

"Hello?"

"Miss Fortune, I've been trying to get ahold of you." The voice was smooth and faintly British. I didn't recognize it.

"Who am I speaking to?"

"My name is Nigel Gordon. I believe you know my brother."

I sank into my chair. Surprise paralyzed me for only a moment; then I reached across the desk for a pad of paper and a pencil. "Mr. Gordon, what can I do for you?"

He laughed. "A more apt question is, what can I do for you?"

I refused to play this game. "What do you want, Mr. Gordon?"

"I have reason to believe that you're looking for my brother and his lovely wife. I thought I might have some information that would help you in your search."

"Why would you think that I'm looking for them? Where did you hear that?"

"It doesn't really matter. I hear many things through the course of my day. Are you interested in the information I have?"

I couldn't hedge here. If he could help me I needed to play this straight. "Yes, I'd be interested. Where do you think they are, Mr. Gordon?"

He laughed again, and it sent a chill up the back

of my neck. "This is not the sort of thing we should discuss over the phone, Miss Fortune. Instead you can meet me at the Belvedere Hotel in three-quarters of an hour. Suite 509."

"I'm not sure I can make it all the way over there that fast. It may take me longer."

"If it does, you'll have missed your chance. I will be waiting for you in my hotel room in forty-five minutes. If you're not there, you'll just have to find Clive on your own."

I wrote down the hotel number he'd given me as I tried to think of a way to stall for time. When a dial tone sounded in my ear, I felt the lead of my pencil snap under my grip. Immediately I dialed Jack's office number. I stuck my finger into the phone dial and cranked out the numbers with dwindling hope. He'd left here less than an hour before, and he'd said that he'd had to meet someone at one o'clock. I couldn't imagine that he would've had time to get back to the office yet. I let the phone ring and ring, but I knew it was hopeless. I'd have to do this on my own.

How exactly had Nigel Gordon heard of me, and how had he known I'd be interested in the whereabouts of Clive and Mary? Another good question was, why would Clive's own brother try to help me find him? I reached in through the passenger window and handed the cabbie the fare. I wished once again that I'd had a chance to get ahold of

Jack, but it was too late to worry about that now. On the ride over I'd had a chance to think about this fortuitous phone call. The questions that needed answers were starting to line up. I shook my head to clear my thoughts. In a matter of moments I'd have a chance to ask the man himself.

I made my way to the elevator and told the operator that I needed to get to the fifth floor. Within minutes, I was knocking on a door bearing the number 509.

I only had to knock once before the door swung open. "You made it. I was beginning to lose faith." He moved out of the doorway to let me pass through.

Once the door was shut behind me, he motioned me into the sitting area of the suite. I picked a chair, smoothed down my skirt, and waited for him to begin. A slight feeling of unease squirmed up my back. I chased it away by focusing on the man in front of me.

"Miss Fortune, I'm Nigel Gordon."

"Let's bypass the chitchat and get right to why you asked me here."

"All right then. I want you to find Clive and Mary, and I have information that could help you do that."

"The question at this point is, why do you want me to find them?"

I heard a door open from the room behind me, and a trickle of dread slid into my belly.

"Actually, I don't want you to find them; I want you to help me find them." Gone was the friendly tone. He stood in front of me, but I felt the slide of cold metal against my neck from behind me. Someone else was here too. I closed my eyes as the gunman I couldn't see pressed a little deeper. I knew going in that this could be a trap, but there had been few other choices than just to take the risk.

"What do you want from me, Mr. Gordon? Surely you don't need to hold me at gunpoint. I can't imagine that you'd feel threatened by an unarmed woman, now would you?"

"Oh, I don't feel threatened; I just think it's friendlier this way. This way I know you'll cooperate without a fuss. I don't really want to hurt you. I mean, it's not in my plans for the day, but on the other hand, I'm a spontaneous kind of man. Things happen and I go with the flow. I suggest that you do the same. All I want from you is a little bit of information."

I knew I didn't have any options at the moment. "Go ahead."

"Who else is after Clive and that little twit Mary?"

"That I know of, me, Soviet intelligence, and the FBI."

"That's what I thought. I don't suppose you have any idea where Clive and Mary are?"

"I wouldn't have come here alone if I had any idea where they were."

"That's true. I only have one more question for you."

"And it is . . ."

"What is the FBI offering as a reward for the gold? I've gotten a sizeable offer from the Soviets, but I have to make sure that there's not a better offer across the table. In cases such as these, it pays not to have any loyalty to either party. The best bidding wars start that way."

The man made me sick, and I'm sure the disgust showed on my face, but it didn't affect Nigel. In fact, it seemed to amuse him.

"My dear, you shouldn't take life so seriously. I'm just making full use of the capitalist system. I can always be bought by the highest bidder. In fact, the only thing that can't be bought is my loyalty. I have none."

"Not even to your own brother apparently."

He smiled again. "It's not like I had any choice in the matter. I didn't choose to be saddled to a buffoon like Clive; it just happened. That's hardly my fault, and it shouldn't preclude me from benefiting from the return of the gold. So I'll ask you again, what is the FBI offering?"

"As far as I know, the reward is listed at ten thousand dollars."

He took a small step back. "I should have known. Cheap Americans." He looked at me as though weighing his words. "You're playing for the wrong team, you know."

I glared at him.

"No, you are. If you're playing for any team but your own, you're playing for the wrong side. Give them your loyalty and what will you get back? They'll cut you out of the deal at the first opportunity and then forget that you exist."

I didn't let the fact that he was speaking my deepest fear show on my face. Instead I reminded myself that I had a contract signed and all I needed to do was deliver.

"Why don't we work together? I'm sure with your background and contacts and my understanding of Clive's simple and predictable mind, we'd find the gold in no time. We could split the reward money from the Soviets, which I might add would still amount to more for each of us than the Americans are offering in total."

I didn't bother to disguise my disgust. "Sorry, Nigel. My loyalty is not for sale, at any price."

He shrugged his shoulders. "Ah, what can I say? I had to try." He lifted his arm and pointed at the man behind me.

I felt the gun pull away from my neck, but seconds later there was a resounding crack on the side of my head. Bright lights flashed behind my eyes before darkness fell, heavy as a stage curtain.

Chapter 15

PAIN BLOCKED my thoughts. My eyes opened and I couldn't quite figure out where I was, but I was pretty sure that what I saw in front of me was carpet. Moving slowly and carefully, I pushed myself up. As my brain cleared I realized that I lay sprawled out on the floor. I was still in Nigel's hotel room, and given the carpet imprint I could feel on my cheek, I'd probably been unconscious for a while.

I boosted myself into a sitting position, but waited there for the pounding in my head to subside to less tympanic levels.

Using the chair, I eased myself to my feet. Once standing, I smoothed down my skirt and tried to brush the wrinkles out of my jacket. I realized how stupid fussing about my appearance was when I could still be in danger, and I let my hands drop to my sides.

A quick glance around the room assured me that I was alone. I must've just been out for a while.

The long cab ride back to the office gave me plenty of time to think and plenty of time to mentally kick myself. I never should have gone over there without Jack. Normally I worked alone and it wasn't a problem, but normally I wasn't involved with cases that crossed international boundaries and involved hostile governments. I'd made a serious tactical mistake.

The cab pulled up in front of the office. I paid my fare and climbed the steps slowly to avoid jostling my brain any more than necessary.

I shuffled up the staircase and felt my heart sink when I spotted Jack leaning against the locked door. He saw me, and I winced. His posture changed from relaxed to tense in an instant. He crossed the few feet that separated us. "What happened?"

Clearly I looked as bad as I felt. There was only a slight crust of blood on my scalp, but the bump was big enough to make my head feel off balance. I suppose the pain-ridden steps I took, trying for as little motion as possible, made it doubly obvious that all was not right.

I grabbed my keys from my purse. "Let me sit down and I'll tell you."

I unlocked the door, nudged it open, and made my way across to the leather couch. Easing into it, I closed my eyes for a moment and tried to get past the whirling. When I felt more in control I opened my eyes again.

Jack stood in front of me, all but tapping his foot in frustration. He was such a fidgeter that I closed my eyes again before he made me dizzy.

Bracing myself for his anger, I recounted my meeting with Nigel Gordon. When I finished I saw that I was right.

"You went to see him by yourself?" He wasn't yelling, but it was close. "What were you thinking?"

"You were unreachable, and I couldn't wait for you. It was an offer with a time limit. I barely made it over there in time myself."

"You shouldn't have gone at all, shouldn't have even considered it."

My jaw tensed. "I did what I thought I needed to do. It wasn't the best option, but it's the only option I had. What would you have done?"

"I would have waited for my partner even if it meant missing out." The words exploded from him.

I stared him down. "Would you really? If you were at your desk and your phone rang delivering the same offer of information, you would have skipped it if I wasn't available?"

Silence.

"Yeah, probably. Maybe, but it's different in any case."

"I don't see it that way. Yes, I took a risk. Yes it turned out badly, but I don't see that I had any other option."

Jack said nothing but walked out of the office. The crash of the door slamming did his talking for him.

I lay back on the couch with a sigh. So, I'd alienated my partner, gotten my head smacked with the broadside of a gun, and all for nothing. I was no further ahead.

By five o'clock I started to feel better. The lump was still there, but the headache was mostly gone.

Just in time for the family dinner. I knew full well that my headache would be raging again once I left my parents' house.

Still I went home, changed into proper dinner attire, careful to avoid touching the sore spot on my head, and took the subway over. When I arrived I was almost too tired and achy to care about my little blind date game, but when I saw a 1945 Chevrolet Venture in the drive, I had to smile.

A maid I'd never met before let me in, and for once I didn't linger at the front door. I walked into the drawing room, fairly sure I knew who was in there waiting for me.

My mother's eyebrows rose at the sight of me. It was only six twenty, making me a whole ten minutes early, and the small smile that crossed her face let me know that she made note of it. Still, a quick look around the room assured me that my guess was right.

My mother thought she'd follow up last Friday's introduction with a Wednesday night blind date. It was the first time I'd ever been happy to see one of the men my mother had set me up with. Not that I was happy to be set up, but I was happy to have the opportunity to make amends.

All through dinner my mother carried the conversation. Jack was open and friendly when talking to her, but just slightly cooler with me. Probably no one else would notice the difference, but I did.

When dinner was over my mother and I moved to the drawing room for coffee. Jack and my father, who were getting along famously, headed for my dad's office. Dad wanted to show Jack his collection of military biographies.

I was waiting for it, but she caught me with a mouthful of coffee before she started in. "Why couldn't you have made more of an effort? He's a lovely man. Intelligent, handsome, from a goodish sort of family. His father is a senator, you know. His mother—well, she's another story; for some reason she insists on running a restaurant. Can you even imagine? It seems as though Jack's father thought it would be a good idea, give her something to do during the time he spent in Washington. What was he thinking?"

My mother interrupted herself from her rambling. "Mostly, and even more important—I think he would understand you, Alexandra." She looked me in the eye, and I was surprised by the seriousness reflected there. "I don't always understand you, but I do care about you. I just want you to be happy and settled, and I think if you gave it a try you might find that you actually like Jack."

She was right about never having understood, but I tried one more time to make her see me.

"I already like Jack. He's a great guy, and in other circumstances I can almost imagine there being more, but it isn't and it can't be."

"But Alexandra, it's been years. You know that a

man like David is not what I wanted for you, but if he'd come home from the war maybe I could have accepted it. But it's been years. He's gone. What are you going to do, be a spinster investigator for the rest of your life?"

"If I have to."

She squeezed her eyes shut in frustration. "Why can't you let this go?"

I looked into her face and tried to really communicate with her. "If I could do anything else, I would. I don't want to live like this, but I don't have a choice. How could I ever marry someone like Jack, a good, honest man, knowing that I love someone else?"

She leaned away, pulled her hands back from mine, and sighed in disgust. "I just can't get through to you."

"And I could never get through to you, so we're even." With that I laid down my coffee cup and headed for the back door.

It was cooler out now. Not cold, but there was a breeze that helped to ease the heat of my frustration. I strode the tree-lined street, and all I could hear was the click of my heels on pavement. I slowed only slightly as I moved onto the pathway through the park. It wasn't dark yet, but the sky had changed to twilight. It was funny—I'd probably crossed the park thousands of times in my life, but the only times I remembered were the times I was with David. That night he'd walked me home in the dark had been a defining moment in my life. Forever after, things were divided into before and after David.

As I walked I heard footsteps moving fast behind me. My breath caught in my throat. I'd been so wrapped up in my memories that I'd lost track of where I was. Of course, I was no longer a naive sixteen-year-old girl afraid of shadows in the dark. I turned, ready, almost anxious to confront whoever was behind me.

I made out his shape in the dimness, broad shoulders in his dark suit with his hat tilted forward.

"Need some company?"

"You haven't had enough of me for one day?"

"What can I say? I thrive on conflict."

"I'm not sure I'm up for another round, actually."

"Let's just walk then."

Jack matched his stride to mine, and we strode through the falling darkness side by side.

"I'm sorry. I should have waited for you."

"Yes, you should have, but I probably would have done exactly the same thing. I was just furious when I saw that you'd been hurt. I kind of lost my temper."

"Kind of? I thought the glass in my door was going to break."

"Don't forget I come from a family full of women. Sometimes the only way to get the last word in is with a slamming door."

I laughed, and we continued our walk in silence for a while.

"So, are we walking aimlessly or are we headed somewhere in particular?"

"The reservoir on the far side of the park is my favorite spot." At least these days it was. "Sometimes I need to just go there and throw in a few stones."

"Lead on then."

We crossed the length of the park in silence, and my mind wandered. When we neared the reservoir I found my thoughts drifting to the past once again.

September 1937

I WANTED TO SEE HIM AGAIN. For two weeks after the incident I lingered as long as I dared at the reservoir.

I'd already decided that this night would be the last time I'd wait. He probably didn't live nearby; perhaps it had just been a lucky coincidence that he was there to save me that night. I'd gone over all of the possibilities in my mind endlessly, yet I lingered.

I took another look around the deserted park and sighed before turning back to the book in my lap. At least I wasn't just wasting time; today I'd brought my homework along with me. I was tucked behind a little clump of trees, but I could see the people as they passed by on the path.

I knew that compared to the possibility of seeing

my rescuer again, the history of the Peloponnesian War wouldn't hold my interest, but I did my best to concentrate. As the light started to fade, I worked faster. I had no desire to be out after dark again, but I still had a few minutes before I needed to go. It took me ten more to answer the last questions of my assignment. As I closed the books and shoved them into my satchel, I finally admitted defeat. Feeling a little foolish for wanting to see him again so badly, I picked my hat up from the ground and put it back on. Ready to go, I pushed myself to my feet. It was only then that I became aware of the change in my surroundings.

The sound of a clipped conversation to my right stilled my movements. Still spooked from my close call the other night, my heart doubled in speed as the conversation increased in volume. I couldn't make out what was being said, but the tone kept me motionless, trying to remain unnoticed.

I closed my eyes and berated myself for getting into a situation like this again. I decided that the better part of valor in this case was cowardice, and that it would be best to wait until the arguing stopped and the people passed by before heading home.

Pleased with my plan, I set my satchel back on the ground.

Suddenly there was shouting.

"No!"

Then a loud pop.

My breath stalled in my chest.

My mind didn't want to believe what I understood instantly. Despite the fact that I'd never heard a gunshot before, I recognized the sound for what it was.

Struck with terror, I couldn't move. There was a loud rustle and then the sound of footfalls on asphalt. I moved just slightly to see through a small opening in the trees. A man was running away, indistinguishable features in the low light of dusk. I turned back to where I'd heard the men arguing. Just a few feet off the footpath I saw another man lying on the grass. I waited for a long moment, my mind feeling strangely out of sync with my body. I waited until I was sure the first man was out of sight, then ran over to the side of the man who'd just been shot.

As I approached I noticed the smell first. A sharp scent like a combination of rust and sea water that stung my senses. I recognized it as blood. His dark suit jacket was stained wet with it, and for a moment I thought I might be sick. I didn't have time to wait for the nausea to pass. Instead I knelt down and placed my fingers on his neck, searching for a pulse. I couldn't find one, but I felt him take a stuttered breath.

Seeds of panic sprouted in my mind. I had no idea what to do. I couldn't leave him here alone, but with that much blood on the ground, I was sure he'd die if I didn't do something.

My decision was made for me when he reached out and grabbed my hand. His sinewy fingers pulled me toward him with surprising strength. Instinct made me try to jerk away. His grip tightened and he drew me even closer still. His hazel eyes were swimming with panic and glassy-eyed shock.

I tried to pull my hand away again. "I have to go and get help. You need a doctor. I'll go get you a doctor." Bubbles of hysteria burst in my brain as I tried to pull my hand from this stranger who was holding too tight. The man shuddered once and then his grip loosened. For a second I remained still, watching for the rise and fall of his breath, but his chest fell once more with a hiss and then there was nothing. His body was utterly motionless. A wave of nausea overcame me and I jerked back, suddenly repulsed by the unresponsive feel of the man's body. My brain was frozen. I couldn't leave him here. I ran my fingers along his neck, trying to make out a pulse, detect movement of any kind, but I knew in the logical part of my brain that he was dead.

I don't know how long I knelt there, waiting for his chest to rise and fall, waiting for any sign of life with one part of me already knowing that it wasn't coming.

The next thing I knew there was a hand on my shoulder, pulling me back, prying me away from the cold, still form on the pavement.

"Let go. You need to let go of him." Despite the fogginess in my mind and the fact that I'd only met him once before, I recognized the voice immediately. He was here.

Chapter 16

"WE CAN SCRAP the idea of Clive turning to his loving brother Nigel in his time of need." Jack's face twisted as he spoke Nigel Gordon's name. I didn't blame him. The man wasn't my favorite person in the world right then either. I rubbed the still-aching knot on my head.

We were back at the office. It was long past a normal person's bedtime, but I didn't sleep and Jack seemed to keep the same crazy hours I did. After our walk through the park we decided to try to come up with a theory or two. At this point we were running pretty low on ideas and even lower on actual leads.

"What are we missing? The story we have is piecemeal. We have a few bits, and we're trying to get a picture of the situation from those." I rubbed my head again.

"What's the biggest missing piece?"

"I don't know if it's the biggest piece, but the one that's bothering me the most is the whole issue of timing. Why now? Why not sometime in the three years since the end of the war? What would make Clive and Mary hock the gold now?" I paced behind my desk. "Do they owe money that needs to be paid back? Are they desperate for cash? Has their situation changed in some way in the past few months?"

Jack shrugged. He had no more answers than I did.

"I think we need to find the answer to that question if we want to figure this out. Unless we stumble across the Gordons on the street somewhere, I think it's our only chance."

"In the morning I can make a few calls and get someone at the Bureau on it."

The idea of having other people do the legwork of an investigation left me with mixed feelings. On one hand, it was thrilling to have access to all kinds of resources that a lowly private eye couldn't even dream of, but on the other hand I didn't like the idea of passing over the reins of the investigation, and I really didn't like the idea of being spoon-fed information from a source I didn't totally trust.

"Why don't you phone now? Get things started on your end."

"Now? It's past one in the morning."

"What? Does the FBI close up at five o'clock? I assumed from the hours you keep that things are running twenty-four hours a day there."

"They are; I just don't usually phone in requests in the middle of the night."

"Any reason not to?"

"No. If it's that important that we start right this minute, pass the phone to me." He sounded irritated, and I didn't blame him. I didn't know why I was pushing the issue other than maybe it kept my hand on the wheel a little.

I reached for the phone, grasped it by the back handhold, and shoved it toward him. He lifted the receiver off the cradle and started the process of cranking out the number. His eyes never left mine. I could tell he knew that I didn't entirely trust the FBI and in turn him, and he was daring me to say as much.

From this end it seemed to take being connected through multiple operators before Jack got through to the person or department he was looking for.

Within five minutes he had placed a request for information and checked whether he had any messages. When he dumped the receiver back into the cradle it was clear he was still annoyed.

He lifted his hat off the desk and jammed it on. "It's time for me to go. I've still got more work to do yet tonight."

I wanted to apologize for being demanding, but I couldn't quite push the words out. "See you in the morning."

"I'll be here." With that he turned and walked out.

I let myself fall into my chair, and I mentally berated myself for angering the ever-placid Jack. Some of the things Nigel Gordon said to me about the FBI had been echoing in my ears all night because they had a ring of truth to them.

I got an hour of sleep on my office couch before heading back home to shower and change my clothes for the day.

When I arrived back at the office Jack was again standing at the door waiting for me. He looked like he possibly got less sleep last night than I did, and I didn't think he'd changed at all. He was still wearing his rumpled suit and appeared to have at least a day's worth of beard growth staining his jaw.

I grinned when I saw him. I couldn't help it. He looked like he'd spent the night lying in a gutter covered by a sheet of newspaper, but somehow he was still handsome. I unlocked the door and preceded him into the office.

"Late night?" I tried to hold back the giggle tickling my throat, but it managed to bubble out. Jack glared at me, which only made me laugh harder.

"I had stakeout duty last night. I haven't slept, eaten, or shaved. I am not in the mood, Fortune." Despite his claim, a grin quirked the corner of his mouth, followed by a half laugh. "Do I look as bad as I feel?"

I couldn't stop smiling. "Worse. Way worse."

Jack sighed. "I've got plans laid out for us today, but I'm going to have to go home and clean up before I can go out anywhere."

"What plans?"

"I got clearance, with much paperwork, favor calling in, and pleading, for you to come in and see the jewelry at the field office. We can go in sometime this morning and you'll get to take a look at the pieces."

I was thrilled by this and wondered for a moment if Jack worked so hard to get me access as a token of trust. Something to show me that my faith had not been misplaced.

Chapter 17

WE STOPPED at Jack's apartment on our way to the FBI field office. That way at least he could shower, change, and shave. As he let me in through the bland doorway of an apartment in a nondescript building, I did my best not to let curiosity overwhelm me. I wanted to find out more about Jack, to see past his government-man veneer, and realized that this might be my chance.

I shut the door behind me with a gentle nudge. Jack turned. "I'll go shower and change; you can wait in here."

"Sure, I can entertain myself."

Jack's eyes narrowed and he suddenly looked less than comfortable. I wasn't proud of the fact that I enjoyed watching him squirm, but considering he'd gone through every book and loose piece of paper in my office over the past few days, I saw this as payback.

Without another word he headed toward what I assumed was the bedroom. I was a modern woman of the forties, not some blushing Victorian, but still I averted my eyes.

Jack's main living area was furnished, but

sparse. Just a couch and a chair, both a little tattered, and one side table covered with old newspapers. By far the most dominant thing in the room was his vast collection of books. They were stacked, shelved, propped, and otherwise scattered throughout the entire room. I crossed to a precariously piled stack to get a closer look at some of the titles. As I read I got a clearer sense of Jack. His books ran the gamut from Sir Arthur Conan Doyle to textbooks on advanced math, from the theory of flight to the history of the first World War.

I moved to his chair where a smaller stack of books lay open, but face-down, most likely his current reading pile. There was a book on the Greeks and Spartans, fitting given our current investigation, and one on the changing face of agriculture. Underneath was a closed slim brown volume with a marker in it. I picked it up and examined the spine. The collected works of John Donne. Poetry? Jack? I flicked it open to the marked page but was instantly distracted from the words by the thing holding Jack's page. It was a photograph, bent and faded and of a woman. Smiling and squinting into the camera, she looked young, in her early twenties maybe. She had a wonderful smile, the kind that was infectious, and the picture was the essence of happy and beautiful. I turned it over to see a faded marking on the back. Maggie 1940.

I replaced the bookmark, taking care not to bend

the edges any further, and set the book back in its place.

Who was that woman, and was she special to Jack? The question flitted through my mind, but I tamped it down. Everyone was entitled to privacy, and despite my snooping, I'd never meant to intrude into Jack's private life. Guilt hummed at my mind. I made my way out of the living room entirely and walked into the kitchen. The sight of his stove gave me an idea on how to make up for my intrusion. I opened the refrigerator. It was clear he didn't actually spend much time or eat many meals there, but there was enough for a makeshift breakfast. As I cooked eggs for him, I tried not to think about the picture and tried not to wonder about the woman.

When Jack emerged showered, shaved, and dressed for the day, his breakfast was ready and I handed him the plate without a word.

He sent me a brief questioning glance before thanking me. I almost wished I'd never come here. Caught up in my own struggles, sometimes I forgot that everyone else had a story too. The photograph made me wonder if Jack's was a sad one.

September 1937

HE WAS HERE.

He put his hand on my shoulder and pulled me back slightly. Away from the body. Away from the darkening blood. My knees were stiff, and I wondered how long I'd been kneeling next to a corpse. A shudder wracked my body, and I tried to push the thought away.

He moved down onto one knee to get closer to the dead man, deliberately cutting off my view, protecting me from seeing the body. He took only a few seconds to determine that the man was dead. A quick search for a pulse and he stood up, guiding me away. Despite the movement, my eyes were fixed on the pool of congealing blood on the concrete path. It was no longer liquid; it appeared to have a skin on it, like gravy gone cold. My stomach rolled over at the thought.

It took a great effort to look away, and when I looked back to my rescuer, he was trying to get my attention.

"Are you all right? Have you been hurt?"

I shook my head slowly, aligning his words one by one in my mind until they made sense.

"We need to phone the police." He put his hand on my shoulder and turned me so I faced him. He kept his dark eyes on mine. "Do you have a telephone at your house?" His voice was intense, and I finally absorbed his question.

"Yes." My thoughts swirled and melted together, too disjointed to do more than answer his question.

"Good, we can call from there."

I was reluctant to leave the body alone. It seemed somehow sacrilegious. "What about him?"

"We can't just stay here. We need to alert the proper authorities. We have no choice."

He draped one arm across my shoulders and guided me from the area. He was strong, but gentle. Still, as he led me away, I felt something tear, sharp and painful. Something of me that would be left on that little patch of concrete.

I didn't remember crossing the park, just the sense of being surrounded and supported by someone I could trust. When we finally arrived at Fortune House it was all I could do to simply unlock the door and show him to the telephone. As he made the call, I sat and tried to think about something else, anything else, or even nothing at all, but my mind wouldn't allow it. All I could see, like a moving picture reel going back and forth in my head, was the panic in the man's eyes fading to nothing. Going blank. Hazel green depths shuttering into opaqueness. A curtain sliding down that signaled the end.

I heard the almost-stranger on the phone, but only random words penetrated. "Shooting . . . dead . . . witness." He turned to face me. "Where are we? I need to give them an address."

I stuttered out directions and did my best to focus back on what was happening in the present.

"We'll be here. I'm David Rubeneski, and the young woman who witnessed the shooting, her name is . . ." He looked at me, waiting for me to supply the information. It was kind of funny to think that despite the fact that this was our second encounter, we didn't even know each other's names.

"Alexandra Fortune."

David relayed the information and then hung up the phone. "They should be here in a few minutes. I told them you were a witness to the shooting, but I never asked—I just assumed. Did you see what happened?"

I nodded. I didn't want to think about it; instead I closed my eyes.

I opened them again when I felt a hand on my shoulder. I turned. David was crouched next to me. He stared, waiting for me to make eye contact. When I did he finally spoke. His promise was low but firm. "I'll be here for you and help you through this. You don't have to be afraid. I won't leave you alone."

When Jack finished his breakfast we headed across the city to the New York City FBI field office. I was kind of disappointed to get my first look at it. The FBI took up the entire twenty-sixth floor of an ordinary office building. Because of my work I'd spent a lot of time around police stations, and I guess I'd been expecting a bigger version of that. Instead, it was a quiet, businesslike office building with a lot of closed doors. The only thing remotely interesting about it was all the security we had to get through to get in. Other than that, I could have been anywhere. Jack had a special pass for me that I had to wear on the lapel of my suit jacket. He led me down a long hallway and stopped in front of an unmarked door just like every other unmarked door we had passed.

He opened the door with a key pulled from his jacket pocket. When the tumblers clicked, Jack let the door swing open. He reached out and held it open, motioning for me to precede him into the room.

It was a small, apparently unoccupied office, maybe twelve feet by twelve feet with a battered metal desk in the middle. A musty smell in the air confirmed it'd been vacant for a while. Lying on the desk was a sealed box about the size of a shoe box.

"That's it?"

"The pins are in there."

I had an intense desire to see them for myself. At that point I hadn't even had a chance to see a photograph of Helen's Gold, so I didn't have a clue what it was I was looking for. I moved across the room and sat in the chair next to the desk. Jack crossed with me and brought out a pocket knife. He flicked the blade and sliced the perimeter of tape sealing the evidence box. He snapped the knife shut and returned it to his pocket. I had to fight the urge to push him aside and open the box myself.

He lifted the lid straight up and off. I could wait no longer. I got up and moved to stand next to him, peering into the box, anxious to get my first glimpse of a treasure that governments were going to such great lengths to obtain. The box was ridiculously big given the size of its contents.

Wrapped in cotton batting were two items about two inches wide and six or seven inches long. I couldn't keep from reaching in to pull one out. Carefully I unwound the cotton. I was surprised by what I revealed. When Jack said *pin* I pictured something closer to a brooch or at least something small. This was different entirely. It was a pin in the same way a hatpin was a pin: a gold ornament with a five-inch spike at the end of it. I moved into the light to inspect it closer.

The ornament at the top was almost square, looking a little like the sail of an ancient ship. There was a row of six craterlike jugs along the top of the square and curlicue embellishments all down the front of the sail. The spike itself was narrow and crooked. There was no question that this wasn't jewelry formed with modern tools. The gold itself looked ancient. Patinaed, so that it looked more like brass that had spotted and darkened with age. On one hand I could see why Clive and Mary were shocked at the prices Robert Follett offered for the crude pieces, but on the other hand, as I held one in my palm, it gave off a sensation of being *more.* I couldn't explain, only that it had a feeling of preciousness. I wondered if I only sensed this because of what I knew about them. I didn't think so. Despite their small size and crude manufacture, I could feel through the tips of my fingers as I traced the pattern that there was more there than just old gold.

Next to me, Jack had unwrapped the other pin, his much simpler in form than mine. The ornamentation at the top was a simple T-arm with the ends curling into a spiral on each side. Again, it was small, but it too had a presence beyond its form.

Jack let me touch and inspect for several minutes. At last I looked up. "Do you want to see everything the FBI has been able to dig up on the gold itself?"

I nodded, even more anxious to know more.

Chapter 18

JACK BROUGHT out a folder that was on the bottom of the box itself. Flipping it open, he bypassed several sheets and pulled out a slim stack of photographs. Without a word he handed them to me.

Pictures of more pieces of the treasure. Beautiful pieces with the same aura of ancientness as the ones I'd just held. I flipped through them quickly, stopping only at the one showing the piece that was clearly the highlight of the collection. The picture featured a dark-eyed, dark-haired woman staring beyond the camera. She was wearing what looked like a cross between a crown and a headdress. It had chains of hammered gold in a band that circled her temples. Along the sides of her face the veil of gold dripped to her shoulders, but where it crossed her face it was shorter, resting like a fringe along her brow. It suited my image of what a mythical queen would wear. The sight of it made me think of great beauties and powerful queens of the past: Cleopatra, Nefertiti, or even Esther from the Bible.

I flipped through the last of the photos, glancing at the gold masks, earrings, chains, and bowls, all part of the collection, but my gaze was drawn back to the diadem. "Do we know what pieces they have?"

Jack shook his head. "We assume he has some of the more elaborate gold pieces or he wouldn't have realized it was worth it to go to all the work and possibly the expense to retrieve them. But we don't know which pieces he has for sure."

He thumbed through the file and then handed me a few pieces of paper. "This is what we've got of Clive Gordon's war record. He served for a little over a year, mostly in France, but he was among the first of the Allied troops who made it into Berlin at the fall. That's when we figure he took the gold, and that's somewhere I think we should start looking."

"Looking for what?"

"I'm curious to know if Clive had any close friends in his regiment—if there may have been someone else who was with him when he stole the pieces."

I let the thought steep. I'd never considered that Clive may not have acted on his own in this, that there may be someone else who knew what happened, but I couldn't discount Jack's theory. "You're right. We need to check that out." I handed the pictures back to him, and he slipped them back into the file. Before he got a chance to replace the file in the box, there was a knock on the door.

We both started. Jack turned and opened the door. A man dressed in a white shirt and dark tie but with no jacket stood in the doorway. He acknowledged my presence with a barely perceptible nod before turning his full attention to Jack. "I need to speak to you."

Jack turned to me. "I'll be right back. Feel free to take a look through this." He passed me the file, and with that he left the office, shutting the door behind him with a snick.

I leafed through the file for a few minutes while I waited for Jack to return, but there was no new information in it. I could tell that it wasn't the official FBI case file. It was probably just a file made up of nonsensitive information that I was allowed to see. That was annoying, but I would simply have to trust that Jack would keep me in the loop with all the pertinent info.

After twenty minutes of waiting, I crossed my

arms and my foot started tapping. I tried to temper the annoyance flooding me by remembering that it hadn't been easy for Jack to get me in here and to get me access to as much as he had, but I was tired of being cooped up in this little office.

No windows, no room to move, nothing to look at. Sick of it, I crossed the room, ready to leave. The knob turned under my hand and I took a quick step back, away from the opening door.

Jack strode in, crossing straight to the desk. He shoved the top back onto the box, grabbed his hat off the desk, and jerked it on before he turned to look at me. "We have to go. Now. Robert Follett was found shot dead in an alley behind the museum this morning."

Chapter 19

JACK DROVE us to the museum. It was hard to believe that two days ago we were there and Robert was alive and well. Now the man was dead. Jack had no details to share; all he could tell me was that a passerby found the body this morning and it appeared that he was killed sometime during the night.

Jack used his FBI credentials to keep the NYPD from moving the body or clearing the site until we got there.

My thoughts were whirling. Everything that had

happened in the past few days revolved around the two pins I'd just held in my hands. And now it seemed likely that Robert Follett was dead because of them. I couldn't imagine any other reason that someone would kill the innocuous man, but I needed to rearrange my thoughts so that I could look at the scene with impartiality.

We pulled into an alley behind the museum but were stopped only a few feet in by a police car blocking the lane. Jack tossed the car into park and our doors opened almost before the vehicle stopped moving.

Though it was a bright sunny day, the narrow alley was shadowy and dark. At least ten policemen stood around. From the number of cigarette butts on the ground I'd guess they'd been waiting around for a while for us to get there.

I stepped around a group of three policemen and brushed off a hand that tried to hold me back. Once I was past them, the body was right in front of me. I tried to avoid looking at his face, instead searching out the bullet holes. There were two holes in his lower chest with dried blood blooming dark and wicking outward, staining his blue knitted sweater-vest.

The familiar feeling of nausea rolled through me. I looked at Robert's face, blank in death, but it was someone else's face that I saw. Eyes filled with panic that drained into nothingness. Eyes that had haunted my dreams for years.

September 1937

The police descended on Fortune House like locusts. They came in full of bluster and demands, but their voices softened when they spoke to me, as though I were a small child. Their questions weren't soft, though. They were sharp and relentless.

"Where were you? Where were the men you saw? What did they look like? Did the man who was shot say anything before he died? In which direction did the killer run off?" The questions hammered down; I was asked the same things over and over again in different order.

Despite the haze in my mind I answered all of their questions. Everything inside me felt numb. I didn't even feel the tears until they splashed down onto my hands.

I rasped my hands across my face, rubbing hard, using the pressure to force the moisture back. Leaning forward, I buried my face in my hands, closed my eyes, and wished it would all just go away. The couch next to me creaked and shifted, and I felt a protective arm cross my shoulders.

"She's told you everything she knows. Leave her alone now. She's exhausted."

I didn't open my eyes; I just sank into the protection David offered. I heard the police officers moving away, and after a moment, the coolness of air against my neck replaced the warmth of David's arm.

"Are you all right?"

I opened my eyes. He was next to me, elbows propped on his knees, his dark brown eyes searching my face for the answer. When I met his gaze he stared for a long moment, then turned away. I wished for a second that I could see his face again, but from my position I could only make out his profile softened by the dark hair that fell across his brow.

"I don't think so. I don't feel all right." I was unable to lie, to say that everything was fine. The layer of pretense and easy answers had been stripped away.

"I'm sorry you had to see that." He moved his head back toward me, and a ghost of a smile crossed his lips. "What were you doing there anyway? I thought we agreed that you were going to stay away from the reservoir after dark." It was said lightly. I wanted to smile back at him, to keep my eyes on his long enough to read the questions that lay just under the surface, but instead I turned away.

"I needed some time alone to think." I couldn't tell him the truth, that I'd been waiting around, hoping to see him again. "I was ready to leave before the sun started to go down, but that's when I heard the shot."

David moved a few inches farther away, then looked back at me. "The police are going to be done here soon. Is there anything else I can do for you?"

The thought of being alone in the house brought a lump of cold nausea to my stomach, but I pasted a smile on my face, denying the fear. "The housekeeper lives in a little cottage out back. So I won't really be alone. I'll be fine."

He didn't believe me. It was obvious from his raised eyebrow. "Do you want me to go get her so she can stay the night with you in the house?"

"No. I don't want to talk about it. I can't tell the story again. Not tonight."

He sighed, but nodded. "Let me just go find out how long the police intend to stay. I can stay with you until they leave."

I agreed, more thankful than he could know. I wanted to cling to him, to let myself be protected, but I knew he had to leave. Without the police there, it would be entirely improper for him to be in the house. But never had propriety seemed so irrelevant.

David pushed himself off the couch and moved into the dining room where the two remaining police officers stood talking. I watched them speak, not really listening. The police were apparently questioning David too. I half listened to hear his answers.

"I was meeting her at the reservoir. She must have gotten there early. When I arrived, the man had already been shot, and she was leaning over him."

The words confused me. He hadn't been there to meet me, and I wondered why he would tell the police that. Too tired and disconnected to try to reason it out, I stopped listening and my mind shut off.

I let my eyes drift shut and relaxed into the peaceful blackness. I took several deep breaths and tried to relax. Slowly my mind formed a picture. The dead man lay on the sidewalk. There was blood on my hands and on my shoes. I wanted to run, but I couldn't move. I didn't know which way to go. The dead man grabbed my ankle, his bony hands squeezing. Terror gripped me and I screamed and tried to get away.

Another hand grasped my shoulder and pulled at me, and my screams turned to shrieks. A gentle shaking motion and deep voice penetrated past my screams.

"Alexandra, it's okay. Open your eyes. I'm here. Wake up. It's all over now."

The words soaked into my brain, and I forced myself to open my eyes. David knelt in front of me, panic swamping his eyes. My heart crashed in my chest, loud as rain on a rooftop, and I struggled against the crushing pressure in my lungs. My throat was dry and scratchy, telling me that my screams hadn't just been in my dream.

"I'm sorry. I think I fell asleep." I felt a blush crawl up my cheeks and tried to avoid the wide-eyed stares of the policemen in the other room. I avoided David's gaze, embarrassed and shaken by my dream. He reached out and held my hands with his own. I stared at my small fingers resting lightly on his wide calloused ones, keeping my gaze down to avoid his eyes.

"There is no way you can stay alone tonight. Let me go and get the housekeeper."

I nodded, relieved that I wouldn't be alone, but David didn't leave. I looked up and found myself staring into his deep brown eyes.

"Alexandra, it's okay to be afraid. The things you've seen tonight would give anyone nightmares."

"Even you?"

"I think that the sounds of you screaming in your sleep will haunt my dreams for a long time to come." He didn't give me time to process his statement. "I'm going to go and get the housekeeper now."

My hands, still held loosely in his, tightened. "Please. Don't leave." I tried to hold the words back, but they escaped despite my best efforts.

David's body tensed, then relaxed. "Why don't I ask one of the officers to do it? That way I can stay with you until she gets here."

Relief swamped me and I felt the tightness in my lungs relax. He took that for assent. Within minutes one of the police officers was back with Mrs. Higgins in tow. She kept Fortune House running like a well-oiled engine. While she'd never been warm or motherly toward me, I still felt safe when I saw her come in. I knew that she would take care of things now.

As she arrived, the police got ready to leave. David went to speak to them again, but never left my line of sight.

"Do you want warm milk?" The gruff question didn't match the look of concern in Mrs. Higgins's eyes. I didn't, but accepted anyway. She bustled through to the kitchen while I watched the police at last take their leave.

David shut the door behind them and crossed back over to me. "I have to go now too. Are you sure you'll be all right now?"

I nodded, even though I was fairly sure it was a lie. I rose from the couch and walked with him to the door. He opened it and crossed the threshold before turning back to look at me.

He held my gaze for a long minute, looked as though he was going to say something, but instead gave me a nod and moved to walk down the steps. My hand on his arm stopped him and he turned back to look at me. Slowly he turned all the way back around.

My breath stalled in my chest and I felt my cheeks heat. I pulled my hand away from his arm. Long seconds passed, my mind blank, unable to remember what it was I wanted to say. David's dark eyes never wavered. He took a tiny step forward. Finally I found my voice. "I just wanted to say thank you for being there tonight." It came out as a whisper.

David shook his head slowly. "I wish there hadn't been a need." He remained motionless, cryptic emotions swirling in his eyes.

I took a tiny step forward, was drawn closer. He pulled his gaze away from me and shook his head again before taking a step back. "Good night, Alexandra."

I wanted desperately to prolong this but didn't know how or why. "Allie. Everyone calls me Allie."

His mouth quirked in a half smile. "You look more like an Alexandra to me." With that he walked away, and I moved back inside and shut the door. The few minutes we'd stood there left me breathless and confused. But for the first time that night, not afraid.

As I stood next to the body of Robert Follett, memories of that night washed over me. The memory of the concern in David's eyes rolled over me like a riptide, pushing me forward only to suck me back.

I rubbed my temples and drew in a deep breath to clear my thoughts.

Jack came up behind me. "Are you okay? I didn't think you were going to come and actually see the body. You could have stayed in the car."

I looked at him and smiled. "It's not my first dead body, Jack. I'm not really the wait-in-the-car type."

He laughed. "No, you certainly aren't."

Chapter 20

JACK POKED around the murder scene for a little over an hour. I mostly stayed out of his way. While I am a private investigator, this was murder. I was not the expert here. I wasn't really sure how much there was to see anyway. Other than the body, nothing caught my eye at the crime scene. Still Jack checked the pavement inch by inch for any sign of a clue.

When he was ready to go, we went around to the front of the museum. We walked in, ignoring the museum staff, and headed directly for Robert's office.

I knew from the last time we were here that Robert's office was a mess, but there was no way we could miss signs that the room had been sacked and searched. Bits of pottery that had been strewn around the desk now lay on the floor, ground into tiny bits. Books were tossed to the floor, some lying open, some closed. It looked as though someone had flipped through the pages of each book, searching for something.

I didn't know what the murderer thought Robert had in his possession, but I had a few guesses. I doubted that anyone believed he still had any of the gold, but perhaps information on the whereabouts of Clive and Mary.

I didn't share my thoughts with Jack; I just stood back and watched him work. He took in the scene from the doorway as though committing the room to memory. From what I'd seen of Jack's ability to recall anything he saw, I didn't doubt that's what he was doing.

"What do you think? Who would kill Robert and why?"

I pondered his question for a moment. "The only

obvious motive I can think of is if someone thought that he knew where Clive and Mary were hiding out with the gold. I mean, he's the one they originally came to with the pieces, and so it stands to reason that they might confide in him where they were hiding out."

"Okay, but it's clear that he was murdered before his office was searched, so it would seem unlikely that he gave his killer the information they wanted."

"What makes you say that?"

Jack scanned the room. "Robert was killed in the alley. He was probably meeting someone there, most likely someone he knew. My theory is that they got him to meet them under false pretenses, and then when they had him alone in the alley, they questioned him at gunpoint. Robert was not a brave man. If he was looking into the barrel of a gun, I don't think he'd hesitate to tell them whatever he knew."

"But Robert really didn't know anything."

"I agree. Anyway, he had no information to give, and he was shot and killed in that alley. The killer then took his keys out of his pocket—we know this because Robert's keys weren't on the body and the police found them inside the museum. They used his keys to gain entrance to the museum and to Robert's office. The search appears to have been a matter of being thorough."

"So you don't think the murderer learned anything, either from Robert or from searching through his office?"

"No, I don't. I think Robert told us everything he knew, and I don't think he's had any contact with Clive or Mary since the day they sold him the gold pieces."

I turned to assess the destruction in the room. "Who do you think would kill him over the vague possibility that he knew something he wasn't telling?"

Jack sighed. "I've got a few ideas, but it's too soon to talk about them yet. Let's poke around a little more, and then I think we should go check out the Follett house. I have a feeling that whoever did this isn't going to rest until they've probed every angle."

"Okay, I'm not sure what I'm looking for, but I'll search."

We spent an hour combing the room for anything that could have been left behind by the perpetrator.

Jack moved back to the doorway and beckoned me over. "Try to see the room as a whole. What does the scene tell you about the person who searched it?"

I'd never looked at a crime scene the way Jack did, but he seemed to see much more than me, so I was willing to give his method a try. I tried to distance myself from the details and get a good view of the big picture. What I saw was the absolute destruction of the room.

"The room has been ransacked thoroughly."

"That's right. The person who did this wasn't rushed; they took the time to check each book, each drawer, every artifact. In fact, I can't see a single thing that they missed. This isn't the work of a flustered amateur. My guess is that a pro did this."

"A pro?"

"Someone who could kill a man at close range and in cold blood and then go on to calmly search his office for something. That's not the mark of your average killer. It's the matter-of-factness of this crime that's bothering me the most."

I saw instantly that he was right. "What does that mean? What kind of pro?"

He just shook his head. "We've seen all there is to see here; let's go check out his home address."

He led the way to the car, and the last thing I saw as we reversed out of the alley was a dark-suited man pulling a white sheet over Robert Follett's face.

Chapter 21

JACK DROVE us across town to the Follett house. I took a moment to hope that Robert's mother wouldn't be there. I couldn't imagine what it would be like to find out that your child had been killed, but to have people crawling around your home, asking questions and poking through his things during your grief would be almost unbearable. Shaking the thoughts and the sympathy away, I realized that Jack was talking to me.

"For their sake, I sure hope we find Clive and Mary before anyone else does."

I nodded. If whoever was after them killed a man for information he didn't even have, I couldn't imagine what they would do to Clive and Mary to get their hands on the gold.

Jack pulled onto a residential street and parked in front of a bland home. I took a deep breath to gird myself before shoving the door open and stepping onto the curb.

Jack came around to where I stood, and we walked up to the house side by side. Knocking on the door, I held my breath. Within seconds the door swung open to reveal a heavy-set woman of about seventy. She had limp grey hair and red-rimmed eyes. She held a handkerchief in her hands and dabbed at her eyes before greeting us.

"Hello?"

"Ma'am, I am Special Agent Jack O'Connor with the FBI," Jack whipped out his badge and showed it to the woman before continuing, "and this is my partner, Miss Fortune. May we come in?"

The woman stepped back and let us pass through into the house. I didn't have a conscious idea of what Robert Follett's home would look like, but the austere cleanliness surprised me. The smell of bleach and detergent hung in the air, and there wasn't a speck of dirt or dust to be found anywhere in the part of the house I could see. I couldn't imagine how a man like Robert could have grown up in an environment like this and still have been such a slob.

Shaking off the irrelevant thoughts, I turned to Mrs. Follett. "I am very sorry for your loss, ma'am." The words sounded hollow and perfunctory, but they were sincere.

She looked into my eyes for a long second, then nodded. "Thank you. It's hard to imagine how God can work this out for good, but I just have to trust that He will."

Surprised and uncomfortable at the words, I moved away a little. "For good?"

She cocked her head. "If you're willing to trust the Father during the good times, you need to also be willing to trust Him despite the evil things. Everything works together according to His good purpose. That is not just a Bible verse, Miss Fortune; it's a promise. And it's all I've got to hold on to at the moment."

I had no idea what to say to this. Wearing faith on your sleeve like this was completely foreign to me. I felt uncomfortable and slightly awed by her statement.

Taking a step back, I tried to shift back into impersonal investigator mode.

"Could you show us Robert's living quarters, please, ma'am?" Jack came to my rescue by reminding the elderly woman about the reason for our visit.

Mrs. Follett showed us downstairs where Robert lived and left us alone in the dim mustiness. It was like being in another house entirely. While the upstairs had been austere to the point of sterile, the downstairs looked as though it needed ten men with strong backs and shovels to clean it out. Down there, there was no smell of bleach; it was more the smell of dirty socks. I longed to open the window to release the stale air, but instead I stood on the landing observing the scene the way Jack had showed me.

We both stood there for long moments before I spoke. "I don't think anyone's been through here."

Jack nodded.

"It's messy enough, but I think that's just how Robert lived. This looks more like his office did before he died."

"I agree. The question is, why didn't the person who killed Follett search here? It's the next logical step. Why go to all the work of killing a man and ransacking his office for information if you're not going to go all the way and search his home as well?"

I didn't have the answer. It didn't make sense to me either.

"Let's go back upstairs and talk to Mrs. Follett. I have a couple of questions I'd like to ask her."

I didn't say anything, just followed Jack back up into the light.

"Mrs. Follett, I know that you've had a terrible shock today, but I was hoping to ask you a few questions that might help us in our investigation."

Mrs. Follett nodded.

"Has anyone besides the two of us been down into Robert's living area in the past twenty-four hours?"

She shook her head, the sadness in her eyes unchanging.

"Has there been anything that you would deem as suspicious happen in the last several days? Salesmen coming to the door trying to get in, or workmen without work orders? Anything that didn't seem right at the time, but that you might have brushed off?"

She pondered this for a moment, but again shook her head. "Nothing that I can think of. The only strange thing had been Robert's behavior. He seemed nervous and upset. He would come home from work and go straight downstairs. He didn't even want his dinner. I told him that he was starting to look unhealthy and advised him to see a doctor. He told me that it was just difficult at work, but that things would be back to normal soon."

I knew exactly why he'd been nervous and upset,

but it would serve no purpose to tell his mother that he had been caught fencing stolen artifacts.

"Okay, thank you for your time, ma'am. We're going to do everything we can to find out who killed your son." Only because I was starting to know him could I hear the disappointment in Jack's voice.

We didn't seem to be much farther ahead in our investigation, and that was discouraging, but I had the feeling that changes were coming our way. Half of the success of any investigation was achieved through perseverance alone. We just had to keep asking questions and eventually we'd come up with some new information.

Mrs. Follett walked us to the door and held it open for us. I wanted to offer her some sort of comfort, but nothing I could say would have made a difference. What did come out of my mouth shocked me. "I'll be praying for you, Mrs. Follett. I don't know if God will listen, but I'll ask Him to give you the strength you'll need to get through this." I couldn't have been more shocked at the words that tumbled out of my mouth if I had suddenly started speaking Japanese.

Jack gave me a sidelong glance, then turned to the older woman. "As will I, ma'am." He reached into his jacket pocket and brought out his badge case again. This time he slid a business card out of it and handed it to her. "If there's anything you need, feel free to call me."

She reached out for the card and pulled it from his fingers. "Thank you, Mr. O'Connor. And there is one thing. I'm not sure if it's important enough for me to mention, but it does seem a bit odd."

Jack's posture changed, subtly, but I saw him go from resigned to alert in a split second. "Nothing is too trivial to mention."

"Well"—she folded the handkerchief in her hands into thirds as she spoke—"there has been a strange car parked a few houses down from here for several days." She pointed out a nondescript green vehicle. "I've lived on this street for over forty years, and I know all my neighbors and what they drive. This vehicle doesn't belong to any of them. It's nothing really, just something I noticed." She seemed embarrassed to have brought it up.

Jack took a small step toward her, reached out his hand, and laid it on her arm. "That is exactly the kind of information that we are looking for. Thank you for telling us. We'll check it out. And please, ma'am, for the next few days, be extra cautious."

With that we walked out the door and down the front steps.

I waited until we were back in the car to speak. "What should we do?"

Jack turned to look at me as he started the car with a roar. "How do you feel about doing a little surveillance work?"

I grinned back at him. "If it gets us closer to a break on this case, I'm all for it."

He shoved the car into gear and pulled out onto the street. "Let's get some dinner, and then we'll come back and watch the strange car to see if it's watching the Follett house."

"Sounds like a good plan to me."

We grabbed sandwiches and Cokes at a nearby deli, then headed back to the Folletts' street. We parked way down from the house and about three cars behind the car we set out to watch.

I could see that the vehicle was occupied and that the windows were rolled down, but beyond that, nothing. We rolled down our own windows and prepared to wait. As darkness fell and lights twinkled on in the houses along the street, I closed my eyes, trying to catch a quick nap.

With my eyes closed my thoughts drifted of their own volition to David.

February 1939

IT HAD BEEN MORE than a year since I'd seen him. I never lingered at the reservoir anymore. Although the blood had washed away with the rain, I still saw the body and heard the shot every time I walked along the path. What had once been my favorite thinking spot was now just a reminder of a night I wished I could forget. I longed to forget everything about it, except one part.

David Rubeneski. I said the name to myself sometimes, just to be sure that I didn't forget him. He'd rescued me twice, then vanished, and I almost had to wonder if he'd ever been real in the first place.

I didn't see him again until a cold, windy February night when no one should've been out. Wind howled and rattled the windows, and the tree branches shook and snapped. I sat on the sofa reading a book, thankful for the fire in the hearth and that I was inside, when there was a knock at the back door. It wasn't a knock as much as repeated banging. It was almost eleven, and the sudden thunder of noise made my heart race.

I was the only one home; Mother and Dad were out at some charity weekend in the country. I raced through the dining room and kitchen to the back door. Fear had me by the throat, but the pounding on the door sounded so urgent, I had to see who was there.

I reached out and grabbed the knob, holding it still, before moving the curtains aside. My pent-up breath left in a rush and my heart raced faster when I recognized his profile. David stood there. Actually he leaned against the door, one arm tucked in close to his side, the other hand raised and pounding on the wood. He rested his head against the door and pounded again.

Pushing the shock away, I unlatched the door and threw it open. David nearly toppled in onto me at the sudden lack of resistance.

"What are you doing here?" I wrapped my arms

around him to steady him. He weaved on his feet as though unable to find his balance. I stared at him in shock. "Have you been drinking?" The question popped out, but taking a closer look at him I realized that this wasn't it. Something was really wrong. "David. Are you okay?" He leaned against me, and it took all my strength to push him far enough away to get a look at him. He still held his arm cradled close to his body, but now I could see that he was bleeding. "David!" Horror flooded through me.

"Alexandra." His voice was soft, like a whisper against my ear. "Can you get me to a chair? I don't know how long I can stay standing."

Immediately I turned and slung his arm around my neck. He leaned into me and I guided him to the closest chair in the living room. The effort of staying on his feet and moving was obvious by his panting breath. He leaned heavily on me, and within a few feet I was breathing just as hard. When I finally got him over to a sofa, I tried to lower him gently, but the impact still wrenched a groan from him.

His eyes were closed as he slumped into the corner of the sofa. I got my first good look at him. His face was pale as wax, and there was a bloom of dark wetness around the shoulder of his woolen coat. I reached out and ran my fingers through it, not the least surprised at the bright red blood coating them when I pulled back.

"David, what can I do?" Kernels of panic jumped in my throat. The sight of blood, from what I guessed was a gunshot wound, made me light-headed. Forcing myself to breathe, I worked at remaining calm. "You're hurt. How can I help?" I shook my head. What was I saying? "I'm going to call you an ambulance. I'll get you to a hospital as fast as I can." I moved to the table next to the couch and picked up the receiver, but David lunged toward me and slammed his hand on top of mine, forcing the receiver back into its cradle.

"No. Please. Don't call anyone. I came here because I couldn't think of anyone else I could trust. I need you to promise that you won't let anyone know I'm here."

"But what am I supposed to do? Let you bleed to death on the couch in front of me?" My voice rose in pitch as bubbles of hysteria forced their way up my throat.

"Just give me a place to stay and maybe you can help me see how bad this wound is. That's it. That's all I'm asking, and I wouldn't be here if I had any other choice."

Jack's voice woke me. I opened my eyes and for a second I couldn't remember where I was. My neck ached and it was now fully dark. I pushed myself up. "How long have I been asleep?" The words came out slurred and gritty.

"An hour or so. I hated to cut short your nap, but it looks like we're going to have to get moving. They've started the car and are about to move out.

We have to follow them if we want to find out who's been watching the Follett house."

The car pulled out onto the street, and all I could make out were its red taillights glowing in the darkness.

Jack followed the car with ease, staying several car lengths back, and it appeared that the people who'd been watching the house had no idea that they were being followed.

The car drove through the city for about half an hour and finally stopped outside a familiar landmark. We were a block away from Clive and Mary's apartment, dispelling all doubts about the intent of the occupants of the car. They were clearly involved in the pursuit of Helen's Gold.

We parked half a block down from the other car. Jack killed the headlights but kept the car running.

"What's the plan? We're not going to sit here all night watching whoever that is up there watching Clive and Mary's place, are we?" Impatience simmered through the words. I'd had about all I could take of sitting around and waiting.

"No, I think it's time to introduce ourselves to the gentlemen in the green car."

Chapter 22

WE WALKED through the semidarkness, avoiding the golden circles of light given off by streetlights and sticking to the shadows as we made our way up to the car. Jack veered off the sidewalk and headed for the driver's window while I moved silently toward the passenger side. As I approached I noticed that the car was running and the windows were rolled all the way down, with the man in the passenger seat leaning out as far as he comfortably could.

I crossed the final few feet to the car door and sought out Jack's form in the dark on the other side of the car. He nodded, and I yanked the door latch and jerked the car door open as hard and as fast as possible. I caught the man in the passenger seat off guard, and he tumbled right out of the seat and onto the concrete. I heard a resounding crack that I guessed was his elbow connecting with the concrete.

From Jack's side of the car I heard heavily accented cursing and the sounds of a struggle.

I didn't let my attention wander, because the man I'd toppled onto the street came up swinging. My stomach shriveled as I watched him stand up. He must have been two hundred fifty pounds and about six foot five. I had to tilt my head back to see him, but I only let myself be cowed by his size for a second. Everyone had vulnerabilities. Huge hammerheads like this guy only had a bit more size on their side.

I ducked as he swung a massive fist at my face. Enraged, he bounced on the balls of his feet and swung again. I skittered out of his fist's trajectory. Seeking out a vulnerable spot, I threw all my weight behind a kick aimed at the outside of his right knee. His leg buckled, sending him down to the pavement with a groan. I covered his distended knee with my foot to keep him immobile.

I saw him reach into his jacket, and I moved like lightning to grab the gun out of his hand before he even had it fully out of the holster. Using it as a prod, I motioned for him to get up. He did so slowly, groaning as he put weight on his knee. I waved him back into the car, keeping the gun trained on him at all times. He complied without a word, but the look of loathing and rage he sent me was truly ugly.

Once he was back in his seat, I closed his door and let myself into the seat directly behind him.

"What do you want from us?" These were the first words spoken. I thought I had an idea of who these guys were, but this man's flat Midwestern accent seemed to belie my assumptions.

Jack yanked the driver's door open and shoved the other man back into the car, then got into the backseat beside me.

I moved the gun from one man to the other until

Jack was settled and took over covering one of the men.

"Why were you watching the Follett house earlier today, and why are you watching the Gordons' place now?" Jack got right down to business.

The man in the driver's seat just scowled, but the one in front of me spoke for both of them. "We don't know who you're talking about. We were just sitting in the car when you came up and attacked us. We should call the police."

"You do that, Boris. I have no problem conducting this little interview from the police station."

"Boris? You have me mistaken for someone else, I fear." The nasal twang in his voice proclaimed one thing, but from the look of skepticism on Jack's face, I'd say that he believed something else.

"You've been watching Mary for over a week now. You were the ones who followed her, spooked her, and you were the ones who ransacked her apartment looking for the gold."

"We don't know what you're talking about."

I took a close look at the two men. They were both tall and raw-boned, but they could both be mistaken for small-town American men. The kind who'd been football heroes in high school and who now owned businesses in small towns with names like Woodpile or Riverside. I'd never given it too much thought, but I'd always assumed that I'd be able to pick out a Soviet spy with no effort at all. In my imaginings they had heavy accents and called everyone Comrade. These two men seemed as American as the stars and stripes. It made a shiver run down my spine to contemplate it.

The guy in front of me matched Mary's description of Overcoat precisely. I shuddered to think of what these men were capable of doing to Mary or Clive, or what they'd already done to poor Robert Follett, in order to get their hands on the gold.

Jack turned to me but kept his gun trained on the back of the driver's neck. "Do you see what I see?"

I had no idea what he was talking about, so I turned to see what he was looking at. His gaze was focused on Clive and Mary's apartment window.

At first I didn't see anything, but after a second, I saw a shadow flit past the window. "They're up there!" I couldn't believe that they would be stupid enough to come back to their apartment.

"Someone's up there," Jack qualified. "Can you keep these two under control if I go up to check it out?"

I saw Overcoat's shoulders tense, as though he was already planning how he was going to overpower me. Jack saw it too and shook his head.

"No, that's not going to work." He sat in silence for a moment, then handed me his gun to hold with my free hand. "I'll just be a sec; I have to run to the car for a minute. I'll be right back. If either of these men moves, feel free to shoot."

I nodded and hoped that I wouldn't be forced to use either gun.

Chapter 23

JACK SLIPPED out of the car, and I heard the pounding of his shoes as he ran back to the car. Neither man moved.

"We are not who you seem to think we are. If you'd just let us show you our identification, we could prove it." Overcoat's tone was soft yet commanding.

I refused to acknowledge his words other than to tell him to be quiet.

I never took my eyes off either man until I heard the click of the door opening and saw Jack slide back in, something shiny glinting in his hands.

He draped one set of handcuffs over my forearm. "I took these out of my pocket when we were surveilling." He went to work securing both of the driver's hands to the steering wheel.

I handed Jack his gun and mine, waited until he was ready, then leaned over the seat, grabbed Overcoat's left wrist, and snapped the shackle onto it. Searching for something to weave the cuff through, I found nothing except the steering wheel. I threaded the chain through the wheel and yanked the man closer to it. I slapped the cuff on his other wrist and then recovered the gun from Jack.

In a hurry now, we popped the back doors of the car open and let ourselves out. I glanced up at the window but saw no sign of the movement we'd spotted earlier. Praying that we weren't too late, we yanked open the door and bounded up the stairs to Clive and Mary's third-floor apartment.

Doing the best I could not to make a racket climbing the stairs, I ended up several seconds behind Jack. When I arrived at the third-floor landing, Jack stuck his arm out, motioning for me to be still. Standing in front of me, he crept toward the apartment door in silence. I noticed then that the door, while mostly closed, was not shut, and that there were scrape marks in the wood, evidence that the door had apparently been levered open.

The idea that it was Mary and Clive in there was dwindling by the second. Glad for the gun I still carried at the ready, I lined up behind Jack along the hallway and forced myself to take a deep breath. Jack turned his head toward me. "On the count of three." He breathed.

"One." His mouth formed the words, but no sound accompanied them.

"Two."

"Three." We burst in through the open door, guns at the ready, prepared for whatever we found.

Moving through the doorway we had a clear view of a living room and a hallway. The furniture in the room was destroyed. Vicious hacks in the upholstery left foam and guts hanging out like entrails. Shelves were emptied, their contents of books and knickknacks tossed to the floor and broken. A mirror on the wall hung crooked and had a spiderweb of cracks darkening it.

Jack and I crept through the room in silence. No one was in the living room, but we both seemed to feel that there was still a hostile presence in the place. Jack motioned for me to follow him down the hall, and we paused just outside the first doorway.

There was a noise, something distinctly out of place in an empty apartment, and my heart tripped, breath backing up in my throat. Jack nodded his head once and we burst through the door. There was very little room to move, as it was a tiny bedroom and most of the floor space that wasn't taken up by a bed and a dresser was covered in rubble. On the opposite side of the bed stood two men. They both wore long black leather jackets and gloves despite the heat. One had black-rimmed glasses, and they both held guns pointed directly at us. Our guns pointed back at them in a classic and dangerous Mexican standoff. I moved along the edge of the bed, two feet farther away from Jack, to get into a better defensive position. I tried to ignore the dread that came from the sight of the gun barrel pointed at the center of my forehead and focused all my energy into controlling the slight tremble in my own gun hand.

The man Jack had in his sights took a small step back, toward the wall, his eyes never leaving mine. His gun dipped slightly, its trajectory more in line with my nose for a second before he brought it back up. The man I had in my sights, the one with a gun pointed at Jack, hadn't moved an inch; he didn't even appear to be breathing.

Faster than I could think, the man raised his gun to the ceiling and pulled the trigger. The sound of shattering glass brought my gaze up just in time to see the light fixture explode. Heat scorched the length of my cheekbone, and another rivulet of fire seemed to scorch the length of my arm. I was stunned for only a second, then looked back down in time to see both men on their way out of the bedroom window to the safety of the fire escape.

Jack leapt over onto the top of the bed and lunged for the window. Missing the second man by inches, he slammed his hand against the windowsill in frustration. I heard the clatter of shoes on metal running down the fire escape. Jack turned back to look at me, probably checking to make sure I was behind him, but I was frozen to the spot. Dazed, I ran my hand down the tingling heat of my face.

"Allie!"

My hand felt slow and clumsy as I trailed it across my cheek, leaving a trail of wet and stickiness behind. Confused, I rubbed at my cheek again. As the back of my hand brushed my face, pain came alive, shooting through the side of my face with the burning intensity of acid etching stone.

Jack looked back to the window for a moment, but it was apparent that the men were out of his reach now. Circling the bed, he came to my side. "That's a deep cut. Let me take a look at it."

I moved my head as little as possible but enough so that my cheek was facing him. The stretch and pull of the broken skin made me wince, and I suddenly became aware of pain in my arm.

Jack took a deep breath and probed his fingers gently across my face. It only took a moment for him to make his assessment. "We need to clean that up. It's deep." He grabbed my hand and led me out of the room.

February 1939

"DAVID, YOU'RE BLEEDING all over the place. We need to stop it." I felt the edges of control slipping through my fingers. "David. What should I do?"

"Get clean towels. And alcohol if you've got any. Bring them back here along with some sort of strips of cloth. I can take care of the rest." The effort of talking seemed to drain him. His eyes closed and his head lolled against the back of the couch.

Forcing myself to leave his side, I headed for the kitchen to get what he asked for. I grabbed a stack of freshly laundered white towels, a bottle of my father's best single malt scotch, and a length of twine from the kitchen drawer.

Supplies gathered, I rushed back into the living

room. David hadn't moved. I deposited my supplies onto the coffee table and shifted closer to him. Terror swamped me as the image of another man covered in blood came to the front of my mind. I reached out and held my open palm to his chest. The feel of solid muscle and his steady breathing relieved my worst fear.

I ran my hand along his face, trying to gently wake him. His jaw was rough with stubble against my hand, and I let myself stare. His eyes were closed and he looked peaceful, but I knew that when they opened, the brown depths would be full of restlessness. Dark hair fell over his heavy brow. All his features were strong, solid. Apparently I hadn't forgotten even the smallest detail since I'd seen him last.

"David, I need your help. I don't know what to do." I jostled his uninjured shoulder, desperate to wake him up.

He turned his face away and mumbled something, so I shook him again. This time his eyes opened.

"Alexandra?" The words came out a hoarse whisper. There was a pause as he looked around. "What are you doing here? I promised I would stay away. Why are you here?"

I made myself smile. "This is my house. You came to me. You need help because you've been shot, I think, but I need you to tell me what to do."

He pushed himself up with his uninjured arm and looked around. Spotting the supplies on the table, he lowered himself back to a semireclining position. "I hate to ask you, but I'm going to need help. I have to get my coat and my shirt off. Can you help me do that?"

I hated the fact that I was blushing. This was no time for propriety. If I didn't work quickly, David could bleed to death in front of me. "Of course. Just tell me what you want me to do."

"Okay, we need to get the coat off. Start with the good side first." He shrugged his shoulder and I helped him slip the jacket off his one side. He was out of breath by the time his arm was clear, and there was a fine coating of sweat along his brow. "Okay, now we have to get the other side off. I'm going to sit up; see if you can tug gently on the sleeve." He took a minute to gather his strength, then levered himself forward. I did my best to pull the coat off, while trying not to notice his hiss of pain.

When his arm was free, I got a better look at the wound. The crimson stain on his Oxford shirt circled a ragged hole in his upper shoulder. I knew we were going to have to get the shirt off too, and I knew it was going to be more painful than removing the coat. There were strings of fabric embedded in the wound from the frayed edges of his shirt. The thought of ripping those out made my stomach lurch.

David's eyes flickered open and he tried to send me a smile. "Okay, time for more fun. I'm going to help you as much as I can, but no matter what happens, you need to get the job done, all right?"

I nodded, feeling sick.

"Once you have the fabric away from the wound, the blood is really going to start flowing again, so you'll have to be ready with some towels. Press down hard to stop the bleeding." He stopped his instructions to take a few deep breaths. "You're going to have to pour the alcohol into the wound then. Front and back. Really douse it. Please." He fell silent for a moment. "I'm really sorry to ask you to do all this, but I didn't have anywhere else to turn."

I didn't answer.

"Are we ready to start then?"

I moved all of my supplies closer and rehearsed the steps in my head. Once I ran through it a few times, I nodded at David.

"I guess I'm ready as I'll ever be."

I started by unbuttoning his shirt, beginning at the neck, until it was wide open. I forced all thought aside except for what came next. David pushed himself forward again, and I removed the shirt from his good arm. Maneuvering carefully, I waited until I was in perfect position.

He took a deep breath and then I slid the sleeve off his shoulder. The threads pulled out and tore open bits of the wound. There was a muffled yell, and David jerked. I froze for a second, then forced myself to continue. Blocking every thought other than getting the rest of the shirt off, I inched it down off his arm. A sudden rush of blood at the newly reopened wound ran down his chest and arm and over my hands. There was another jerk and then he slumped to the side. I turned my eyes to him, relieved that he'd finally passed out. I grabbed the stack of towels and put one between the couch and his shoulder, and one on the front of the wound. Blood welled, bright red, but I covered it with the brilliant white towels. I pressed, as hard as I dared, knowing that it was the only way to slow the blood loss.

David moaned quietly and tossed his head. I had to gear myself up for the next bit. Grabbing the bottle of scotch, I brought it toward me and flicked off the lid one-handed. Holding it by the neck, I brought it toward where my hand was pressed. The noxious scent of oak and whisky assaulted my senses. I pulled back the cloth, and blood welled immediately at the cease of pressure. Tipping the bottle, I dumped alcohol directly onto the wound. David's entire body went stiff and he cried out, but his eyes never opened. I was sweating and nauseous, but couldn't stop now. I levered him over, removed the cloth from the exit wound, and poured the liquor into it too. David was unresponsive this time, and for that I was thankful.

I set the bottle down and pressed the towels back onto the cleaned-out wound. I grabbed the kitchen twine and proceeded to wrap the wound in yet another towel, and then I tied the whole thing together with the string. When the twine was knotted, I leaned back and let out a deep breath. David was quiet, no sign of movement.

Relief washed over me with the force of an ocean wave. Exhaustion followed right on its heels. I sat down on the sofa next to him, let my head fall back, and let my mind empty. Sleep came immediately.

Jack cleaned out my cuts as best he could, wrapped my arm in a washcloth, and gave me another cloth to hold against my cheek. We shut the door on Clive and Mary's apartment and went back to where we'd left the Soviets. All that greeted us was an empty parking space.

He turned to me. "I forgot to take their keys."

I had to suppress a laugh. I tried to picture the two men driving while handcuffed to their own steering wheel. "I hope they didn't have to make too many left turns."

Jack grinned and I tried to ignore the giggles rising in my throat at the thought.

"Let's just call it a night. Why don't you take me back to the office?"

Jack looked worried. "You should probably get those cuts checked out by a doctor."

I pulled the cloth from my cheek and felt for wetness. "I'd rather not. I think the bleeding has almost stopped. You did a good job cleaning it out, and I just want to lie down on my couch."

"We'll see. I'll take another look in better light and we'll decide if you need to go for stitches. That's all I'm willing to promise."

"Fair enough. Lead on, Agent O'Connor."

Chapter 24

IT FELT LIKE weeks since I'd been in the office instead of hours. I unlocked the door and flipped on the lights. It had been a quiet ride home, a combination of reflecting on everything that had happened and trying to ignore the pain on my cheek and on my arm.

As soon as I had the door shut behind us, Jack put his hand on my shoulder and turned me toward him. He tilted my face for a better look and probed gently with his fingers. "I don't know. It's stopped bleeding for the most part, but it's still pretty deep. I think maybe you should get it stitched."

I moved away from him and walked toward a small mirror that hung on the wall. The whole side of my face was red, and there were little streaks of dried blood smeared along my skin. The cut itself was maybe two and a half inches long, but it was more of a slice than a cut. The skin edges seemed to pull together of their own volition. "I'm going to leave it the way it is. The most they can do for me at a hospital is stitch it. It doesn't seem to need it. As long as I don't do a lot of smiling or laughing in the next few days, I probably won't have too bad of a scar."

Jack looked horrified. "I hadn't thought of that. It's going to scar."

I smiled a little. Not enough to cause the cut to split open again. "Yeah, I'm pretty sure."

"I'm so sorry, Allie. I never should have gotten you involved in this."

"Believe me, Jack, there are worse things in life than a scar."

"Still . . ." He looked pained.

I decided it was time for a drastic change of subject. "This is going to seem nosy, 'cause it is, but I have to ask."

Jack watched me in silence.

"Who's Maggie?"

His head jerked back and his breath huffed out. After a minute, he moved to sit on the couch. "How do you know about Maggie?"

Confession time. "I happened to see a picture of her in your apartment the other morning."

Jack was silent for a moment. "That's what the breakfast was about." The realization dawned in his eyes. "You felt bad because you'd been snooping."

My face heated. "Guilty."

He laughed, there was a second of silence, and then he sighed. "Maggie."

I moved to sit in a chair across from the couch.

"Maggie grew up in the house three doors down from mine. I'd known her since she was five years old. She was a year younger than me, and a girl, so she was of no consequence in my world until the day both her parents died in a car accident." He took his hat off and pulled the brim through his fingers. "She was fifteen years old and all of a sudden she was an orphan. My aunt and uncle, who lived right next door to us, took her in. It seemed like the best thing for her. She could stay in the same neighborhood, continue going to the same school; basically it would help her keep as much of her life intact as possible after losing her parents."

Jack laid his hat aside and sighed in frustration.

"It didn't really turn out that way. Maggie was a good kid, but she isolated herself. With all the depth of character of a sixteen-year-old boy, I was just glad she didn't get in my way.

"Then one day things changed. It was the last day of school before summer. I was walking home, stopping to buy a celebratory Coke at the corner store. I took a shortcut through a small bit of forest. There was this clear little pond in the middle of it, and I had the idea that I was going to drink my Coke and hang out at the pond for a while. Except, when I got there, someone was already there."

"Maggie." I said it for him before I could stop myself.

"Yeah, she was sitting at the pond, crying. The horrible thing was, at first I was only annoyed that she'd wrecked my plan; I didn't care what she was upset about."

Jack looked disgusted with himself at the memory. "It turned out that she'd gotten straight As on her report card, and it struck her that she had no one to show them to. My aunt and uncle would have been happy, but it wasn't the same, you know?"

"Yeah, I think I understand."

Jack was silent for a moment.

"So what did you do?"

"I shared my Coke with her."

I smiled. "That's sweet."

"Well it occurred to me at some point as we were talking that she wasn't an annoying eleven-year-old neighbor anymore. In fact, all of a sudden I couldn't believe that I hadn't noticed her in years."

A broad smile crossed my face, and I winced as I felt the edges of my cut pull apart. "And did you share more Cokes with her after that?"

Jack laughed. "As many as I could afford. We were together until we graduated. She took her nurse's training after high school, and I always assumed that we'd get married eventually."

"But that didn't happen?"

"She signed up to serve as a nurse in the war. One day everything was fine; the next she tells me that she's going to work at a field hospital in free France. I was furious. I didn't want her going over there, putting herself in danger. I was already working for the FBI then, and I knew exactly how bad things were over there. We had a massive fight, and she told me that I'd never asked her about the future; I'd just assumed that she'd want whatever I wanted. She told me that she'd always wanted to

175

use her nursing skills as a missionary. That working with wounded soldiers and spreading the gospel were exactly what she wanted to do with her life. I was hurt. And terrified for her."

Jack's voice faded into a long stretch of silence.

"Did she make it through the war?" I was afraid even to ask the question.

"She did, but she never came back. She stayed in Berlin, tending to the wounded and sick there. She sees it as her own personal mission field."

"Is she ever coming back?"

"I have no idea. I got a few letters from her during the war and one after, but nothing in years."

"And yet you still use her photograph as a bookmark?"

Jack raised his eyebrow at me. "Do you really want to compare the lack of promise in our love lives?"

"Not a chance. Consider the subject dropped."

I racked my brain for a safe topic. "Okay, I have a question for you. How did you know that the two men in the car were the Soviets?"

"The FBI has files on all known and suspected foreign agents operating in the city. Those two are well known to us. The two men in Clive and Mary's apartment, on the other hand—I don't know who they were. I'm going to have to do some digging for answers on that one."

"So, if you know that those two men are Soviet agents, why doesn't the FBI arrest them?"

"Almost all foreign agents work through their home country's embassy, and so they have diplomatic immunity. It's a lot harder than commonly thought to get people like our two Soviet friends off our soil."

"So it would seem." I shook my head. "The most disturbing part of seeing them up close is how much they looked and sounded like everyone else."

"They go through years of training so that they can blend in with everyday Americans."

I suppressed a shudder. "You have no idea who the other two guys were?"

"I didn't say that. I said that I didn't know. I have lots of ideas. I'm going to swing by the office tonight on my way home and pull a few files. See if I can't match faces to names and nationalities." He rose, flipped his hat with his fingers, then shoved it on. "I'll come by in the morning and let you know what I've found out."

I stifled a yawn and nodded. "Sounds good. I have some bookkeeping stuff to do first thing in the morning, and then I guess I'm free."

Jack headed for the door. "Take care of those cuts, Fortune. And just for the record, I still think you should have gone to the hospital."

"Your opinion has been duly noted."

As soon as I heard Jack clattering down the stairs I crossed to my desk, opened the top drawer, and pulled out a bottle of aspirin. Fishing out two tablets, I crunched them dry, hoping that they would take effect faster that way. I grabbed the blanket off the back of the couch and lay down. Exhausted from nearly a week of one to two hours of sleep a night, I had the feeling that I would be able to sleep tonight. The day's events had tired me, and more than anything I just wanted to shut off my mind for a while. Perhaps if I woke up refreshed I'd have a whole new perspective on the case.

My face and my arm were still throbbing, and it was hard to find a comfortable position. In the end I had to lie flat on my back, staring at the ceiling, counting the water marks on the ceiling for hours until I finally fell asleep.

Jack pounded on my door at about nine a.m. I'd been up for hours and was feeling rested and productive for the first time in days.

I'd spent the morning cleaning up the office, getting my books balanced, and phoning around to get a quote on painting my office.

By the time Jack walked in, I was ready for a break. He crossed the room in two strides and tossed a rolled-up newspaper onto my desk. His face was stormy, not at all the happy-go-lucky expression I was used to.

My heart lurched as I picked up the paper. I could only assume that it wasn't good news. The front page said it all.

CURATOR MURDERED
FOR ANCIENT TREASURE

I scanned the article, shocked at how much information the reporter had. The specific nature of the treasure wasn't mentioned, but Robert Follett's murder was tied to "the search for a treasure that multiple parties, including several governments, were trying to get hold of."

My breath hissed out in a rush. "How did this reporter put everything together so fast? They must have had an inside source to get a story this close to the truth."

"The FBI is looking into it, but I can think of several reasons that someone who's looking for the gold would do this. It's like calling a game of poker. Everyone has been sitting around staring at each other, trying to gauge what everyone else knows, trying to bluff about their own resources, but someone has decided to raise the stakes and shake things up."

"And for us? What does it do for us?"

Jack shrugged. "The same as it does for everyone else. It destabilizes things. Whether circumstances fall in our favor isn't something we can predict at this point. All I can say with certainty is that things have just gotten a lot more complicated."

I pushed away from the desk and paced the room. "Okay, so we might as well ignore this new development and keep on in the same direction with our investigation. Until something changes, I guess we have to just keep working at it."

Jack nodded. "Also, I have some information on the two men from last night."

"Which ones?"

"The ones inside the apartment were East German intelligence officers."

"East Germany?"

"Yeah, Soviet-controlled Germany. It's not official yet, but it's only a matter of time before Germany is split into East and West. Allies control the Western half and the Soviets control the Eastern half. We don't have a lot of information on the whole East German intelligence system, but they seem to be made up of half German nationalists and half Soviet enforcers. My guess is that it would be a massive coup for the German nationals to get Helen's Gold back. I don't think they're working with the Soviets either. Despite the fact that their nations are technically allies, it looks to me like they are competing with each other on this particular mission."

"Okay, so we've got another player added into the mix here. Who do you think killed Robert Follett then?"

"If I was going solely by instinct, I'd say the East Germans. The Soviet agents would probably have hesitated about killing a man only peripherally involved in the matter, but the East Germans are well known for their cold efficiency. It's exactly how they would handle the situation."

"Which does not bode well for Clive and Mary."

"No, it doesn't. If the East Germans find them before we do . . ." He took a deep breath. "Let's just not let that happen."

I told Jack that I needed about half an hour to finish a few of the things that had been piling up on my desk. He nodded, asked for a pen and a pad of paper, which I handed over, and then proceeded to make notes about something. We worked in near silence for close to an hour, and when I finally leaned back in my chair to stretch my kinked muscles I felt much better. Running my finger along the cut on my cheek, I noticed that while it felt sore, it was a lot less painful than it had been. I took a deep breath. All of the day-to-day details of my work that I'd been getting behind on had been feeding my tension. Plowing my way through a few of them made me feel much better.

I was just about ready to start tidying up my desk when the office door flew open. Glass shook as the door slammed against the wall behind it. My head flew up in time to see the giant Soviet from last night burst in, followed almost immediately by his partner.

Jack looked up from his notes, apparently not surprised to see them. I, on the other hand, was flabbergasted.

The huge Soviet crossed the room in two angry strides and tossed a handful of silver metal onto my desk. The crash it made as it landed made me jump. The remains of Jack's handcuffs were hacked into pieces. Apparently someone had needed to cut the two Soviets out of their car with lock cutters.

"We wanted to return these to you along with a message. Stay out of our way if you like breathing." The tall guy seemed to be the spokesman for the two of them. The other guy mostly just stood around snarling.

Jack got to his feet. "Is that a threat?"

"It's a prediction of your future. You and your *partner*" —he pointed to me and smirked—"are way out of your league on this. You should go back to your desk and file some more paperwork. Stick with what you're good at. And the little woman over there should go back to her sewing circle. Things are about to get rough."

Anger flooded me, but I tamped it down. I was used to this kind of bullying tactic. The expression on Jack's face went from annoyed to vicious, but he seemed to have an ironclad grip on his temper. "The little woman over there had you on the ground writhing last night. Does that mean you should go back to basket weaving?"

The Soviet's face turned nearly purple at the comment. Nothing like deflated male pride to accelerate fury. I thought back to Jack's reaction to being bested by me outside of Mary's apartment. He'd been annoyed at being beat, but not furious that it had been at the hands of a woman. And now, it seemed like he was almost proud of me.

The Soviet took a step toward Jack, as though trying to intimidate him, but Jack didn't give even the slightest indication of being intimidated. He looked almost lazy as he stood there. Bored even.

"If you know what's good for you, you will stay out of our way." He repeated the threat. "And give up the hunt for the gold. We're going to get it, and we're going to send it back home to Soviet Russia, where it belongs."

"There are a lot of people who think it belongs somewhere else. You're going to have quite a fight coming from the two East German agents we found in Clive and Mary's apartment yesterday."

I turned to look at Jack.

He watched the Soviet pair intently for any reaction. He wasn't disappointed.

"East Germans? What were they doing up there?"

"It seems that they had a pretty busy day. I'm guessing they started with murdering Robert Follett and ransacking his office, and they ended it with breaking into Clive and Mary's apartment right under your noses. It would be a full day for anyone. My guess is that they're after the gold, like everyone else."

"You're lying. There are no East Germans after the gold. We would have seen."

Jack laughed. "I wouldn't worry about it too much. Reports of your incompetence will take a while to get back to Russia. Although, once your superiors find out how badly you've bungled this mission, I'm guessing your next mission will be more along the lines of latrine duty in the Gulag."

The quiet Soviet's face had gone white, but there was still a little bluster in the voice of the giant.

"Doesn't matter. We will find the gold first. That's all that my superiors will care about." The more agitated he'd become, the more of an accent I could hear in his voice.

Jack delivered the final blow. "You're never going to find the gold until you find Clive and Mary. You getting anywhere with that?" He knew they probably had less information on that than we did. It's what the whole investigation was hinged on. Nothing else really mattered, other than getting to Clive and Mary first. Jack took a step toward the Soviet. "You getting any good information out of the brother?" he said, referring to Nigel Gordon.

There was a second of silence before Jack went on. "Yeah, that's what I thought. He doesn't have the first idea where to find them either. And with the whole story being plastered across the front page of the *New York Times* this morning, Clive and Mary are going to go so deep underground that you're never going to find them. Explain that to your superiors."

The Soviet took a step back. "We came here to

tell you to stay out of our way if you know what's good for you. I'm going to tell you again, just to make it clear. We will do whatever we need to, to get this gold. Whatever needs to be done."

With that, the two men turned and walked out of my office, slamming the door behind them.

I sank to my seat, drained. "One of these days someone's going to break that glass, and I am going to be very upset."

Jack sat back in his seat and laughed.

"Why did you tell them all that?"

"Two reasons. I wanted to watch their reactions and see what they knew, and I also wanted to shift their attention off of us and onto the East Germans. If we can take the East Germans out of play by sic-cing the Soviets on them, we will be free and clear of both of their influences."

I nodded. "That's what I thought. I was watching for their reactions too. They had no idea."

Jack picked up his notepad again. "Nope. It was a shock for them to find out that there were more people chasing this gold. And a nasty shock to find out who it was." Jack pulled out his pen and made a note on his paper. "Still, it doesn't really matter who's in the game; all that matters is who finds Clive and Mary first. There's no ribbon for second place in this race."

Chapter 25

WE SAT IN silence for a few minutes. Me staring at the ceiling, thinking, Jack scribbling more notes on his papers.

The phone rang and I answered it, still feeling distracted. The person on the other end asked for Jack. My eyebrow went up, but I handed it across the desk to him, and he held his hand out as though expecting the call.

A series of grunts and uh-huhs ensued, followed by, "Ten minutes. We'll be there."

He handed the phone back to me, and I slid it into its cradle.

"You going to tell me what that was about?"

"Remember when I said I was going to get the FBI to find out more about Clive and Mary? That file is ready. Someone is going to hand it off to us at my mother's restaurant in ten minutes. Which means we need to get going."

"At the restaurant?"

"It's a good spot. I go in the front, the contact comes through the back; my mother is used to it, and we'll get a free lunch out of the deal."

I grabbed my hat from the coatrack, shoved it on, and threw Jack's to him. "Let's go."

The walk took us the full ten minutes despite the fact that I was moving as fast as I could without breaking into a run. Jack merely strolled, and I wanted to throttle him for being so calm. Easygoing and laid-back was fine sometimes, but other times it was wholly inappropriate and really annoying. With the events of yesterday and all of the things that had happened already this morning, my nerves were humming with the promise of a breakthrough.

Every fiber of my being told me that we were getting close, and the closer we got to Clive and Mary, the closer we got to the gold. And the closer we got to the gold, the closer I was to finally having an answer. After so many years of having no answers, I could almost taste it.

February 1939

WHEN I WOKE, David was still asleep beside me. With the light coming in the living room windows I saw that he was pale, but peaceful.

I got off the couch and took a second to stretch out my cramped muscles. Falling asleep sitting up did not make for a good night's rest. I looked over my shoulder at the grandfather clock in the corner. Five thirty.

I rushed to David's side and shook his good shoulder lightly. "Hey, you've got to get up. The housekeeper will be here any minute."

His eyes flickered open and he tried to sit up, but groaned at the movement and slumped back against the couch. "What?"

"Mrs. Higgins starts work at six. Sometimes she's early. We've got to get you out of sight."

His eyes opened and he was fully awake in an instant. "I can't leave just yet. I can't afford to be seen. Is there anywhere I could hide? Just until she's gone for the day? After dark, I swear, I'll leave and won't bother you again."

"No, it's probably best that you don't leave yet anyway. You're still looking rough, and you definitely lost a lot of blood. I think more time to rest would do you good."

I racked my brain trying to think of a safe place he could hide. Only one place came to mind, but it was completely improper. I shouldn't have even considered it. On the other hand, the man had already spent the night at my house, without the benefit of a chaperone. It probably wasn't much of a stretch to let him stay in my bedroom for a few hours.

I crossed back over to the couch and stretched out my hand. "Do you think you can make it up a flight of stairs?"

He grimaced. "I guess we'll find out." He grasped my hand, and it took all my strength to pull him up. He wavered for a second, then found his balance. I moved to his side, ready to help steady him, but he waved me away. "I'm fine. I just got a little light-headed when I stood up. Lead the way, Miss Fortune."

I took him to the base of the stairs, but once there, I couldn't imagine him being able to make it all the way up. "Look, I think you should lean on me. If I'm a few steps behind you and you start to waver, there's nothing I can do to stop your fall."

He let out a pain-filled laugh. "If you're standing behind me and I fall, you won't have to worry anymore. You'll be crushed."

"All the more reason to let me help you up the stairs."

He nodded and gave me a wide, if weary, smile. My heart fluttered at the sight, so I looked away. I went to his side and he slung his good arm around my neck. Slowly we made our way up the stairs, bumping up against the length of each other as I steadied him. I kept my face partially averted so that he didn't see me blush at the accidental contact. His bare skin was warm under my fingers, but not with the scorching heat that would indicate a fever. In fact, his skin was no more heated than my own. I tried not to dwell on the fact that my arms were wrapped around his bare arms and back, but I couldn't stop the embarrassment that flooded me.

By the time we got to my room, I was sweating. David was big, strong, and very heavy. I felt like I'd spent an hour running, not ten minutes getting up a flight of stairs. With my free hand I shoved open the door and escorted my injured guest inside.

My room was large. Luxurious by almost any standard. I had a large sleeping area, a huge closet, and even an en-suite bathroom. Unfortunately, it was also decorated solely in pink and white with gold trim. It was the perfect bedroom for a nine-year-old. At almost eighteen, it was more than a little embarrassing. I maneuvered David over to my bed. He looked afraid to touch the sparkling white bedspread, so I gave him a little push.

"No, no. I might get blood on the blanket." Apparently the thought of this terrified him as he tried to lever himself up, vastly increasing the chances that he'd tear open his wound and actually smear blood everywhere.

"Lay still. I've got to go back downstairs and clean a few things up before Mrs. Higgins gets here. I'll try to bring up something for you to eat."

David lay on the bed, angled toward me, propped up on his good elbow with his injured arm cradled against his chest. "I feel bad that I've brought all of this trouble down on you. I'm sorrier than you could possibly know." His eyes echoed the remorse in his voice.

"You've saved me on more than one occasion; it only seems fair that I get to return the favor." With that I turned and headed back downstairs, shutting the bedroom door behind me.

I sighed when I spotted the bloodstain on the back of the sofa. Expecting Mrs. Higgins to arrive any minute, I grabbed a blanket from the linen closet and draped it over the stain, hoping to hide it. I heard the back door open and decided that it was probably best to tell Mrs. Higgins the truth, or some of it.

I heard whistling, so I headed for the kitchen. "Morning, Mrs. Higgins." I didn't bother to inject morning cheer into my voice.

"Oh, goodness, girl. What are you doing up at this time of day?" She laid her hand over her heart in surprise but didn't wait for me to answer. "I suppose you had another of your sleepless nights. Did the dreams wake you up?"

She meant the reccurring dreams I'd had since witnessing the shooting. "No, I ended up falling asleep on the couch for part of the night."

She nodded absently as she grabbed her apron off the hook and went about tying it around her ample middle.

"I'm just going to fix a breakfast tray for myself and see if I can't get a few more hours of rest."

She stopped what she was doing immediately. "No. I'll do that, Miss Fortune. There's no call for you to be doing my job. Go wait in the living room, and I'll have it ready for you in a minute."

"I'm feeling extra hungry this morning, so if you wouldn't mind, could you make sure there's lots of food? And then I'll just take it up to my room with me."

"Of course, Miss Fortune."

I moved to the living room and waited for her on the sofa. I hadn't been lying; I really was exhausted, and I waited for the breakfast tray with my eyes closed.

"Here you are. I gave you a double portion of

everything, so you'll have to have a mighty fine appetite to get through it all."

"That's perfect. Thank you so much. And I just have one more favor to ask of you."

She propped her hand on her hip and waited for me to elaborate. "And that is?"

"Could you just leave this blanket here? I managed to fall asleep for a little while last night on this sofa, and I think I might try it again tonight if I have trouble. It's just easier if everything is there for me if I come down in the middle of the night."

She didn't seem to think this was a strange request, and so I took the tray from her arthritic hands and made my way back upstairs.

I paused at the entrance to my room. It felt strange to walk into an occupied room unannounced, but everything had to appear normal. Knocking on my own door would definitely be perceived as odd.

I turned the knob and slid the door open. With my tray balanced neatly, I walked into the room as though I was the only occupant. I avoided looking at the bed, set down the tray on my bureau, and then turned to shut the door behind me. I took the first easy breath in what felt like hours and then turned back to where I'd left the tray. "I've got lots of food here, so you won't starve." I moved to face him, only to find him lying flat on his back, injured arm resting across his chest, fast asleep. I believe there was even a hint of snoring.

Stifling a laugh, I pulled the folded blanket at the end of the bed up and over him. I let myself take a lingering look at him. It had been more than a year since I'd seen him last, but in the past twelve hours, all of that time seemed to disappear. Despite the injury he looked strong and dependable. I felt a blush stain my cheeks when I realized I was staring at a sleeping, shirtless man.

I turned away, searching for anything that would distract me. I couldn't deny the fact that I was attracted to him. From the first, I'd been captivated by him. Even way back then, when we'd first met, when I was sixteen years old, there'd been something about him that made my heart lurch. And it had only gotten stronger in the intervening year or so.

I crossed to the upholstered chair in the corner and took a seat. I picked up a book I'd been reading and tried to settle my thoughts with fiction. It wasn't long before the book got too heavy to hold up, and I let it fall as I dropped off to sleep.

We got to the restaurant and I followed Jack to the table closest to the kitchen. His mother waved at us, and her eyes widened when she spotted me, but there was no comment and no one came over to our table.

"Do you do this a lot? Meet a contact here?"

He held up a finger, telling me to wait for a second. He rose and walked through the kitchen door, returning right away with a basket of bread.

"Yeah, fairly often. I mean, I figure that I have to eat somewhere, so it might as well be here. My family is used to me coming in and out, so it's not a big deal." He picked up a piece of bread but didn't take a bite. "Coming here with you, for the second time in a week, appears to be a bigger deal, though. At least to my mother and sisters." He sighed and I wondered what it would be like to have a family so involved in your life. It was probably a combination of comforting and annoying.

Jack proceeded to eat three-quarters of the basket of bread all by himself, as I was too nervous to eat.

His mother made her way over to our table a few minutes later. "Are you two staying for a proper lunch?"

Jack shook his head. "I'm waiting for someone, and we have lots to do today, so it will have to be a quick meal."

She shook her finger at him. "Rush, rush, rush, that's all you ever do. You will need to slow down, enjoy a nice meal with a pretty girl . . ." She trailed off, looking at me.

She could not have made me more uncomfortable had she insisted I stand on the table and sing a song. I glanced helplessly at Jack, and he looked annoyed. "I've told you, Allie and I are working together. This is a working lunch, not a date."

His mother huffed. "Well, it's not like you bring a lot of women by, so how am I to know?" She walked back toward the kitchen and called over her shoulder, "I will bring you lunch. A fast, business lunch." She sounded as annoyed as Jack looked.

My stomach tightened. "I hope she's not mad."

Jack shook his head. "She's not. She thinks I'm a fool for not trying to turn this into a romantic lunch, but she's not mad."

If possible, I was even less comfortable now.

"Don't worry about it. She just wants to see me happily married with a dozen or so children, and I'm not obliging her at the moment."

I laughed. "I understand that. My mother has been setting me up on blind dates for five years. I've never yet wanted to see any of them a second time, but I guess hope springs eternal."

Jack grinned. "You're wrong."

I shot him a confused look. "What do you mean?"

"I was your date this Wednesday, and I've seen you every day since then." He laughed.

"You're right. After five years of a perfect record, you come along and mess everything up."

We grinned at each other for a second, then Jack sighed. "It would sure make things easier, wouldn't it?"

I didn't pretend to misunderstand. "Yeah, probably, but easy isn't always right. I've thought about it, though."

He laughed, but this time the laugh had no humor in it. "I have too. It seems that we've both doomed ourselves by needing what we absolutely cannot have."

I didn't want to ask, but the question popped out of my mouth anyway. "Do you think, if things were different . . ." I trailed off, not wanting to put the question fully into words.

"I don't know, maybe. But maybe we're too much alike. I just don't know."

Desperately needing a change of subject, I said the first thing that came into my head. "Where is that guy? It's been over half an hour."

Jack looked as relieved as I felt to put that line of conversation behind us. "Don't worry. He'll get here."

Jack's mother brought us our lunch of chicken piccata a few minutes later. She placed mine in front of me and smiled, then turned and thunked Jack's down and glared at him before retreating to the kitchen again.

I had to laugh, but it didn't seem to bother Jack at all. He just dug into his lunch and, after a moment, I did the same.

I was taking the last bite of my chicken when a man in a suit and fedora charged through the swinging kitchen doors, deposited an envelope next to Jack, and walked back out.

Surprised at the brusque exchange, I raised my eyebrow, but Jack didn't even seem to notice. He just set down his fork and knife and tore into the envelope.

I held my breath as he skimmed the file. "So, what have we got?"

Jack ignored me for a moment, then tossed the pages across the table to me. I picked them up as Jack spoke.

"We've got leads on a cabin they own upstate, hotels they've been known to frequent, places they've been on holiday, and also it looks like Clive entered the United States from Great Britain a little over two months ago. They don't have all the information yet, but it appears that he took a quick trip to London."

I took a sip of my water and laid the papers back down. "We have some new leads to work on."

Jack pushed his chair back, shoved the papers back into the envelope, and led me to the door. "Lunch was great, Mom. I'll see you at dinner on Sunday," he called over his shoulder, then held the door open for me to precede him out.

Chapter 26

WE WALKED BACK to the office, and this time Jack didn't dawdle. It appeared he was every bit as eager to get back to work as I was.

We divided the list. Since we needed two phones, Jack headed back to the field office and I got to work immediately. I started with the hotels they'd stayed at. It took a while to get through, but none of the hotel employees I talked to had seen anyone matching the description of either Clive or Mary. If we turned up no other leads, I'd have to go to each of the hotels, with photographs, but at this point I put them on my "tentative no" list.

Their cabin was harder. The FBI hadn't listed a phone number, and I wouldn't have wanted to call them anyway. No point in alerting Clive and Mary that we knew about the place. Instead I phoned the general store, the gas station, and the post office in the small town closest to their cabin. I figured that if they were there, one of the employees in those places would have seen them.

I struck out in all three places. The owner of the general store knew who I was talking about, but said he hadn't seen Clive or Mary since some time last spring. The postmistress was very officious and refused to discuss any of her patrons with me. Sighing, I hung up frustrated. The gas station yielded slightly more promising results, but even that was only a tiny crack of hope. The gas attendant on duty was new. He didn't know any of the customers by name yet and suggested that I call back when the owner was in. He had owned the station for fifty years and knew the name and vehicle of nearly everyone who stopped in for fuel.

I took a break after that, hoping that inspiration would strike for who to call next, and I hoped that Jack was having more luck than I was. He'd taken the half of the list with the passport office on it. With his FBI credentials, he'd have a much easier time getting information about Clive's travel than I would. I probably should have given him the task of trying to get information out of the post office too. He might have done better. Then again, given the postmistress's cantankerous tone, I wouldn't count on it.

It was past five o'clock by the time I'd followed up on every lead on my list. I'd saved the least promising leads for last, so I was pretty discouraged by the time I laid my list aside. I'd had no real breakthroughs, and I only hoped that Jack was doing better.

When he knocked on the office door I was thoroughly frustrated. I'd read the entire file over again, but nothing had jumped out at me. I tried to swallow the feeling of hopelessness.

I saw immediately that Jack had perhaps had less success than me. His expression was dark and frustrated.

"Anything?" he asked.

I shook my head. "You either?"

He took off his hat and threw it down onto the desk. "Confirmation of what we'd thought, but no new information at all. I was able to find out that Clive traveled from New York to London for a total of seven days, over two months ago."

"It seems very likely, then, that he got the gold when he was there. The timing fits perfectly. One of my biggest questions about this case has always been why they waited for three years to try to fence the gold. If it wasn't in his possession until two months ago, it makes perfect sense." I paused, thinking for a second, and then continued.

"And it also makes some of the other pieces fit together. Like why Mary worked so hard. When she was my client I saw how long the hours were that she worked. From sunup to sundown every day. Clearly they needed the money, and so maybe Clive went to London to bring the gold back hoping that he could hock it for enough money to get them on their feet again. From the look of their apartment, Mary's clothes, and a few other little things, I think money has been very tight since the war."

"Yeah, that makes a lot of sense. Clive must have thought that the gold would be enough to give them a fresh start, but he had no idea that it was worth enough to make them wealthy beyond their wildest dreams."

"It might do that, but right now it looks like they might not live long enough to enjoy it."

We sat in silence for a moment. I couldn't help thinking about how a few stolen bits of gold might end up costing both Clive and Mary their lives. If we didn't find them before the Soviets or the East Germans did, their chances of survival were hovering around zero.

Apparently Jack was thinking along the same lines. "We have got to find them. Fast."

We were interrupted from our thoughts by the

shrill ring of the phone. Frustrated, I yanked the receiver up to my ear and barked, "Yeah?"

"Miss Fortune, I need to speak with you."

My heart stalled in my chest. "Who is this?" I thought I knew, but I had to be sure.

"This is Mary Gordon. I'm in a bit of trouble, and I may have been acting too hastily when I terminated our professional relationship."

February 1939

WHEN I AWOKE again, I actually felt rested. I checked the bed and gasped, shocked to find it empty. Shoving myself out of the chair, I scanned the room for David. Not spotting him, I wondered for a moment if I'd dreamt the whole thing. I crossed to the bed, and the rumpled blankets told me that I hadn't.

Then I heard water running in the bathroom. My breath came back with a rush. I closed my eyes for a second as the panic drained. When I opened them again I realized David must have been awake for a while. The breakfast tray was half empty. Apparently he ate half the toast, half the oatmeal, half the eggs, and drank half the milk. The precision in sharing made me laugh.

I went to the tray, grabbed a slice of the toast, and took a bite. The sound of running water faded into silence. The breath backed up in my lungs when I heard the door creak open.

David stepped out, and the first thing I noticed was

that his hair was wet. He still had my unwieldy bandages attached to his shoulder, so I doubted he'd had a shower. Instead he'd probably just stuck his head under the tap and let the water run. He looked better, had more color in his cheeks, and seemed much stronger and more in control than yesterday. I couldn't imagine helping this David up the stairs. Nerves fluttered through my stomach and my mouth went dry.

David stared back at me for long moments without a word. "I tried to get cleaned up as best I could." His eyes held mine, and I was aware of his words only dimly.

"How long have you been up?" It was an inane question, but it was something, and I'd take what I could get.

He smiled and looked over to the chair where I'd slept. "A while." A small smile played at the edges of his mouth.

The break of eye contact allowed my brain to start functioning again. I stepped forward. "My bandages are pretty ridiculous. I should probably look at your wound and find something more suitable. I'll need to make sure there's no sign of infection."

I started to walk around him to go into the bathroom, but he held his hand out for me to wait. I stopped.

"I owe you an explanation. What this is all about and why I came here."

A shudder quaked my heart. I didn't want to talk; I

wasn't ready to know. "Let's clean that out first, and we can get into all that later."

He seemed hesitant but after a second followed me into the washroom. I motioned for him to sit on the edge of the toilet seat, and he did so without a word. Feeling both in control and desperately out of control, I got out a few washcloths.

When I laid my hand on his shoulder and reached to untie the knot holding the bandages on, David's breath hissed out.

"Am I hurting you?" I couldn't imagine how as I'd barely touched him.

"No." The word came out jagged and hard. "Let's just do this, okay?"

Not sure why he seemed so grim, I fiddled with the twine until I had the knot undone. I peeled the towel back slowly, noting that there was a lot of blood on it but none of it fresh. Letting out a sigh of relief, I pulled both cloths all the way off. When they were off, I sucked in a deep breath. The wound looked awful. A fleshy hole surrounded by bruised skin and dried blood. In fact, there was dried blood all over his upper chest and shoulder. I wet one of the washcloths with warm water and wrung it out, then turned back to David. I was ready to clean off all of the bloodied skin, but his hands wrapped around mine to stop me. He held me still for a second, then took the cloth from my hands.

"I can do that." It came out quiet but firm. He cleaned the skin surrounding the wound with little fuss, giving the wound itself a wide berth, and he was done in seconds.

"Okay, I still have to wrap it up again, but it doesn't look red and there's no heat coming from it, so I think you've missed the chance of infection." I said the words, but my thoughts were hazy and slow. All I could think was that I had never seen such beautiful eyes in my life.

David nodded and set the washcloth down on the counter. I bandaged the wound again; this time it was less bulky and clumsy. When I finished, I became aware that I'd been holding my breath. There was a hiss of air from David when I took a step back too.

I watched as David flexed and rolled his shoulder. He rose and I took one more step back, but the bathroom was too small to go far. I still found myself inches from him. Our gazes locked, and there was nothing but the two of us and my thundering heart.

David didn't move, or at least I didn't think he did. Instead it was me that moved closer. Drawn, I couldn't stop myself from leaning toward him. He closed his eyes as though seeking inner strength, but when he opened them again, I saw more than regret and restraint in them.

Closing the space between us, David wrapped his good arm around my back and inched me toward him. His breath on my cheek made my knees weak. I lifted onto my tiptoes, wanting, more than anything, for him to kiss me.

He lowered his head until his mouth was a hairs-breadth from mine, then stilled. He lifted his good hand and stroked it through my hair once before finally touching his lips to mine.

At the contact I leaned forward an inch and I felt his fingers twine and tighten in my hair.

Behind my closed eyes I felt the world spin. He moved away for a second. My eyes flew open and I found myself staring into eyes darker than a midnight storm. He held me away from him for an endless, desperate second before leaning in again. This kiss was sharper, stronger, and more demanding than the first. My heart squeezed so tight I could hardly breathe, but it wasn't until I ran the back of my hand down his cheek that the tension eased. He breathed out, pulled me away to lean his heated cheek against mine.

I was glad his arm continued to hold me up. My mind was a kaleidoscope of colors and sensations, but most of all it was just David. I pulled away to look at him. His eyes were hazy, and a deep red flush colored his cheekbones, but he continued to hold me so gently, running his fingers through my hair. I closed my eyes, let out my breath, and held on to the moment.

Chapter 27

I STARED AT the phone in shock. Jack looked up from the notes he was rereading. Using my hand to cover the receiver, I mouthed the word "Mary." His eyes went wide, and I pulled my hand off the mouthpiece.

"What can I do for you?" I decided to play it cool. The last thing I wanted was to scare her off with a bunch of questions.

"I assume you read the paper this morning?"

"I did." I offered nothing else.

"How much do you really know about what's going on?"

I thought for a moment before answering. It was a thin line I had to walk. "I think I know most of it. At least who's after you and why." I left it at that.

She laughed, but the laugh was completely devoid of humor. "Well, it's possible you know more than I do then."

I decided to go with my gut. "Mary, do you know how much trouble you and Clive are in? Do you have any idea how dangerous it is for you two if anyone finds out where you are?"

"I'm beginning to get the idea, but I can't seem to figure out what to do about it."

"I'm going to be blunt. You need to get the gold into the hands of the only people who can protect you at this point."

"And that would be?"

"The FBI. They're after you, and the gold, but as far as I can tell, they are the only ones who seem to care that they don't get the gold over your and Clive's dead bodies." I figured bluntness was the only tack I could take right then.

Her breath whooshed out, and I heard her take in a ragged breath. "Can you meet me? I need someone to talk to that I know isn't trying to kill me, and then you can help me work out a plan for handing the gold over."

I felt like a golden apple had just dropped into my lap, but I could also feel sweat prickle around my hairline, reminding me that to go anywhere near Mary put my own life very much in danger.

"Are you in a safe place now?"

"Yes, I think so."

"Then let me come to you." I held my breath.

"No. No. I'll meet you somewhere in the city."

I closed my eyes and gritted my teeth in frustration. "Mary, if you are seen by anyone, you'll be putting yourself in unbelievable danger. Robert Follett is dead, and he hardly had a thing to do with the whole mess you're in."

Mary let out a vicious laugh. "There would be no mess if it weren't for Robert. If he could have just kept his mouth shut, none of this would be happening."

I had no answer to that.

"I'll meet you tomorrow morning. I'll call you at seven a.m. and let you know where."

"Okay, but I'm going to give you my home number. Call me there. Obviously this needs to be kept as quiet as possible." I rattled off the numbers, and there was a moment of silence.

"I'll call in the morning. Be sure that no one follows you."

"I will." I paused for a second. "And Mary, be careful."

She made a sound of agreement, and the next thing I heard was the dial tone in my ear. I replaced the receiver with a soft click.

Jack just stared at me, waiting.

"She wants me to meet with her tomorrow. We're going to arrange a way to hand over the gold and to get her and Clive out of harm's way."

Jack leaned back in his chair and let out a breath. "That turns the whole thing on its head now, doesn't it?"

February 1939

STUNNED, I STAYED wrapped in David's arms. Thoughts, like swarming bees, wanted to intrude on this moment, but I shoved them aside, instead holding on to the peace I felt. I knew the feeling would be fleeting.

The kiss had knocked me flat. Never had I felt such emotion or confusion or rightness all at the same time. I lifted my head from his shoulder and pushed myself away to see his face.

I wanted to see if he was feeling the same sense of rightness that slid through me. As I caught sight of his eyes, suddenly the ground beneath my feet felt unsteady. Instead of the mixture of happiness and shyness that bubbled through me, I saw an entirely different mix of emotions coursing through him.

Anger, regret, pain.

He still held me with that same intense gentleness, but it was at war with the blaze of regret I read so easily in his eyes.

"What? What's wrong?" I couldn't control the tremble in my voice. I kept my gaze focused on his, trying to understand, to decipher David's reaction to what had passed between us.

He didn't answer my half-formed question. Instead he wrapped his hands gently around my arms and led me to the bed and sat me down. The second he let go, he stepped away, and the emotions that been visible solely through his eyes seemed to stream through his entire body. His fists and his jaw clenched; every part of his body tightened.

"This was a mistake. It shouldn't have happened." The words came out harsh and brittle.

I turned my face away, trying to force down the tears I felt rising.

"I need to leave."

"It's still light out. You said you needed to wait until after dark."

"I'll have to take my chances." His gaze darted around the room. Crossing to the French doors, he tossed them open and walked out onto my balcony. It was about a twenty-foot drop to the ground, but he looked almost desperate enough to attempt it.

I reached out and put a restraining hand on his arm, and he went completely still. "Why are you doing this?"

He turned to face me and took a step backward until he was leaning against the iron balcony railing. "I never should have come here. I've put you in danger; I've taken advantage of your trust, and now this. You should have thrown me out when you found me at your back door."

Annoyance crackled from my voice, but it only just covered the hurt. "And what? Left you to bleed to death in the snow?"

He moved away in disgust, apparently annoyed with both of us now. "You are so naive. You let a bleeding near-stranger into your home without demanding a reasonable explanation for why he's got a gunshot wound. You take a man up to your bedroom to hide him from whoever's chasing him, never asking a single question. You don't know me; you don't have a clue about who I am or what I'm capable of, and that is the definition of *naive*."

"Fine, maybe I am naive. But I was also right. I trust you completely." I moved so that he had to look at me. "I'm glad you came here. I'm glad to see you again, and I don't regret anything about the last two days."

His eyes softened, and I saw the recrimination in them. He shook his head slowly. "That's the problem. You will."

He was right. He said I would regret the time I spent with him, and despite the fact that he walked away without looking back, I didn't really believe him. I thought the hours we spent together would be a shiny memory with a tarnished ending, but I never believed that I'd come to a point where I wished I'd never met him.

It wasn't the tears that I spent on him, or the hurt I carried like a thorn in my heart because of his sudden rejection. It was because of a newspaper headline.

After spending a long, sleepless night wondering what happened to turn everything on its head, I went downstairs to get a cup of tea. Watery sunlight streamed through the windows, and I heard the thunk of a newspaper hitting the front door. Letting in an icy blast of air, I plucked the rolled paper out of the snow and brought it in. If nothing else, it would serve to distract me from unproductive thoughts of David.

I unrolled it and the bold, black headline screamed up at me:

STILL NO SUSPECTS IN
CENTRAL PARK DOUBLE MURDER

My heart plummeted as I scanned the article. The night David turned up at my front door, bleeding, there had been a double murder, a shooting, in the park. By the reservoir. The police had no suspects but were saying that it was probably tied to organized crime. A blood trail leading away from the scene of the crime made them believe that the shooter had been injured. Police were watching local hospitals for a gunshot victim who might be tied to the double homicide. They assumed the suspect would be armed and dangerous.

My mouth went dry, and I felt the paper drop from my numb fingers. Not bothering to pick it up, I crossed to the sofa where a blanket still covered the blood stain. I shoved it back and stared at the rust-colored circle. Had a murderer lain here? Had I cleaned out his wound, helped him up the stairs, and sheltered him from the police? A murderer with ties to organized crime?

The image of David, the hero, and this new information wouldn't fit. How could the man who'd rescued me and protected me in my most vulnerable moments be a cold-blooded killer? Why would he try to warn me about himself if he were the man the police said he was?

My thoughts swirled, but I went to the kitchen and got a bucket of warm water, soap, and a scrub brush. I spent more than an hour scrubbing all traces of the blood from the fabric. When I was done there was little more than a large damp spot remaining. I took the bucket and brush back to the kitchen. The tears flowed. This time, I couldn't stop them. I went back upstairs to bed. All evidence of David's presence had been erased, but nothing could erase the last two days.

Chapter 28

IT WAS POURING rain and getting dark by the time I finally decided to go home. Jack drove me and dropped me off at my door with a promise to return the next morning at five a.m. He said he was going to head back to the field office and get a team and a plan together for whatever came up the next day.

The nerves in my stomach were stretched so tight I couldn't eat supper or even think about sleep. Instead I drank tea and sat curled in my apartment window, watching cars splash through the puddles as they raced through the dark streets. I tried to plan, to work up various scenarios in my mind and how to react to them, but my mind was buzzing with what had happened and I couldn't seem to put two coherent thoughts together.

Unsettled to the point of feeling sick, I got up from the window and paced the apartment. Something besides the uncertainty of tomorrow gnawed at me. I couldn't name the restlessness fighting inside me, nor could I tame it.

I eventually moved so that I sat cross-legged in

the middle of my bed. I took a deep breath and tried to let all of the tension in my body go. I consigned thoughts of Mary and Clive and the gold to later. Something else was wracking me, and I needed to push everything out of the way to find out what it was. I don't know how long it took for me to dig past the chaos in my mind, but when I did, I realized that I was angry.

Furious. And terrified.

Everything in my life that mattered hung on a knife blade tonight. If things went badly, lives could end, dreams would die, and I would lose every last vestige of hope in my life.

A small voice inside me told me I was wrong. That hope could never be extinguished.

If there is no hope left that David is alive, or worse, if there is no way for me to ever know if he's dead, there will be no hope in me, I argued with the voice.

A picture of Mrs. Follett grieving her son sprang to mind.

The voice continued to speak. *People die. Everyone dies, and yet there is still hope. If David is dead, there will still be hope, but it's hope in something different. Hope in something greater than the circumstances of life.*

I tried to remember what Mrs. Follett had said; it seemed important that I remember. Something about trusting God during the bad times in life as well as the good.

This was about God? The logical part of my brain rebelled at the idea. Years before I'd given up the idea of a bearded old man who controlled the world with His fingertips. It had never made sense to me that a God who could create an entire universe could not prevent terrible things from happening. The two ideas couldn't seem to coexist, so I had walked away from the belief.

Except that my whole being seemed to scream now that there was more to it. I didn't want to listen. Wanted to clap my hands over my ears like a child, but that did nothing to quiet the voice inside of me.

If God wanted me to have hope, why wouldn't He send me a sign that David was alive? That would give me hope.

That's not the kind of hope that lasts, the voice argued. What if something else bad happened? Would hope disappear again? Could life always be directed by circumstances, or was there something bigger that kept hope alive?

I pushed myself off the bed, trying to get away from the thoughts. I put the kettle on the stove, crashing it onto the element, searching for anything that would distract me. But it didn't work. The voice pounded at me from all directions. *What is hope? Where is your hope?*

Frustrated and a bit afraid, I paced around the apartment, but nothing could tear my thoughts away from the questions.

I picked up the phone, thinking I could call Jack and silence my thoughts by planning for the morning, but they just got louder.

What if there is no morning? What if this is all there is? This moment, right now. Do you know where the real hope is?

I was shocked at the answers that came. No. I don't. I have no idea where the real hope in life is. That's why I haven't slept in years; that's why I live every day like I'm not really living.

The real hope is an assurance that Someone other than you is in control, Allie. The thought came to me as though whispered into my ear.

All the chaos in my mind stilled. Soft as a whisper but clear as rain I heard it.

Your hope is in Me. Hope in a love that is stronger than even your love for David, and hope that there is a forgiveness big enough to cover the regrets that haunt you.

April 1939

THE AIR GREW warmer with the promise of spring, but the chill hadn't faded from my bones. The day I found out about what really happened in the park, my heart iced over. I hadn't called the police; I hadn't told anyone what had happened; I hadn't done anything. I just pretended that everything was all right, that nothing had changed. That I hadn't fallen in love and had my heart broken by a murderer.

With only a few months of school left I had decisions to make. What I wanted to do with my life. My mother was pushing me to visit relatives in Europe, spend time traveling, become a woman of the world. I knew she was worried about me, had seen the transformation in me, and she hoped a change of scenery would help me. Oh, how I wished seeing the castles and cathedrals of England would cure what ailed me.

It was a clear and starry spring night when I stood out on my balcony, staring out into the blackness. Sleep was once again elusive, and I'd taken to standing out and staring at the wide world beyond the iron railing. The last year had proven to me that the world beyond Fortune House could be frightening and dangerous. Feeling both hemmed in and protected, I couldn't decide if I wanted to get away or stay tucked inside the confines of my childhood home. Trying not to think of anything at all, I let my mind wander. Thoughts of David, never far from the surface of my mind, popped up, but I squashed them back down. The air was cold, and after a while it changed from brisk and refreshing to damp and chilling. I turned to go back inside but stopped when I heard my name called from below.

Hand on the knob, I didn't need to turn to look. I knew that voice. I heard it in my dreams when I did manage to sleep. My head told me to turn the handle, go inside, and lock the door, but I couldn't make my body obey. Instead I turned and moved to the railing to see him again.

"Alexandra, I need to talk to you."

My eyes closed at the sound of my name, but not before I caught a glimpse of him on the lawn below.

"I need to explain. Tell you the truth about what happened that night."

I pulled the cold night air around myself, and when I spoke, my words came out frigid. "I know what happened. You killed two men in cold blood. What more is there to say?" I tried not to look at his face as I spoke.

There was a moment of silence. "I know what you saw in the papers, but I need to tell you my side of the story."

"I don't care about your side. You told me that I would regret what happened between us, and you were right. I do. Every day."

The words hung like a bank of icy fog. "I know I should have told you everything before I walked out, but I had to get away. Things were getting all tangled up. Can you understand that? Give me a chance to explain."

"David, just go. Before I call the police." Regret and betrayal knotted together in my gut. How could I have been so wrong about him? "Nothing you could say matters. You killed two men and you took advantage of my trust." My hands had begun to shake, so I folded my arms across my chest.

"For everything that happened, I am sorry. Sorrier than you could possibly believe. I never meant to hurt you."

His face, illuminated in the moonlight, looked sincere.

Suddenly anger rose in my throat, choking me. I'd always seen what I wanted to see when I looked at him, but I wasn't going to let him fool me this time. This time I wasn't a naive teenager. The desire to believe him, the desire that tugged at me to trust him, made me furious at myself and at him. I threw words designed to hurt over the railing at him. "You know what I wish, David? I wish you'd died that night. I wish I'd just left you to bleed to death in the snow."

I pulled my gaze away from him, staring straight ahead into the blackness instead. The frozen air had wrapped around me, so that my entire body felt numb, but I could still feel the hot tear trail down my cheek before landing on my hand, cold as ice.

I turned and opened the French doors. The air inside was warm and welcome, but I wished for a second that the cold numbness would never wear off.

If there were a single moment that I could take back, one action I could erase, it would be the exact moment I passed judgment on David. It's the moment that has haunted me for more than five years.

What if he's dead? What if you never get the chance to make things right? What if there is never going to be an opportunity to apologize? The thoughts hammered me. It was the fear that had driven me beyond reason and beyond sense to find David.

But what if he couldn't be found? How could you find forgiveness for something when there's no one left to do the forgiving?

I sank into my couch and rested my head in my hands. I felt as though I teetered on the top of a cliff. I felt as though God Himself were speaking into my soul. "All things work together for good. David's disappearance, your life, all of it, have been woven together to get you to where you sit tonight. The choice is before you. Will you trust in Me? Put your faith and hope into an eternal God who loves you? Or will you continue to rely on yourself? I offer forgiveness to those who ask it, and I offer hope to all those who will receive it."

My hands started to shake. "There is nothing in the world I need more than hope and forgiveness." I said the words aloud, and my heart felt like it was cracking open. For the first time in years, I lowered my head and prayed.

After my night of turmoil I woke to the clean scent of the streets after a storm. The pounding rain of last night had left the world outside my window sparkling, and it was an echo of how I felt. The hurts and fears and regrets were gone. In their place was a contentment that I couldn't explain. I knew today could be a major turning point in my life, but I finally felt as though I had the strength to accept whatever happened.

I got up closer to four than to five, but felt rested and clearheaded. There was a knock on the door at five after five and Jack stood there, looking again as though he hadn't slept.

"We've got a team assembled. Whenever you've got a location, I've got people standing by to get into place. That way we can take her in, get her to safety, and get the gold with as little fuss as possible."

I shook my head. "Mary's not stupid, and I have the feeling that she's not going to surrender herself into FBI custody. It seems to me that she's got some sort of a plan worked out in her mind."

Jack didn't seem to be listening. "Yeah, but we're not going to give her a choice."

I had a feeling that things weren't going to work out exactly the way Jack envisioned, but I wasn't going to press the matter. Time would tell.

Jack made his way past the front hall to the living room. He spotted the couch and moved over to it. Falling into it, he slumped forward and scrubbed his face with his hands.

"Want coffee?"

"More than life itself. Please." He leaned against the sofa arm, and I had to smile at how spent he looked.

"I've got some made. Just a minute."

He sat up and looked toward me. I went to the kitchen, poured him a cup, and brought it back.

"You seem awfully alert this morning." He sent me a quizzical look, then took a sip of coffee. "Must be nice."

I went back to the kitchen to get my own coffee cup.

We talked a little, but mostly sat, lost in our own thoughts. When the phone finally rang, we both jumped. I crossed to it, breath tight in my chest, and paused for a second before picking it up.

"Mary?"

"Who else would it be? I've got a meeting place for you."

"Are you sure it's somewhere safe?"

"It's the best I could come up with. Nowhere is particularly safe for me or Clive at the moment. But this is probably the best option."

I shook my head. "When and where?"

I had a sinking feeling in my gut when she told me her plan. I looked at Jack and shook my head. This wasn't going to make him happy.

"Are you sure?" I couldn't argue with her too much, as it was a good plan. For her. "Okay then. I'll be there. Half an hour. Right, I'll wait for you to find me." I set the receiver down and sighed.

"What?" Jack looked tense and frustrated.

"She wants me to meet her on the subway. Seventh line express at Central Park North. I'm supposed to just get on and let her find me."

Jack's face screwed up in frustration. "That is the worst possible scenario. There's no way to get all our people in place in half an hour on a subway car."

"Clearly she thought things out; it's a good plan for her. She can find me, move around, and she's surrounded by people. She's not a woman who stands out. She stands a very good chance of going unnoticed."

Jack gritted his teeth in frustration. "This is not what we need. We need to bring her in, get the gold, and get her and Clive to safety."

"Well, I don't know how to fix this so it's easier for you, but I have to get going now if I want to get there in time. I'm going to have to call a cab as it is."

"I need to use your phone so I can advise the team about the updated situation."

I nodded. "Go ahead."

"I'm going to be on that train. I'll get on a few stations ahead of you and then just wander the cars until I spot you. At least then I can observe and be there as backup in case things don't go as planned."

I'd been trying not to think about all the things that could go wrong today, but standing next to the woman who was probably the most hunted person in the entire city wasn't exactly safe. Still, there was so much at stake that I really didn't have a choice.

I grabbed my hat from the rack and my purse from the table. "I'll see you when I see you then. I've got to move now if I want to catch that train."

Jack nodded but didn't speak, as he was on the phone trying frantically to make the necessary arrangements.

I shut the door behind me, leaving Jack in the apartment, and clattered down the stairs. Despite the early hour, waves of heat bounced off the pavement and pounded full force into me as soon as I reached street level.

The sidewalk was already filling up with people starting their day. I rushed to hail a cab. Within minutes I was off the street and being whisked toward the Central Park North subway station. It was a familiar spot, as it was one of the closest stations to Fortune House. I'd been riding that line for years. I wondered for a moment if there was any way Mary could have known that, but dismissed it as impossible.

The cabbie screeched to a stop and I got out, tossed his fare through the window, and shouted my thanks. I had only minutes to catch the right train. Everything depended on me getting there in time. I paid my fare and pushed through the turnstile, breathing heavily from the exertion and the nerves of the morning.

I didn't relax until I stood on the platform and checked my watch. I'd made it with four minutes to spare. I took a deep breath and tried to exhale some of the tension tightening my chest.

With nothing to do but wait, I realized that the possibility of Jack getting on the train before me was almost nil. It was very possible that I'd be on my own.

The thought didn't make me as nervous as I would have thought. I'd dealt with Mary before and had always been able to hold my own, and if everything went well, that's all this morning would be. Me convincing Mary and Clive to hand over the gold and surrender themselves into federal custody for their own safety.

My thoughts were cut short by the scream of the train coming into the station. The herd of relaxed people on the platform transformed in seconds as they rushed forward, eager to be the first one on the train, as though that would get them to their destination faster. My stomach flipped as I searched the faces around me for the Soviets or the East Germans. Not spotting them, I let the crowd suck me onto the car as the doors opened.

The car was full, but I'd been told not to move, that Mary would find me. I searched the faces around me, expecting to see her, but no one looked familiar.

Slowly the car emptied a bit as people moved from car to car, spreading out, searching for more room. A few seats emptied, but I chose not to sit, but instead to hold on to the bar above my head so as not to come face to face with Mary while in a position of weakness.

The train started to move and I held on tight. Within seconds we were up to full speed and I was hurtling into a situation I couldn't control. I looked around me, as unobtrusively as possible, searching out people who were moving around, but none of them was Mary.

Trying to tamp down my impatience, I stared out the window. There was nothing to see, but the mindlessness of it soothed me.

The train stopped again, letting more people on, but there was still no sign of the woman I'd come to meet.

Getting a little nervous that I'd somehow gotten on the wrong train, I tapped my fingers on my leg. What was I going to do if I got all the way to the end of the line and there was still no sign of Mary?

There was a bump on my hip as the train moved, and I turned to apologize to whoever I'd knocked into. It was a woman, short and frumpy with her head down, paying no notice to her surroundings. Ready to dismiss her and go back to my waiting, my brain clicked in and I realized the woman, who was now several feet away from me and headed to the back of the train, was the woman I'd been waiting for.

Chapter 29

MARY HAD NO need to worry about being recognized. What I'd said to Jack earlier about her being a woman who went unnoticed was dead accurate. In fact, she seemed to realize it and accentuate it. She was dressed in a greyish-brown dress that neither flattered her nor gave anyone a reason to give her a second look. Her hat had a wide brim and she kept her head down, so it was hard to even pick out definable features. She'd dressed to her advantage, and she pretty much disappeared into the crowds of people around us.

I watched her as she kept walking to the back of the train. She never looked back, never gave me any indication that she wanted me to follow her, nothing. I waited until she'd gone through the doors to the next car before I traced her path through the door.

She passed through five cars before she finally stopped. If I hadn't spent three days tailing this woman, I might have wondered if it was really her. But I'd learned her walk well enough in the early days of this investigation to be sure that I was trailing the right woman.

Finally when we came to a car that was nearly empty, she stopped. She didn't turn around, but kept her back to me, and I caught up to her, walked past, and then turned to face her.

"It's been a while, Mrs. Gordon." I kept my voice low.

She raised her head, and I could finally see past the brim of the hat. She looked rough. As though she'd been neither sleeping nor eating for several days. Her skin was sallow and her normally bright eyes were dull. "Yes, it has. We've been out of town for a while." She stared at me for a long second. "What happened to your face?"

I ran my finger along the edge of the slice. "I ran into some friends of yours. They weren't very nice. But enough about me—let's talk about you. Now that you're back in the city, what are your plans?"

It made sense to speak in generalities even though there didn't appear to be anyone paying us the slightest bit of attention.

"They're quite fluid at the moment."

I took a quick check behind her to make sure that no one was watching us.

"What about Helen? Will you be returning Helen's things?"

Mary's eyebrow arched up. "I haven't been assured that it's the best course of action at the moment. Why don't you tell me what's been going on since I left?"

I decided it was time to be more straightforward.

"I saw Clive's brother a few days ago. He was wondering where you two were. In fact, he was going to great lengths to find out." I needed to make it clear that Nigel Gordon was not seeking them out in the name of familial relations. "He was interested in Helen's things as well. He seemed very eager to get them."

Mary's expression betrayed her true feelings for Nigel, and they were far from kind. "Nigel and I have never been close. I think I shall do my best to avoid him while I'm in the city."

Information transmitted and received. It wasn't going too badly. "You should also know that your cousins from Russia and the ones from Germany have been trying to get in touch. They seemed a little rude to me, so it might be a good idea to avoid them." Okay, I'd just informed Mary of all the parties out to get her and Clive. Now it was time to get what I came here for.

"In fact, there are so many people who want to see you, you probably won't have time to return Helen's things. Why don't you just pass them along to me and I'll see that they get where they need to go."

Mary looked past me, not meeting my eyes. "It's really not that simple. I have to be sure that once those things are out of my hands, Clive and I are going to be kept safe. Those things of Helen's are all we have to bargain with at the moment."

I held back a growl of frustration. Mary was not getting the fact that she was in far more danger with the gold than she was without it. Still, I had to keep trying. I wished for one second that Jack were here right now to help, but wishing didn't change anything. I was on my own. "Why don't you come out for lunch with me and some friends. We can meet anywhere you'd like and maybe help you figure out what you're going to do."

I knew as soon as the words were out of my mouth that I'd made a mistake. The mention of "friends" had tripped me up. To this point she hadn't known that I was working with the FBI, but I'd all but broadcast the fact to her with my little slip of the tongue.

"I'm not interested in meeting with your friends."

It was time to get tough. "My friends are probably the only ones in this entire city who aren't using a photograph of you as target practice. My friends are the only ones who can help you out of this. Everyone else that knows what's going on is looking for a way to kill you." I lowered my voice even further, to the point where Mary had to strain to hear me. "You are all out of options, Mary. Anything but surrender to the Feds is suicide."

Mary's eyes hardened, and I realized I'd pushed too hard. She straightened up. "Thank you for your advice. I'll be in touch." With that, she circled around me and walked to the back of the car. She pushed through to the next car, and just as she entered, the train came to a stop. Before I could react, she bolted out the open door and disappeared into the crowd on the station platform. I tried to get off, but the crush of people trying to get on blocked my way.

I slammed my hand against the window when the doors closed and the train began moving again, killing all chance I'd had of catching up to her.

I got off at the next station and took another train back home. Entering my apartment with an oppressive feeling of failure, I sighed as I unlocked the door. I took a second to wonder what had happened to Jack, but I had the feeling that the unexpected meeting place and little notice had caught us all off guard.

Sitting on my couch, I buried my face in my hands. I'd messed the whole thing up. A smoother negotiator would have been able to talk Mary in gently, get her to hand over the gold, and get her and Clive into protective custody. But as usual, I had the negotiating skills of a bulldozer. "Do it my way or you're going to die." I spoke the words aloud and shook my head at the poor decisions I'd made so far.

Mary had come to me because she trusted me, and I'd made a muck of the entire opportunity.

The doorknob rattled and there was a knock at the door. I strode to the door, my frustration at my own incompetence morphing into seething rage.

I threw the door open to Jack, who stood there looking exactly as frustrated as I felt.

I moved aside so he could come in. "Where were you?" The words came out far harsher than they should have.

"I missed the train. I missed it by inches, and all I could do was stand there and watch it go." He bit the words off, eyes flashing with a dangerous kind of anger.

A warning in my brain told me to tread carefully, but my mouth didn't heed it. "Well, that was helpful. I lost Mary, and you didn't even show up. We're certainly quite the team, aren't we?"

"You lost Mary?"

I glared at him. "Do you see her in the apartment with me?" His eyes narrowed and the planes of his face hardened. I wanted to stop the words coming out of my mouth, but they tumbled out despite my brain's frantic effort to shut me up.

"How could you lose her? She was ready to come in, and now she's gone?" His eyebrows disappeared into his hairline, and he looked as though he were about to explode. An internal struggle played out on his face. Several times his mouth opened as though he were about to say something, then snapped shut. Finally he took a deep breath and headed for the door. "Where did you last see her? I'm going to go out and look for her."

The last of my anger fizzled out, and I just wanted to take back the last two minutes. "Jack—"

"The last place you saw her, Allie." He didn't look at me; he looked beyond my left shoulder and kept his hand on the doorknob.

"She got off at the Lincoln Center station. I don't know anything beyond that."

"Fine. You stay here in case she calls back and wants to meet again. I'm going to go out and see if there's any way to find her before she ends up dead."

Chapter 30

GUILT AND WORRY nagged at me, and Jack walked out before I could work up the nerve to apologize.

Standing around, doing nothing but waiting was the worst thing possible for my frame of mind. I kept picturing Mary in her frumpy grey dress lying on the ground in a pool of her own blood. The images then shifted to another body lying in the dirt, but this time, the face was David's.

I cleaned my apartment and stared at the phone, willing it to ring. When I was finished cleaning, I moved to the window, staring out at the street below, checking every face, looking for Mary. It was unreasonable to hope that she'd come here, but with nothing else to occupy my mind, I was willing to give unreasonable a shot.

After an hour of fruitless waiting, I moved to check and make sure the phone was working. Out of the corner of my eye I caught sight of a flash. It was really nothing more than that, a flash, but it put a jerk in my stride. I stopped and strained my line of sight to identify it. Again, the sun shifted from behind the clouds and something flashed. Like light reflecting off glass. I followed the glare and my breath hitched when I saw its source. It came from a doorway kitty-corner to my apartment building. Only just visible from my window, it was directly in line to watch the front door of my apartment. The glare came from sunlight bouncing off a man's glasses. A man I recognized. It was one of the East German agents, and he was staring directly up at my window. I was fairly sure he couldn't actually see me, but I ducked out of his line of sight anyway.

Heart thumping, I tried to think this new development through. I took another look through the window, and now that I knew just where to look, I could spot the man with no trouble. He was alone, and he'd barely changed position. He still stared straight up at my window.

I backed away. If he was alone, then where was his partner? There were only two possibilities I could think of. Either he'd followed me to my meeting with Mary this morning, or he had followed Jack when he left several hours ago. Either way it wasn't good.

I had no way of contacting Jack. If he, by some miracle, did happen to find Mary, he'd be leading the East German agents directly to her. Panic trickled into my gut. I couldn't leave my apartment because I needed to stay near the phone in case Mary or Jack called, but they were both out there with no idea that either Jack or I may have led the East Germans right to her.

I walked to the door and put my hand on the knob, debating the risk of leaving to go out and search for them myself. I turned the knob, still debating, when the shrill ring of the phone stopped me cold.

I raced across the room and snatched up the receiver. "Hello?"

A male voice I didn't recognize answered me. "Is this Miss Fortune, the private detective?"

I sighed, annoyed. I wasn't sure how a client or potential client could have gotten my home phone number, but it was the worst possible time for him to call. Determined not to tie up the line, I said, "Yes, this is she, but it's not a good time to talk right now. Can I call you back in the next day or two?"

"This is Clive Gordon, and I'm wondering if my wife is with you."

I sank down onto the couch. Clive Gordon. I'd never met or spoken to the man, but he had as much part in this whole debacle as Mary, possibly more. "She's not. I met with her this morning on the subway; then she ran off and I was unable to catch up with her."

Clive's voice rose. "And how long has it been since you've seen her?"

I looked at my watch. "It's almost eleven, and she got off the train at about eight. So three hours or so." Tendrils of alarm wound their way through my mind. "When was she supposed to be back? I assume you two had a plan of some sort."

"It was more of an outline, but I expected her back by nine or so. When ten o'clock came and went with no sign of her I started to worry in earnest."

"You're right to be worried, Mr. Gordon. Your wife is in danger. She has a lot of people on the lookout for her. In fact, I think one of them is watching my apartment at the moment."

"Who is it?"

"It's a known East German intelligence officer. The truly frightening part is that his partner isn't with him. If he's somehow picked up Mary's trail, she's at risk. We believe that these two men are the ones who murdered Robert Follett."

Clive gasped, and once again I regretted my penchant for brutal frankness.

"I'm sorry, but I have to be honest. There are people scouring the city for her that will kill her to get the gold. The fact that she hasn't been seen in three hours is not a good thing. Look, Clive, the facts as they stand are that you and Mary are in huge danger. The only option you've got at this point is to hand over the gold to the FBI and surrender yourselves to them for protection. Your own brother is working with the Soviets to find you. Why don't you bring the gold to me, and we can get the full force of the FBI and the NYPD out on the streets searching for Mary. At this point we can only hope it's not too late."

There was silence on the other end of the line. "Despite my . . . rather questionable past and long-held dislike for the FBI, I must admit that I agree with your assessment of the situation. And the fact that there appears to be no other solution."

I felt like maybe I'd been given a chance to make up for this morning, but I had to think about how to do this. "Okay, I can sneak out of my building without the East German seeing me, so what if you met me at the Central Park North subway station too. I can be there in twenty minutes. Can you meet me on the platform then?"

"I believe I can get there on time. How will we recognize each other?"

I thought for a moment. "I'll have a yellow rose in the lapel of my suit jacket. How about that?"

Clive made a sound of agreement.

"Okay, it's going to take me a few minutes to get out of here unnoticed, so I'll meet you at eleven thirty."

"I shall be there, Miss Fortune."

I hung up the phone and took a second to think the situation through. I was going to have to leave the apartment, but I could at least leave a note for Jack to let him know the updated situation. I scrawled a note, grabbed my purse and hat, and exited, locking the door behind me.

The landlord of my building lived in the basement, next to the boiler room. I flew down the stairs and rapped on her door.

Mrs. Grogenski opened the door and sent me a questioning look through her thick glasses. "Oh, Miss Fortune, what can I do for you?" She squinted at me, and I was fairly sure I'd woken her up from a nap.

"I'm really sorry about this, Mrs. Grogenski, but is there any way I can go out your garden door? It's an emergency, and I would really appreciate it."

She looked confused, but nodded and let me in. I crossed the room to her window. Looking out, I spotted the East German, still peering up at my window. One of the perks of the landlord suite was that it had a private entrance at the back. Mrs. Grogenski had a small garden there, but more importantly, the exit led out to the back alley, well out of sight of the man watching me. I could cut across to the next street, hail a cab, and get to the station, and he would never even know I was gone.

I stepped away from the window and crossed to the door. A cement stairway led to ground level, and when I emerged into the sunshine I breathed a deep sigh. Plucking a yellow rose from one of the rosebushes, I tucked it into my lapel pocket and headed for the station.

Chapter 31

I MADE IT TO the station five minutes early. I was still unsure whether I should have left the apartment, but I figured if Clive was agreeable we could get back there fairly quickly. The chance of missing a phone call from either Jack or Mary was fairly low. It was a risk I had to take.

The platform was emptier at this time of day, and I didn't see anyone who appeared to be waiting for me when I arrived. Breathing a deep sigh of relief, I looked over my shoulder again. I'd checked and rechecked for someone following me on the way over. I'd had the cabbie take a circuitous route here, yet I still couldn't shake the fear that I was going to lead a hostile agent right to Clive. It felt almost surreal going through the same motions to meet Clive that I'd gone through earlier that morning with Mary.

A train arrived and there was a swirl of humanity with a group of people getting off and a group getting on. I leaned against the wall and peered at the station entrance, checking for Clive.

Instead I saw him coming off the train. I recognized him immediately; he was either Nigel's twin or they just looked remarkably similar. I took a reflexive step back. My experiences with Nigel hadn't been pleasant, and an instinctive part of me didn't trust Clive either.

He didn't smile when he saw me, but he did acknowledge me with a nod. I didn't bother to speak, just headed back outside and hailed a cab. Clive followed and stood behind me, passive and defeated looking. I could only imagine the stress of the last week. Despite the fact that he was a criminal and a con man, I felt a bit sorry for him.

I gave the cabbie my address and he headed toward my apartment. As though we'd arranged it, neither of us spoke until we were out of the cab.

"Aren't we going to go into the building? Or are we just going to loiter at the back of it?"

I pointed toward the below-ground entrance. "It would be a bad idea to go in through the front door. The men watching it might be surprised that they missed me leaving. The last thing we need is them knowing you're here."

"Good thinking. I must admit I'm not an expert at all this intrigue. You are quite the modern woman, aren't you, Miss Fortune?"

I didn't answer, just led him up to my apartment. I unlocked the door and was disappointed to see that my note was exactly where I'd left it and Jack apparently hadn't returned. There was no way to know if Mary had called, but there was nothing else I could have done.

"Make yourself at home in the living room; I'll be right there."

I headed for the kitchen and banged a few pots around as though making coffee. I pulled the little revolver I'd taken from the Soviet from my cutlery drawer.

I walked into the living room with it pointed directly at Clive's heart. My suspicions about him were confirmed when I saw his gun pointed directly back at me.

"Ah, Miss Fortune. You wound me. What gave me away?"

"You were probably a good con man in your day, but I think you've lost your touch."

He looked truly affronted. "Explain that remark."

"You laid it on too thick. 'I must admit, Miss Fortune, that I'm not the expert in all this intrigue . . .' It was too much. You forgot that I know what you are. I felt myself being conned."

He seemed disappointed, but his aim didn't falter. "You do know how to deflate a man. I will admit that since the end of the war I've gotten a bit out of practice. People just don't have enough money to go throwing it away, and the confidence game business has been a little slow. So I made you suspicious and you came at me with a gun? That seems a bit extreme."

My eyes widened. "After the week I've had, it seemed only prudent. And apparently I was right."

He nodded. "We appear to be at an impasse then. You have your gun trained on me; mine is aimed directly at your heart. Which one of us is going to lose focus first?"

"I must warn you—imminent death has a great way of focusing my thoughts, Mr. Gordon. Although if you lower your gun I can promise you the original deal I offered. Protection from the FBI and no jail time." It was annoying to be caught in this bluff. And both of us were bluffing, no question. I wasn't ready to shoot Clive, and if he was going to shoot me, he would have done it already. But now that our guns were out, we appeared to be stuck.

"And such a generous offer it is. But you see, my dear, that still leaves me with nothing. And that is the crux of the problem. I quite abhor being . . . how shall I put it? Skint. I really prefer having a bit of weight in my pockets. Money makes life much more fun. And so, I'm waiting for a better offer."

I raised my gun hand a little higher. "Don't tell me that you've put your trust in the Soviets. Why would they pay you for the gold when it would be just as easy to shoot you and then take it?"

"I've considered that possibility. And I have taken steps to ensure that I am the one in the position of power."

"Do tell. And I hope it's a good plan, as it will be the only thing keeping you from bleeding out of multiple gunshot wounds once they have the gold in hand."

He covered his mouth with his hand and affected a gasp. "You really have the most dreadfully active imagination, Allie. May I call you Allie? The situation seems to call for informality."

"I've always said that if you're holding someone at gunpoint you should at least be able to call them by their first name, Clive."

He nodded at me, as though saying touché. "I have a plan that will hand off the gold to someone who wants it rather desperately, in exchange for more cash than I could spend in a lifetime. And that's a lot of money, as I long to cultivate expensive tastes."

"Care to let me in on the details of your grand plan? It seems we both have nowhere better to be at the moment. And while you're at it, why did you call me? Why are you even here?"

"Since we do seem to have time to kill, I guess I might as well. I called you because that's what Mary asked me to do if she wasn't back by ten. And as to the master plan, I have contacted the Soviets and told them that I will sell them the gold. They can cut my brother out of his finder's fee, and their government will be pleased. Mary, on the other hand, has contacted the East Germans and promised to sell the gold to them. Both parties think they will be the ones to get the gold."

"Okay, I'm starting to see the fool part of your foolproof plan. Why don't you enlighten me about the part that's going to keep you with a pulse?"

"Ah, my dear. I thought you would have figured it out by now. There is a third interested buyer. The East Germans won't hurt us until we hand over the gold; the Soviets will also restrain themselves. We will give them both a time and a place for a meet, and while they are busy waiting for us to show up with the gold, we will have already divested ourselves of the treasure for a sum large enough to shock you and will be on our way to a place that no one will ever find us."

I shook my head. "You'd better hope that that's true. 'Cause they won't stop looking. Ever." I took a second to wonder where Jack was. His return would turn this whole situation around. Although, at the moment, hope was looking a little dim.

"You worry too much. As soon as we hand the gold over, we shall bow out of the picture and barely be missed. Of course we might just find a way to alert the Soviets and the East Germans as to the name of the gold's new owner. At that point, it would no longer be our problem, and all attention will be off us."

"Who is this poor soul that has made the mistake of getting into dealings with asps like you and Mary?"

He laughed. "That's the best bit. It's the only person who knows me well and still consistently underestimates me."

It dawned on me. "Nigel." I took a deep breath. "You would do that to your own brother?"

His eyes narrowed and for the first time in this discussion he looked truly annoyed. "Don't be naive. He has already tried to sell me out to the

Soviets, and I'm sure his endgame in this situation includes my death as well. Unfortunately for him, he doesn't realize that I've got every angle covered."

I sighed, finding it hard to believe that there could be such betrayal between brothers. "Surely he doesn't have the money to buy something like this?"

"Oh, no. Of course not. He would simply be buying it for someone else. Like a broker. But that would be of little consequence to the Soviets or the East Germans."

"So, why would he risk it? They're all going to come looking for him eventually."

Clive shook his head as though disappointed that I didn't get it. "Every proposition has risk. He thinks the monetary benefits outweigh the risks in this one."

I shook my head. People would do ridiculous things for money. "So, what now?"

"We wait to see who drops their gun first. Or, we wait until Mary gets here and you run out of luck."

"Mary?"

"She had a few last-minute details to take care of, and then she's going to make her way over here. So really, you've already lost this battle; it's just a matter of time."

"She never intended to turn herself in this morning; this was just an elaborate version of bait and switch?"

"It was. See, that's what we're good at. It's a gift, figuring odds, predicting how people will react under certain circumstances, the long con . . ."

"Okay, in the spirit of sharing we've got going here, why don't you tell me about how you got the gold? I've done a fair bit of research, and it's one thing I couldn't figure out without your help."

He smiled a tiny smile as though recalling a particularly pleasant dream. "It was fate. There is no other explanation for it. Through a bizarre set of circumstances I ended up with a group of British soldiers in Berlin as the war came to a close."

I interrupted him. "Define *bizarre*."

"I got separated from the men in my unit when they came under heavy fire, and I somehow ended up in Berlin. But that's not an important part of the story."

"You deserted your unit when they were in battle is more like it," I muttered.

Clive glared at me, but went on with his tale. "Anyway, I was in Berlin and the Germans had finally given up. It was anarchy in the streets. It was easy for me to wander and not be noticed. It was like harvesttime in an orchard. I was merely picking cherries from the low-hanging branches. No one knew what was going on, there were valuables everywhere, and no one was really minding the store, so to speak. So I helped myself. A little cash here, some jewelry there, anything of value that could fit in my pockets.

"I mostly took things that people wouldn't notice until later, but then fate smiled upon me. I happened to walk by the Berlin Zoo and I saw a whole bunch of Soviet soldiers bringing crates and boxes up out of a bunker and loading them onto a truck. Now, one thing I'd learned from my time in Berlin was that where there were Soviet soldiers, there were valuables. They had direct orders from their commanding officers to take anything of value, load it up, and send it back to the Soviet Union. So I figured if the Soviets were there, surely there must be spoils to be had."

He paused. "There were men bringing the crates up from the bunker, and there were men loading them into the trucks. There must have been more men bringing them up than loading, because there was quite a stack waiting to be hefted into the truck. I just picked a smaller-sized, easy-to-manage crate and walked away with it. No one noticed a thing. I didn't open it until I was a long way off, and I have to confess it was initially a bit of a disappointment. There were about ten pieces of gold jewelry in there. They weren't overly pretty, and, to be honest, I thought for a while that I'd made a poor choice when I'd picked out the box. Nonetheless, I am one who likes planning for the future, so I told myself that the gold would come in handy when I got back home. I shoved the pieces in my duffle and carried them around with me until I made it back to England.

"Now, it was illegal for American soldiers to bring such things back with them, so I came up with a plan. I decided that I would rent a safety deposit box from a bank in London, stash the gold, and come back for it on my own when I had the chance. And that's what I did. I truly had no idea how much the pieces were worth until our dear departed Robert nearly fainted when he saw them."

I shook my head. The whole story was almost too fantastic to believe. "One last question."

"Of course. There are no secrets between us now, my dear."

"Why did you wait so long to retrieve it? I've been wondering almost since the beginning, why now?"

"Excellent question. You see, money has been a bit tight since I got back from the war, and we've really had no cash to spare for a trip overseas, but about two months ago, we received a letter in the mail. The rental on my safety deposit box was about to expire, and I realized that the time had come to go and get my little war mementos."

I sighed, then raised my gun a bit higher. My arm was aching, but I did my best to ignore it.

My heart sank in my chest when I heard knocking at the door, followed by the sound of the door opening. Clive's smile was triumphant. "As fascinating as this conversation has been, my dear, I am afraid it is coming to an end. My lovely Mary has arrived, and we will now outgun you. I promise, out of the respect I feel for you, I shall make your death as painless as possible."

Making sure my aim was true, I turned my head just enough to see the door creak open.

Chapter 32

December 31, 1939

NEW YEAR'S EVE. The start of a new decade, a decade that, thanks to Germany's invasion of Poland, promised war and tragedy. I tried to shove the depressing thoughts aside and have fun. Two friends from school had dragged me out to the dance hall saying that I couldn't be alone on New Year's Eve. I didn't feel like sitting in a cavernous room filled with loud music, boozy laughter, and cigarette smoke, but I didn't want to spend all night alone in my apartment either. I tried to paste a smile on my face for the sake of the girls.

I'd found and rented an apartment of my own several months ago, despite my mother's protests at the unseemliness of it. I lived above a private detective's office and got a job as his secretary and girl Friday. The secretarial work itself was dead boring, but his cases fascinated me.

I sat with my back against the wall, all alone at our table. I'd waved off all invitations to dance but laughed at the antics of the other New Year's Eve revelers.

Glancing at the clock, I was relieved to see it was almost eleven thirty. Once the countdown to the New Year was over I could slip away quietly and catch a cab home. Pleased at my plan, I looked around the room for my friends. My heart tripped when I saw a familiar-looking figure standing in the shadows. I turned my eyes away and gave myself a mental shake. That hadn't happened in a while. For months I thought I'd seen him everywhere I went, but finally I had convinced myself that David was out of my life for good. I looked back to the figure I'd seen, determined to prove to myself that it was only my imagination, but there was no one there. Taking a deep breath, I decided to go outside for some air.

I skirted the tables and the dancers, making my way to the front of the building. As I got closer to the doors I could almost taste the fresh air. Inhaling a crisp lungful as soon as I had the door open, I felt more content than I had all evening.

Wondering if I shouldn't just try to catch a cab now, before the post-midnight rush, I looked out at the street. Movement at the corner of my eye caught my attention. I turned, and lost my breath when I saw who stood there.

David. I hadn't imagined him.

He stood about ten feet away looking back at me with unreadable eyes. Neither of us said a thing. His hair was a little longer than the last time I'd seen him and falling over his forehead, but he looked much healthier. He was dressed in black, and there was no smile in his eyes. "I spotted you inside. I decided to leave before you saw me."

I felt awkward, and he was clearly uncomfortable, but I couldn't get past the shock at seeing him again. "You don't have to leave. I was about to call a cab to take me home anyway."

His eyebrow quirked up. "Headed home before midnight?"

"Not much of a party girl. I didn't really want to come out tonight to begin with. I would rather have stayed at home."

"But your boyfriend wanted to go out?" His tone was neutral.

I couldn't believe I was standing here talking to him like this. Like he was some random acquaintance. "No. I'm here with a couple of girlfriends. And you? Are you here with a date?"

I closed my eyes for a second. I couldn't believe I'd asked. Standing outside in the shadow of the dance hall, this whole scenario seemed so unreal.

"No. I'm here alone. I head overseas in the morning, and I didn't want to spend my last night stateside, alone."

I wouldn't let myself ask. I didn't want to know where he was going, or anything about his life. Instead I stared out into the street, watching cars race by.

We stood in silence for a long moment.

"Where are you going tomorrow?" I couldn't help it. The questioned burned at me until I asked. I watched him out of the corner of my eye.

"France."

My heart sank like a stone. Germany with its guns aimed in so many directions had Europe holding its breath. Despite everything I knew about David, I didn't want him over there, in the middle of it. And somehow I knew he would be in the middle of it.

A cheer drifted out from inside the building and reminded me that it was probably mere minutes from the New Year.

"Alexandra, I shouldn't even ask, but would you dance with me?"

I hesitated.

"I'm sorry. I know it's not right; I just hoped that we could put the past behind us for this one moment."

A war waged within me. There was nothing I wanted more than to pretend that everything was all right. I turned to him. "Let's pretend we just met. Two strangers at a party. We'll probably never see each other again after tonight." The words came of their own volition, but once they were out I couldn't regret saying them.

We walked back inside the building, and this time the music didn't seem so loud, the smoke didn't feel as thick, and I could think of nowhere on earth I'd rather be than right there. In that moment. He led me out onto the crowded dance floor. The band played a slow song and couples all around us swayed to the music. He held out his hand, waiting for me to decide. I placed my hand in his, and he pulled me closer. I held my breath. Dancing with David Rubeneski. Despite my claim to the contrary, I couldn't pretend that he was a man I'd just met. Instead I was acutely aware that I was being held by the first and only man I'd ever loved. He held me gently, one hand entwined with mine and one hand resting at the slope of my waist. My arm stretched way up to rest on his shoulder.

A couple dancing next to us bumped me, pushing us closer. I watched his eyes close. He bent his head and whispered my name into my ear. I'm not sure how I even heard him above the music and laughter around us.

My breath backed up in my chest, and for a second I wanted to run away. He seemed to feel the tension flood my body. "Please. Don't leave yet. Let's just finish the dance." Again, it was whispered, but his voice at my ear drained all resistance.

He continued to speak, almost to himself. "You have no idea how much I wish things had been different, that I could have explained. I tried so hard to stay away from you, but I couldn't. And then I did the one thing I promised myself I'd never do. I hurt you."

The band had started a new song, but I couldn't pull away.

"I've relived every moment I ever spent with you at least a thousand times, and there hasn't been a night since I saw you last that I haven't dreamed of you. And every time I dream, I do it differently, trying to change the ending, trying to make things right, but it never works. I always lose you. And I wake up still in love with you."

My heart felt like it was going to pound right through my chest. I forced myself to take a deep breath. "It doesn't matter. Not how you feel, or how I feel. I can't forget what happened, who you really are."

His breath came out in a rush, as though I'd punched him in the stomach. He leaned his head down until our foreheads touched. "I wish I could make you understand. I would give anything for you to believe in me."

I didn't have a chance to respond as a roar went up from the crowd around us. I felt disoriented as the partygoers began the countdown.

Ten.

I tried to pull my hand from David's, but he wrapped his fingers tighter around mine.

Nine.

Eight.

My eyes stung with tears, and I pulled my hand off his shoulder to rub them away.

Seven.

Six.

Five.

Giving up, I laid my hand back on his shoulder, savoring the solid warmth I felt.

Four.

Three.

Two.

This was it. The moment when things could be different. I reached my hand around to the back of his neck and whispered into his ear. "I never forgot you either."

One.

The frantic cheer of Happy New Year poured down around us, but I barely noticed. Instead all I saw was the shine in David's eyes as he leaned down to kiss me.

I took a deep breath and tried to prepare myself for the inevitable. The door opened, and it was all I could do not to gasp when Jack walked into the apartment. He saw me, and for a second the shock registered on his face, but almost instantly his hand went to his holster and he whipped out his gun, aiming it directly at Clive. I turned my head back toward the man who'd had a gun trained on me for the better part of an hour. I almost laughed at the look of shock on his face.

"What's going on here?" Jack didn't look at me but instead kept his eyes focused on Clive.

"Jack O'Connor, meet Clive Gordon. Clive, this is Jack, the FBI agent in charge of the Helen's Gold investigation. I think his arrival means that the odds are now in my favor." I lowered the gun to relieve my aching arm, then switched it to my other hand and went back to aiming it at Clive's heart.

"Oh, I see. This is an unfortunate turn of events, isn't it?"

"Not for me." My voice was a shade away from gleeful.

"No, I suppose not. But unfortunately I'm not quite prepared to surrender myself to the FBI yet, so unless you have plans to shoot me, I am afraid the situation hasn't really changed."

Jack narrowed his eyes at Clive. "Tell me what's going on, Allie."

I racked my brain, trying to figure out a way to sum it all up. "Clive and Mary had no intention of giving the gold up to the FBI and used me this morning to find out what the FBI knows and to find out if they're even close to catching up with them. They've promised the gold to both the Soviets and the East Germans, and they plan to deliver the gold to neither one. Clive here called me and told me that he was ready to come to the FBI for protection, so I went and met with him, but obviously, I have since discovered that he didn't have good intentions. He thought you were Mary coming through the door, and he planned to kill me once they had me outgunned." I looked to Clive. "How did I do?"

"You summed up a complicated situation admirably, my dear."

Jack shifted his gaze between me and Clive and shook his head in disgust. "Okay, I'll decipher all of that later. For right now, I'm going to put you into protective custody for your own safety." He reached into his coat, I assumed to pull out his handcuffs, but his hand came out empty.

I sighed. "You used them on the Soviets. Let me guess—you haven't had a chance to replace them yet?"

"Right."

"Well, there's a roll of thick twine in the hall closet over there, if that would work."

Jack nodded. "Cover him for a minute, would you?"

I didn't bother to respond, just brought my gun hand up a few inches and realigned it so that if the revolver went off, it would hit something vital.

Jack walked out of the room, and I heard the closet door open. I thought I heard another noise coming from behind me but dismissed it from my mind when I didn't hear any more.

Jack made a lot of noise, shifting things in the closet, looking for the promised twine. I tried to visualize the closet. "Third shelf, left side, behind the sewing kit."

There was another second of silence. "Third from the top or third from the bottom?"

I sighed, then sucked in a deep breath at the feel of cold steel aimed at the side of my neck.

"I'm sorry to interrupt this little treasure hunt, but I believe it's time for Clive and me to get out of here." Mary's voice came from behind me, but I didn't dare turn around to look.

"Jack!" It was supposed to come out as a shout, but it came out as more of a hoarse whisper. Still, it brought him running.

He stopped instantly when he saw the situation. Mary grabbed me by the hair with her free hand and pulled me closer to her. "Put your gun down and I won't shoot her."

Jack kept his gun hand steady, aimed at Mary's head. Unfortunately, Clive now had his gun pointed at Jack, and I'd lost mine at the shock of Mary's arrival.

"Goodness. Circumstances do change quickly around here, don't they?" Clive remarked, jovial as usual.

From behind me, Mary jerked hard on my hair, bringing tears to my eyes. "I told you to drop your weapon. I've never liked Miss Fortune here, and I really wouldn't have any compunction about putting a hole in her. It's your choice, but don't fool yourself into believing I won't do it."

Jack held his gun steady for several long seconds before raising his hands in a gesture of surrender.

"Put your gun on the ground and kick it over to me." Mary barked out orders, and Clive looked as though he were enjoying a really good show on television.

Jack did as she asked, and I held as still as possible. As soon as Mary was in possession of Jack's gun she pulled at my hair again. "You're coming with us. Having a hostage should make this whole process easier. It will keep Jack here from shooting us in the back anyway."

Clive scurried across the room until he was next to his wife. "Wonderful timing as usual, my dear."

"Oh, shut up, Clive."

He didn't seem particularly offended at the snappish comment. He just moved out in front of her and made his way to the door. Mary backed out, keeping me as a shield in front of her. Jack watched helplessly, a storm of frustration crashing in his eyes.

Mary said nothing more. She backed us all the way to the door, shoved me out, and slammed it behind her. She pointed her gun directly at my head. "If you want to stay alive, don't get in my way, don't slow me down, and don't annoy me." With that she gave me a hard push in the small of my back, and I had to scramble down the stairs in order to avoid falling down them. When we got to the bottom she pushed her gun into the base of my spine and ran me out to the car that was idling in front of my building.

Chapter 33

MARY SHOVED me into the car, pushed me across, and got in next to me. The second she slammed the door shut, Clive stomped on the accelerator and took off down the street.

"Not to question a good turn of events, but what

took you so long, my dear? It was getting quite uncomfortable in there. I was starting to wonder if I wouldn't be spending the night in jail."

"I had a little trouble getting here is all. Now let's just concentrate on getting to the ship."

Clive focused on the road, and no one spoke. Mary was paying just enough attention to me that I couldn't imagine being able to overpower her and wrest the gun from her grip. Instead I plotted. *Ship* probably meant we were headed to the New York harbor. I couldn't think of a way that information would help me, but it was best to be prepared for anything. I knew that the minute he could, Jack would have a team of agents out searching for me, but it was a big city and he didn't really have a clue where to start looking.

Still, he was looking for me, and that gave me hope.

From the front seat Clive whistled a jaunty tune. The man was unbelievable. Every day was a sunny day in Clive's world.

I leaned back into the seat and closed my eyes. Unsure of how to pray, I settled with a simple "God, help me" and figured I could leave the details of it up to Him. After all, He'd have a better plan than I did anyway.

The car sailed through the city, zigging and cutting through traffic. A sudden thought occurred to me, and it was all I could do not to sit straight up and turn to look behind me.

The East Germans, or one of them, at least, had been watching my apartment, which made it likely they'd seen Mary enter, only to watch all three of us leave moments later. It was probable that they were there somewhere, behind us, trailing our route through the city. I wasn't sure if that was good news or bad news for me personally, but it was definitely bad news for Clive and Mary, who were still unaware of the probability. If Mary had made arrangements with the East Germans, telling them that she would sell them the gold, then it was apparent that they weren't content to take her at her word.

"So, what's the plan, Dearheart?" Clive stopped whistling but never slowed as he made his way east.

Mary rolled her eyes, apparently as sick as I was of Clive's relentless good cheer. "You've got a meet with the Soviets scheduled for nine, I've got a meet scheduled with the East Germans at nine, and we're going to hand the gold over to Nigel and get our money at three. Our ship starts boarding at two thirty and sets off at four. We will be long gone before anyone realizes that we're even missing. I've arranged to have notes delivered to both the Soviets and the East Germans alerting them to who has the gold. I don't think we'll have any trouble with anyone searching for us after that."

Clive laughed. "It's perfect. If only we could

watch it happen. That would be even better, but you can't have everything, I suppose."

We were getting close to our destination; I could detect the scent of the water. "Why do you need me then? Why not let me go? You'll be long gone by the time I can do anything to stop you."

Mary shook her head. "It would be wise to keep your mouth entirely shut, Miss Fortune. Remember what I said about annoying me." She waved her gun at me, and I let the issue drop.

"Right, so I'm going to need some directions soon, darling. There are a lot of boats in the New York harbor."

"Ships. They're called ships. Ours is called the *Cassiopeia*, and it's the first left after this turn, and then it's all the way at the end. We'll have to walk from there."

Clive found a spot to park and shut the ignition off. Mary yanked me out of the car by my elbow. There didn't seem to be a lot of people around and the ones that were, were far enough away that I wasn't sure they'd be able to hear me if I screamed. Feeling a lot like I was being shanghaied by pirates, I was wedged between Clive and Mary and forced to walk.

"Smile and pretend you want to be here. We're having a lovely day out by the water. Don't make me shoot you." Mary's gruff threats were getting old, but I had no plan at this point, so I didn't protest.

The *Cassiopeia* was a smallish ship compared to some of the mammoth passenger ships I'd seen. It appeared to be a commercial vessel that probably took on a few dozen passengers to make a little extra money.

The gangplank was down, and the two of them marched me up and onto the boat itself. Mary seemed to know where she was going, and she found a passage that led down into the belly of the ship. Yanking out her gun again, she let Clive go down first, then motioned for me to precede her. "Don't let her take an unnecessary step, Clive."

By the time I was at the bottom, Mary was almost on my heels. I had no real chance to escape. I fought back a groan of frustration and reminded myself that an opportunity would present itself. I just had to be ready.

Mary led us down a long corridor. She stopped at a door that looked remarkably similar to all the other doors, so I couldn't tell how she knew this was the right one, but the key in her hand fit the lock, so she must have been right.

The door swung open and revealed a cramped room that was as spare as it was ugly. There was a bed, a washstand that sat underneath an unframed, spotted mirror, and a tiny porthole. The only thing in the room that didn't look as though it belonged was a dark blue trunk with a brass lock that rested at the foot of the bed.

"Sit on the bed and don't move." She didn't look at me or acknowledge me in any other way, just turned to Clive and started speaking. "I got our trunk here earlier—had to pay one of the sailors to let me on early, but it will save us time in the end. We should just get back here a few minutes before the ship disembarks, and the last thing we need is to be struggling with our things, trying to get it all on in time."

Clive grinned at her. "You are a brilliant woman who keeps all of the details straight. You are the best wife a man could have." He moved to kiss her, and I felt like standing up and shouting that she was holding a hostage, preparing to set her brother-in-law up to be killed, and she was a known criminal, but I didn't think Clive would see my point.

He kept his arm slung around her shoulder for a moment. "Now, I have to admit, I'd like to see the gold one last time before we hand it over. Where have you stashed it?"

Mary didn't react to the question for a moment, then just pointed to the trunk.

"Ah, one last quick peek and then we'll be done with this whole interesting, if slightly panicked, time in our lives." He flicked open the latch and shoved up the lid. Clothes were piled along the top, the only things I could see from where I sat. Clive started to dig. "Now, I don't suppose you can remember where in the case they are?"

"Right at the bottom." Mary took a step closer, watching over his shoulder.

"Of course it is. Isn't that always the way?" Clive continued to shift things around, and it occurred to me that neither one of them was paying attention to me. Mary seemed very interested in Clive's search, and so I shifted position, getting ready to move. The chance of escape was slim from inside this room, but an opportunity could present itself and I was going to be ready.

"I can't seem to find it. Could you look, Mary?" Clive took one last poke into the trunk, then moved to stand up. Mary took a step back, raised her gun hand, and swung with a level of force I wouldn't have believed could come from such a small woman. The sound of metal crashing against skull resulted in a dull thunk that made me cringe.

Clive's eyes opened wide for a second, then faded closed, and he toppled forward onto the floor. Mary took a step back, watched him for a moment, then looked up at me.

I was frozen to my spot on the bed. For the life of me I couldn't have moved if the door opened and a map to freedom had appeared in my hand.

"Okay, plans have changed. We're getting out of here."

"What are you *doing*? Don't you have any loyalty at all, woman? And I thought Nigel was the allegiance-switching megalomaniac." A thought dawned on me. "You're not in league with Nigel, are you?"

Mary's face wrinkled in disgust. "Of course not . . ." She trailed off. "Never mind. You're just the hostage. I don't need to explain myself to you."

"Well, I sure hope you know what you're doing, 'cause that's going to be one furious man when he wakes up."

Mary shook her head. "By the time he wakes up, he's going to be on his way to Africa, so it's not really going to matter. He'll forgive me when I show up in Africa with fistfuls of money." She moved over to Clive's prone body and pulled something out of his pocket. Car keys. "Okay, we're leaving now, and you are worth only slightly more to me alive than you are dead, so don't mess around, don't talk to me, and do not do anything stupid."

My eyes widened at the depth of the treachery in this family, but I preceded her out of the room. Once we were in the corridor, she moved to close the door behind us.

I walked in stunned silence off the ship, down the gangplank, and back to the car. This time Mary motioned for me to get into the driver's seat. She tossed the keys at me, and almost automatically I got into the car and started the engine.

"Head back into the city. Once we're closer, I'll tell you where I want to go." I didn't say anything, just put the car in reverse and turned back to the main road.

I tried to remind myself of the ultimate goal here. It wasn't to get away from Mary; instead it was to follow Mary to the gold and to find a way to get it into the hands of the FBI. That was the only winning outcome for me, and I needed to imprint that fact on my brain. I was beginning to have serious doubts that Mary would actually shoot me, and she certainly wouldn't shoot me while I was driving, so I took a deep breath and tried to force myself to relax. Mary may have had the gun, but I was in control of the two-thousand-pound piece of metal we were both seated in.

"You don't honestly think you can win at this little game you're playing, do you? Mary betrays everyone, dupes everyone, and makes off with the gold. You aren't naive enough to think it's that simple, are you?"

Her eyes narrowed and sparked. "You have no idea what you're talking about. I'm just trying to stay alive. Clive was the one with the big plans. He was going to plan and plot and outthink everyone. I think his favorite part of this whole scheme was that he would end up besting his brother. Clive was the naive one. He got so caught up in his plans that he convinced himself his plan was foolproof. He's always been like that. He'd set up a con and he'd have all these grand plans, but he couldn't see that people don't always react the way he thought they would. And I was always the one left behind to clean up his messes. I have kept that man out of jail and kept him alive more times than I can count."

"So, you're trying to tell me that you knocked Clive out and deserted him on a ship that's leaving for Africa because you're protecting him?" The disbelief shone through my voice like a beacon.

"Not that you'd understand, but I'm doing this for his own good. He will forgive me when I come to find him in Africa, holding the money we're going to get from the Russians."

"The Russians?" I asked.

"I wouldn't sell it to the Americans for any price, and the East Germans would put a bullet in my head and then just take the gold. I'm going to sell it to the Russians, take my money, and get on a ship bound for Africa tonight. He shouldn't be there longer than a day without me." Unlike Clive, Mary didn't seem gleeful as she shared the details of her plan; instead she looked grim.

I shifted into the right lane, getting ready to take the turn that would lead us back into the city. I shoulder checked, then crossed.

Mary was nervous. Her leg was tapping, and when I looked closely I saw that her hand trembled. Just the slightest bit, but it was there.

From what I'd heard of their plans, the East Germans and the Soviets would realize that they'd been betrayed by a little after nine o'clock tonight. At the latest. The question would be, when would Nigel realize, and would he then alert the Soviets to Mary's change of plans as though he'd been on their side all along and had never planned to broker a deal with the Gordons for someone else?

Allegiances seemed fluid in this case. Promises made, promises broken, new allegiances formed. My head ached just trying to keep up. There wasn't a scrap of loyalty to be had with any of them.

I checked the rearview mirror again and smiled to myself a little.

January 1, 1940

THE EUPHORIA lasted for only the first moments of the New Year. I held on to him and tried to block out reality as it crashed over me in waves.

"He's a murderer. He killed two men," the voice in my head taunted.

David must have felt the shift in me, because he pulled far enough away to look at me. He studied my face, and I saw the precise moments he witnessed my doubts. He closed his eyes. When he opened them again, they were carefully blank. "I know it's hard to trust me. I understand that."

I wanted to argue with him, to tell him that I wasn't doubting him, or to defend my doubts as reasonable, anything to quantify my confusion.

He took a notebook out of his pocket and fished around for a pen. He scribbled something on a sheet of paper, ripped it off, and shoved it into my hand. "If you want to find out what really happened, go to this address and ask to speak to Andrew McDowell. Ask him about me, and he'll tell you everything you need or want to know."

He took another step away from me. "I'm leaving on a ship called the *Aurelia* at noon tomorrow. If I you don't come to say good-bye, I'll assume that you've made your decision about me."

With that, he turned and wove his way through the crowd, and in seconds I'd lost sight of him. I stood alone in the crowd of revelers, bewildered, with nothing but a crumpled note in my hand.

Chapter 34

I DROVE JUST under the speed limit. I was in no hurry to get wherever it was Mary wanted to go. I'd guess that the drive from my apartment to the harbor had taken at least an hour. Every minute that I could delay us was another tiny scrap of advantage that shifted from Mary to me. I thought about Jack for a second. I knew he'd be frantic at the thought of me with Clive and Mary, but if there was anyone in the world who could actually do something about it, it would be Jack. I just had to trust that he had his end covered.

Going on a hunch, I changed lanes and took the next turnoff. Mary sat up straight and shoved her gun in my face. I snarled back at her. I was getting mighty sick of that gun.

"Where are you going? Why did you change directions?"

"I didn't change directions. The road is closed up there, and I assumed you didn't want to take a diversionary route that was thirty miles or more out of our way."

She stared at me suspiciously, then relented a bit. "You'd better get us back to the city, fast."

"I'm working on it." I didn't let myself smile, but I'd just been proven right. Mary didn't know where we were. As someone who did most of her travel either on foot, on the subway, or by taxi, there was no real reason for her to know her way around the outer edges of the city. Unfortunately for her, I was now convinced that I could head for Canada, and other than the time it took to get there, she'd be none the wiser until she spotted Niagara Falls. Another check mark in the Allie column. Despite her gun, the odds were starting to even out between us, and she didn't even realize it.

Of course, there was another factor, one that Mary had no inkling of, that could tip the balance either way. Or it could once again turn the situation on its head. I tried not to think about it, but just to concentrate on the task at hand. I was taking back roads, working my way into the city, but I was headed for the FBI field office. I figured that if I kept our route to obscure neighborhoods and away from visible landmarks, I could keep Mary in the dark for a good long while. Another glance over my shoulder and I realized that my plan, for all its cleverness, was not going to work.

Since our abrupt departure from my apartment we'd had the East Germans on our tail. I figured they hadn't given up and gone home when we were on the boat, so I'd kept my eyes open for them on the drive back into the city. Spotting them once we got under way, I realized that they could be a kink in my plans. Either they would continue to follow us at a distance, in which case my plan would still work, or they would decide it was time to force Clive and Mary's hand, and in that case, it would be anyone's game.

Instead of maintaining a nice, comfortable distance, they were now gaining on us and not attempting to conceal it. Mary saw me looking over my shoulder, and this time she looked too.

"Who is that?"

I suppose the sight of a big black car racing toward the back of our car on an otherwise deserted road couldn't be missed by even her.

"Those are the two East German agents who have been following us since you took me hostage back at my apartment."

Mary's face paled, and the slight tremble in her hand turned into a visible shake. "What do they want?"

I rolled my eyes. "Well, Mary, they could just want some company, they could want to race us, or maybe they want the gold you promised them. And this probably looks like a great opportunity to get it from you without even having to pay you for it. For them, it's a win-win. They get the gold and they just shoot you."

"I'm not the only one they're going to shoot."

I didn't answer, as I was very much aware of the fact that it was just as easy to kill two people as it was to kill one. Three actually, I mentally corrected myself. They'd already killed Robert Follett in the pursuit of the gold.

"What are our options?"

I turned to stare at Mary, not sure when she'd decided that we were on the same side. Of course, any side that didn't end in being shot was a good side to be on.

"I'd say we only have one. We can try to outrun them. We're only a few miles off the more well-traveled roads, and we'll have a much better chance there."

"Stop yapping and step on it then."

January 1, 1940

I HAD TO WAIT until morning to go see Andrew McDowell. His address was scrawled, barely legible on the notepaper David had given me. It was an unfamiliar address to me, but the cabbie seemed to know how to get me there. When he pulled up in front of a police station, I was sure he'd taken me to the wrong place.

I checked the address on the sheet against the

numbers printed on the door, and my heart did a weird kick when they matched.

Why would David send me to a police station?

The cabbie cleared his throat, and I yanked myself out of my thoughts. Handing him his fare, I stepped out of the vehicle and shut the door behind me. I stared up at the building with nerves writhing in my stomach.

The cabbie rolled down his window behind me. "You okay, lady?"

"We're about to find out." It was said more to myself than to him.

I asked at the desk to speak to an Andrew McDowell and was directed to another desk in the middle of a large room full of people. I sat, waiting for McDowell to show up, trying not to stare at everyone around me. Uniformed police officers walked by, and suited men sat at desks, pecking at typewriter keys with pencils and yelling into telephone receivers.

I waited for half an hour before a tall man, about forty, walked up and introduced himself. "I'm McDowell. What can I help you with?"

"I was given your name by a friend. David Rubeneski. He told me that you could answer some questions for me." I felt awkward, and McDowell looked surprised.

"And your name would be?"

"Alexandra Fortune."

He leaned against the corner of his desk with a thoughtful look on his face. "Tell you what—there's a diner around the corner. Why don't you meet me down there in, say, fifteen minutes, and I'll tell you whatever you want to know, because I don't think this is the place you want to have this discussion."

I sighed and resigned myself to having to wait a little longer for answers. "That would be fine. I'll meet you there in a quarter of an hour."

He nodded and I took a moment to hope that after this I would finally have the answers I needed.

Chapter 35

I STOMPED ON the gas, and there was a deep roar from the engine and a few-second lag, then a burst of speed that pushed both Mary and me back in our seats. It was a gravel road, and I heard loud pings as rocks hit the car's undercarriage. The rearview mirror showed that we were going about the same speed as the other car now, as they were no longer catching up to us. I had never traveled these particular roads, but I knew that if I just kept heading west, I'd eventually end up back in the city.

I coaxed the car a little harder, and the speedometer needle flickered its way up to sixty-five miles per hour. There was a little swing to the rear tires, just a hint, but it was enough for me to back off of the gas a bit.

"What are you doing? You need to go faster, not slower." It was a sign of how distressed Mary was that her voice had risen to a shriek.

"It's not going to help us make our escape if we crash. Something to remember about driving; control is always more important than speed."

"Just what I needed, a know-it-all, full-of-fear private detective. Why did it have to be your office I walked into that night?"

"Okay, since we're either about to die in a fiery car crash or be shot to death by East German agents, tell me the truth. Was it simply a coincidence, or did you target me specifically?"

From the corner of my eye I saw her turn to stare at me.

"No word of a lie—it was a freakish coincidence. I knocked on the first door that had lights on."

I shook my head, but only slightly, as all of my concentration needed to be on the road ahead. I held my breath as I took a set of curves without even slowing down. My hands ached from the death grip on the steering wheel, but a look in the rearview mirror told me that I needed even more speed, as the East German car was gaining on us.

"Okay, in the spirit of insanity and curiosity I've got a question for you. Why were you so eager to jump back into this whole thing to help me? I fired you over a week ago. I can't imagine that you thrust yourself into danger for all of your ex-clients."

I winced. Good question. "After you fired me, I made a deal with the FBI. They are giving me something I want in exchange for the gold. They figured I had the closest connections to you and Clive, and I had the best chance of recovering it. We made a deal."

Mary laughed. "You're in it for the money just like everyone else." She sighed with apparent disgust.

I made a sound, trying to decide if I should explain, but I stopped myself.

"No. Don't make excuses. I'm just surprised, that's all. I wouldn't have expected someone like you to be willing to sell out a client for money."

Despite the terrifying speeds, the horrible men chasing us, and the fact that I couldn't respect Mary less if I'd tried, her assessment of me hurt. "It wasn't cash, but that makes no difference. Yeah, I sold you out, after you fired me. But I was also trying to protect you."

She looked skeptical. "Maybe, but you sold me out nonetheless."

I had to agree, but the thought flew out of my mind when I caught sight of the road ahead. Or more appropriately the lack of road ahead. There should have been a sign, but there wasn't, nothing to warn drivers that the road ended but the sight of the great deep ditch where the path should have been.

"Hold on!" The words came too late. I hit the brakes and knew immediately it was the wrong thing to do, but nothing could stop the out-of-control fishtailing. I pulled my foot off the brake and did my best to keep the car steady, but it was out of my control now. I felt the back end lose grip, and I knew it was over. Bracing my head with my arms, I yelled at Mary to do the same. The last thing I heard was her screams stop as her head hit the windshield seconds before the car went off the road.

The first thing I saw when I opened my eyes was a man's face peering at me from upside down. I tried to focus my thoughts and make sense of the scene, but it wasn't until my body started registering pain that it all came into clear focus. I was upside down, my neck and shoulder pressed against the roof of the car at a strange angle. I tried to clear my thoughts. I hadn't been out long, as I could hear the wheels still spinning fruitlessly in the air. I took a second look at the face staring at me and confirmed that it was the bespectacled East German agent. I closed my eyes and blew out a breath of frustration.

"This one is alive." His accent was thick and harsh, and he continued to stare at me as though I were a bug he was trying to identify.

"This one is not awake yet, but I believe she will be fine." The voice was much quieter, as though coming from much farther away, and I assumed he was talking about Mary. My head hurt too much for me to turn and see for myself.

January 1, 1940

THE DINER WAS mostly empty, with only a few people in booths sipping coffee. I picked a table toward the back and watched the door, waiting for McDowell and answers.

He arrived a few minutes later and made his way directly to where I sat. He signaled the waitress for a coffee and folded himself into the seat across from me.

"So you're the Fortune girl." He took a sip from his mug and studied me over the rim. "I've heard a lot about you. You've found yourself in the middle of more than one of our operations over the last few years."

I looked at him in total incomprehension.

"You witnessed a shooting in the park, didn't you?"

I nodded. "How did you know that?"

"It was the second time David had to extricate you from the middle of an active investigation."

"I don't understand."

"David's my partner. For the past two years we've been working on an undercover operation involving organized crime. The shooting you witnessed was mob related, as was David's shooting last year. The two men found dead in the park had brought David out to the reservoir to kill him. They'd discovered his identity, and he had to shoot both men and run for his life. I understand that he came to you for help when he was injured. I've never had a chance to say thank you, but I will now. You saved my partner's life that night."

I leaned back in my seat and tried to take in what I'd just learned, but McDowell didn't stop to let me adjust my thoughts. "I don't know all the details of what happened that weekend; David never wanted to talk about it, but I do know that he wasn't able to tell you what really happened to him. I think that bothered him. Letting you assume the worst."

I pushed out of my seat. I knew all I needed to know. The only thing I could think of now was getting to David, apologizing, and letting him know how I really felt.

"What time is it?"

McDowell looked startled, but checked his watch for me. "Twenty after eleven."

My heart lurched. "I'm sorry, but I have to leave. Thank you for meeting with me and clearing all of that up."

He rose with me, looking confused for a second, but then his face cleared. "He leaves at noon. You'd better hurry if you want to say good-bye."

I smiled at him, picked up my purse, and rushed toward the door. The harbor was half an hour away if the cabbie moved fast, which was just enough time to tell David that I'd be waiting for him when he got home.

I hailed a cab immediately.

"I need to get to the harbor as quickly as possible,

and there's a big tip if you can get me there in under twenty minutes."

The cabbie's eyes lit up at the prospect either of the cash or of racing through the city. I leaned against the plush seat and practiced in my mind what I was going to say to him when I got there.

The East German yanked open the driver's side door. I had no strength or breath in me to fight when the man reached in, hooked his hands around my arms, and dragged me out of the car.

Once he dragged me out of the vehicle, he dumped me on the grass. I lay there, dazed and wondering what was going to come next. Mary had the gold somewhere. They would get it, and then they'd most likely shoot us. Being in the hands of the East Germans was probably the worst-case scenario imaginable. Not only was there a very good chance they'd kill us, but there was almost no chance Jack would be able to find us. Not with all of the creative driving I'd done. I wasn't totally sure myself where we were.

I heard a yelp from Mary's direction, then a whispered conversation. I thought about trying to get up and make a break for it, but I was fairly sure that I couldn't even manage the get-up part, never mind the running. I took a deep breath and tried to shove myself up into a sitting position with my uninjured arm. My head whirled and my mind fogged over for a moment at the effort.

"Stay where you are." The command was shouted from several feet away, and I sagged back against the grass. One of the men came over to my side and hovered over me, blocking the fading sun. His hat was silhouetted against the circle of light, and he looked like a nightmare come to life.

"Get up." The words came out flat, with no expression, but the tone made my head swim. It wouldn't bother this man at all to shoot me. The instinctive knowledge filtered through and left me cold. I got my hand under me and shoved myself up again. I tried not to show how weak I felt, but a quiet moan escaped. Immediately I felt his hand grasp my upper arm, and he hauled me to my feet. Every part of me moaned this time, and my shoulder, the shoulder he'd just wrenched, the shoulder I'd hit when he unbuckled me, wanted to weep.

Still, I didn't give him the satisfaction of seeing me weak; instead I turned toward him and glared. "Get your hands off me."

He looked past me as though I were invisible, but the hand that circled my upper arm tightened mercilessly. I used all my strength of will not to squirm under the pain, and finally his grip eased.

"Get into the car." He barked the words out and immediately led me toward their vehicle, still running, parked on the side of the road. He opened the back door and shoved me in. My legs were barely clear when he slammed the door shut.

I took a second to even out my breathing. Every sinew of my body hurt, but my shoulder screamed at a pitch that dwarfed the other complaints. I took a second to rub it with my other hand, but it moved in a sickening direction that took my breath away. Pulling my hand back, I tried to concentrate on something, anything else.

I peered out the window and saw Mary being forced to her feet every bit as roughly as I had been. She looked bad. She was bleeding from a cut on her head. Blood trickled down the side of her face and dripped off the edge of her jaw. She had a dazed, unfocused look, and one of the East Germans led her toward the car as though she were on a leash. She walked, unprotesting, although at one point she stumbled and fell onto one knee. The man didn't even slow; he just yanked her along until she hopped and regained her footing.

Aside from the pain in my body as a whole and my shoulder specifically, I at least had a clear mind. I had serious doubts that Mary did. She'd knocked her head against the windshield, and I was pretty sure that it was going to take a while for her to be able to give me a hand in the coming-up-with-a-plan department.

The door squealed open and Mary was shoved in next to me. The door shut and the two East Germans got into the front seat. The one in the passenger seat, the one with glasses, turned toward us, aiming a gun at me from the back of the bench seat.

I fought back a sigh. I'd had so many people pointing guns at me today it was starting to get predictable. Or expected, anyway.

The man stared at me for a second, then shifted his gaze to Mary. "You will give us the gold."

Mary didn't even turn toward his voice; she just stared into space, apparently not even hearing him.

"Where is the gold?" The voice got loud, and this time it seemed to penetrate Mary's haze.

"I don't have it."

My heart plunged with her answer. I had no doubt she was telling the truth. She didn't appear capable at the moment of lying. She simply stated the facts.

"Where is it?" His voice got dangerously slow, and the fear I'd been trying to hold at bay tumbled over me.

Mary didn't respond. She seemed to have retreated into her dazed state again. The gun turned toward me.

"You will take me to the gold."

I raised my uninjured hand in a gesture of surrender. "She's the only one who knows where it is."

He squinted at me as though debating whether I told him the truth, and I watched as his finger slid up and down the pistol's trigger. I stopped breathing. After five interminable seconds he moved his weapon back to Mary.

"Where is the gold?"

Mary slid her gaze in my direction. "Her office. It's in her office."

I had no idea what she was trying to do, if this was a plan or if she was just delirious, but I knew that if I wanted a chance of surviving the next hour or so I'd better play along. No matter what, it would be easier to stay alive and get help once we were back in the city.

Chapter 36

MARY ALTERNATELY dozed and moaned all the way back into town. The East German in the passenger seat kept an eye and a gun trained on us for the full hour that it took to get back. The two men didn't speak to each other, and the silence made me even uneasier. It was exactly what Jack had said; they were professionals in the worst sense of the word. Taking us hostage was no big deal to them because it was just part of their job. The same way shooting Robert Follett had been part of their job.

My head ached, and it was hard to think logically, but I kept trying to figure out why Mary had directed them to my office. Surely she realized they were going to be less than pleased when they realized that she'd been lying. It had probably been a move born of desperation and a brain that had recently been slammed against a windshield. I tried to think of anything that I could turn to my advantage in the office, but I knew that chances were pretty slim. Even under perfect circumstances these two men were to be feared, and these circumstances were as far from perfect as I could imagine.

The car slowed and downshifted as we approached my building. "Miss Fortune, you will give me your keys so that there is no ill-fated attempt at escape when we get out."

The breath hissed out from between my teeth. Frustrated, I tried to focus my thoughts. My loss of my keys was first and foremost the loss of a potential weapon. Anything hard and pointed could be used as a projectile if there was enough force behind it. I wasn't squeamish; if it came down to life or death I would have no problem stabbing one of these men with a set of keys. Unfortunately, that weapon was about to be confiscated. I reached into the pocket of my suit jacket where I'd stuffed them when I'd brought Clive back to my apartment. That seemed like eons ago. I grasped the key ring and handed it over to the man. He kept his gun pointed at me and took the keys with his other hand. Frustrated again with the total lack of opportunity to change our circumstances, I sighed, and he pulled them out of my grasp.

The driver parked the car, and both men shifted to face us. "We are here; now where is the gold?"

Mary jerked awake, and she looked alert this

time but confused. She looked at me, then noticed the two narrow barreled guns pointed at us. Her eyes went wide, and I could see just from looking at her that the details of our predicament were coming back to her.

"Where is the gold, Mrs. Gordon? This is the last time I shall ask you politely."

Fear rippled across her face. She licked her lips. "I hid it inside Miss Fortune's office." She opened her mouth as though to add more, but decided against it.

I could only pray that she had a plan, that she wasn't telling the truth.

Almost as soon as the words were out of her mouth the two agents got out of the car, whipped the back doors open, and hauled us from the car to the bottom of my office building's steps. The driver held his gun to my throat, so there was no opportunity to call out, and he held me so that if anyone passed by, they wouldn't be able to see that I was being held against my will. Every thunk of my heels on the steps was another step closer to being trapped in my office with no gold and two very angry East German agents.

January 1, 1940

THE CABBIE earned himself a great tip when he got me to the harbor by fifteen to twelve. He let me out, and I watched him pull away before I walked down the row of gangplanks. I searched out names on the prows, looking for one marked *Aurelia*. Not spotting it, or any other ship that appeared to be loading passengers, I broke into a run.

I scanned both sides, but none of the vessels were the *Aurelia*.

Cold dread filled my belly. I searched the area for anyone who could give me directions to the ship and to David, but in my heart, I already knew.

A man passed me and I turned to him. "I'm looking for a passenger ship called the *Aurelia* that's supposed to leave at noon today."

The man shook his head. "These are all commercial vessels. The ship you're looking for is probably where the passenger vessels are docked. It's a few miles from here"—he looked at his watch—"but you won't get there in time. It's five to twelve now."

I think I mumbled thanks, and I moved to the gangplank of the closest ship and sat down. Arms wrapped around my chest, I cried. I'd been given one last chance to make things right with David, and I'd missed it. When I didn't show up to say good-bye to him, he was going to take that as my final good-bye, that his reasons didn't matter, that I never wanted to see him again.

I felt the hope drain out of me as I realized what I'd just lost.

They marched us up the stairs, and I desperately tried to make eye contact with Mary, hoping against hope that she'd signal me, anything to let me know she had a plan, anything to show me that she was lying about where she'd stashed the gold. Unfortunately, she never looked my way, and my terror mounted with each step we climbed.

The flight of stairs didn't take long enough, and within moments we found ourselves standing in front of my office door. The black stenciled letters on the glass said "A. Fortune," and for once I figured I should have just gone with Miss Fortune. It seemed to sum up a lot of my life. Shaking my head, I took a deep breath.

The bespectacled East German inserted my key into the lock and shoved the door open. It was a little past sundown, and shadows coated the office, making it appear cavernlike. I let one of the agents search for the light switch, prolonging the moment of truth for a few additional seconds.

It wasn't long enough. Suddenly the lights flooded on and illuminated the bare room. There was nothing but an expanse of wood floors and space. Every bit of furniture was gone.

Mary gasped. One of the Germans turned to her, gun shoved right against her temple. "Where is the gold? There's nothing in here."

"I don't understand. I was here a few days ago. How could everything be gone?" All three of them looked at me.

"I'm having the office painted. Everything is in storage." The paint pans, ladders, and rags in the middle of the otherwise empty office made the explanation seem superfluous to me, but from the looks of incredulity on their faces they still didn't understand.

"Where?"

My patience, despite the situation, was wearing thin. "I have no idea. The painting company takes care of everything. They move all the furniture, repaint, and fix the place up; then they bring everything back. It's all part of the service."

"How could you do this?" Mary's voice came out as more of a screech.

I glared at her. "It's your fault actually. Yours and Jack's. You came in here and looked around as though this office were a shanty, and I started to think that maybe the place could use some sprucing up. Then Jack told me that the office looked unsuccessful. I was offended. I decided to do something about it. So, it's your own fault if the Germans kill you now. Maybe you shouldn't be so snotty and rude next time you hire a private investigator." I realized the words coming out of my mouth were ridiculous, but I was past the point of caring.

Mary lunged for me, looking as though she was ready to draw blood. The East German holding on to her arm jerked her back.

"If there is no gold here then we don't need you any longer. We need to find where this painting company has taken the furniture." The East German holding Mary clicked back the hammer on his pistol.

There was a loud bang to my left, and we all looked toward the noise. The door burst open, bouncing off the wall behind it, and shattered the frosted glass. I gritted my teeth. I always knew that someone was going to break that glass someday.

In the doorway stood the two Soviet agents who were becoming as familiar as old friends. They had their guns aimed in our general direction, but their attention was taken up by the barrenness of the office.

"Where's the gold?" one of the Soviets shouted, then pointed his gun directly at the East German agent's head. "We know you're here to get it. Where is it?"

"Ask the painters. Apparently they have it now." Mary should have just kept her mouth shut, as everyone turned to glare at her.

"The painters?"

"The night I came to Allie's office I realized that it was the perfect place to hide the gold, as no one would ever think to look there. Including Miss Fortune here. So I hid it in her couch and have been waiting for a time when I could get it back." Mary sneered at me. "Some private investigator you are."

I glared.

"And now the couch is gone, who knows where, and a million dollars' worth of gold is in the hands of a bunch of painters."

I felt a small niggle of satisfaction. It hadn't been intentional, but I had kept the gold out of the hands of all of the sleazy con men and vicious foreign agents who wanted to get at it. It was possible that one of these people would kill me and Mary now, but thwarting them all did bring some satisfaction.

Chapter 37

SO IN THE SMALL, barren office stood Soviet agents, East German agents, a con woman, and a private investigator. And at least two of us looked like we'd just gone nine rounds with a prize fighter.

Mary's eyes slid to mine, and I nodded slightly. I knew what she was thinking. Up until now there had been no real opportunity to make a break for it, but with the entrance of the Soviets, both sides had their attention focused away from us. Instead they were glaring and pointing guns at one another.

Unfortunately, even without being guarded closely, it was still going to be difficult to get away from these men without ending up full of holes. We were outgunned four to zero, and both Mary and I were injured. Whatever plan we came up with was going to have to be an incredible stroke of genius. Still, we had a better shot now than we'd had five minutes ago.

I was approximately five paces from the door. Even in my injured state I could make it there and out in a matter of seconds. I had to assume the same of Mary and just hope that the knock on her head hadn't compromised her ability to run. I watched the standoff taking place to the side of me. The Germans had their guns aimed at the Soviets, and the Soviets had their shiny black pistols pointed right back. They glared at one another with unconcealed distaste. Clearly hostilities ran deep under the surface, despite the fact that they were supposed to be allies.

Mary and I stood near the middle of the room, with our backs to the window, facing the door. I had the bones of a plan worked out in my mind, and I turned to catch Mary's eye. My plan didn't have the stroke of genius I'd been hoping for, but I gave it a 30 percent chance of actually working, which was still better than the 100 percent chance of being shot if we did nothing.

I took a quiet step backward until I was within striking distance of the ladder. I sucked in a deep breath, then shoved it over. It went down with a clatter, right through my office window. The explosion of broken glass made everyone but Mary and me jump. The Soviets didn't even look; they both fired instantly in the direction of the noise, and the Germans, thinking they'd been fired upon, shot back at the Soviets. I saw it out of the corner of my eye as Mary and I ran for the door. Gunshots went off behind us, but I didn't stop to look, didn't turn around, but instead kept my eye on the goal. Getting through that door meant freedom, and nothing else mattered.

I reached the door in four strides and pulled it open. Mary was right on my heels, and she shoved me through. I turned to lead the way down the stairs, aiming for the relative safety of the street.

Except the stairway was blocked.

Blocked solid with people. More people with guns. My heart sank, and the adrenaline that had given me the strength to make a break for it crashed. All I felt was despair. I'd tried, and I'd failed.

Someone grabbed me by the shoulder, and I cried out at the wave of pain that coursed through my body. My eyes blurred and I nearly tripped as they shoved me down the stairs. Pushed from hand to hand, I found myself at the bottom of the staircase. My dazed mind couldn't make sense of the fact that I hadn't been shot yet. Mary was shoved down the stairs the same way, and she bumped into the back of me. I jerked at the contact.

I had no strength left to run, and no time to think, but I took a deep breath, trying to scrape together just a bit more determination. I turned to grab Mary's hand and drag her out of the building. We could try and get help on the street; we just had to make it out to the building's front door. Mary looked worse than I felt, half her face covered in rusty, dried blood, with new fresh tracks of red trailing over top. I yanked her hand to get her going, but something caught my eye. The men on the stairs, the men with guns, were in uniform.

Uniforms I recognized. Feet cemented in place, I gazed in wonder up the stairs. They were moving now, charging up the staircase. Some of them were in NYPD uniforms; some of them weren't, but it didn't matter. The only thing that counted was the fact that the cavalry had arrived. Jack was responsible for it, I was sure, and the relief made my knees wobble. Fatigued beyond measure, I almost didn't see Mary's reaction to the sight of our rescuers. Out of the corner of my eye I saw her body tense as though she was still going to make a break for it. To her, the FBI and the NYPD were the enemy too. And for good reason. They would arrest her and send her up to Rikers Island. I turned my body as I watched her get ready to run. I had almost no energy left, but I had just enough to stick my foot out and trip her as she made a break for it.

Probably as exhausted and as injured as I, Mary toppled to the cement and didn't move. Using my last bit of strength, I crossed to her and sat down on the small of her back. "They'll be coming to get you any minute—I promise."

"I'm your client. You have to let me go." The words were barely audible, as I was probably squishing her lungs.

"Yeah, well, you broke rules one and two, and you definitely broke rule number three, so you can just forget it, Mary. A piece of advice: Never mess with a P.I. We take it personally."

Chapter 38

JACK DROVE me to the hospital himself. An ambulance came for the two Soviets and one of the East Germans, but the other one needed only a white sheet and a body bag.

Mary had been arrested, then taken to the hospital, and Jack had all but carried me to his car and driven me to the closest emergency unit. In the car, I recounted the short version of what had happened since I'd been taken hostage.

I was seen right away in the emergency room and told that my shoulder was dislocated. Thank goodness they put me out before they relocated it, but I woke hours later with it feeling almost as good as new. The rest of me felt battered, bruised, and sore, but I was still strong enough to want out of the hospital.

"The doctor said you should probably just rest overnight." Jack had been trying to convince me to stay, but he didn't seem surprised when I walked out anyway. He'd gotten special clearance to see me because of his FBI credentials, but I'd sent him right back out of my room until I was out of my hospital gown and decently dressed. My grey suit might have been dirty, wrinkled, and bloodstained, but it was much better than what the hospital offered. Feeling much more in control and almost exultant, I walked out four hours after I was carried in.

Jack pulled the car around to the front of the hospital, and I got in. Echoes of pain shivered through my body. Not extreme, but enough to remind me of the events of the last twenty-four hours.

"Why don't I take you home now? A good night's sleep would do wonders for all of your aches and pains."

Apparently he saw the wince as I got into the car. "I had at least three hours of sleep already."

"General anesthetic does *not* count. And having your shoulder relocated is not my idea of a relaxing experience." His voice was tight, and he kept his eyes on the road. Deliberately not looking at me.

"Jack, I'd never be able to sleep. We need to see this through. Right to the very end. We need to get the gold, and then—I promise—I'll rest."

He said nothing, but his hands relaxed somewhat on the steering wheel.

"Okay, I need to know. How did you find us?"

"When Clive and Mary took you from your apartment I put out an APB on all three of you. You were top priority for the FBI and for the NYPD. I couldn't stand around waiting to hear something, and I knew it would be useless to drive around the city looking for you, so I did a little digging and found our good friend Nigel Gordon."

"Where was he?"

"I found him at a hotel close to the one where he met you. I interrogated him, and he told me that the Soviets had backed off on their search and instead were just watching the East German agents. I knew that the Germans were following you, so if the Soviets were following them, they would lead me right to you."

"Oh, for pity's sake, it sounds like the Macy's parade. How did you find the Soviets?"

"Pure luck. I put out a BOLO—be on the lookout—on them, and they were spotted a few blocks from your office. I had a feeling that this was it, and I got a team out there. We were just ready to make an entrance when the shooting started."

I let out a laugh. "It was a desperate attempt to make something happen. Our situation was looking pretty bleak when they discovered that the gold had been moved. I suppose if I'd just waited, there might have been no need for the shooting."

"There was no way for you to know. I'm proud of you. You made something happen. If I hadn't been there, it would have been your only shot. You did good, kid."

"Where are we going?" I hadn't thought to ask, but Jack seemed to have a destination in mind as he wove his way into a part of town I didn't know well. From the glow of the streetlights I saw that the buildings were a little rundown, and some appeared to be deserted.

"I called your painting company, and this is the address they gave me for their warehouse. Your furniture should be inside one of these buildings. An employee will meet us and let us in."

I looked at my watch. "Someone is going to meet us out here at eleven o'clock at night?"

"One of the perks of being with the FBI. Very few people argue with me when I suggest that they come out to meet me. No matter the time."

I shook my head and laughed.

"Okay, that's the building there, and there's a car idling right in front of it." Jack pulled up to the curb and shoved the car into park. I was out as soon as the vehicle had fully stopped. The gold was somewhere inside this building. I had to force myself to keep my breathing steady. Even two nights ago, this moment would have meant everything to me, the promise of what the gold would bring me, but it didn't carry the weight it once had.

It still carried the weight of my dreams and all of my secret fears, but it didn't carry my hope anymore. I'd finally realized that hope didn't depend on circumstance, but that it depended on eternity. A God who loved me in spite of my failings and who cared deeply about my hurts.

We walked up to the front of the building where

a young man, maybe twenty, stood. Without a word he unlocked the door, opened it, and handed the key to Jack. "Just lock the place up when you leave and put my keys in the mailbox. I'll get them tomorrow." With that the man jumped back into his car and took off.

Jack shook his head. "Aren't you glad you entrusted all of your furniture, files, books, and a million dollars' worth of gold to this company? Clearly security is a big priority for them."

I said nothing, just preceded Jack into the warehouse, but I had to agree with his assessment. I was less than impressed with the care they were taking of my things.

Shaking my head, I brought my thoughts back to what was important. Finding the gold.

Chapter 39

MY FURNITURE was stored along the far wall and clearly marked with "A. Fortune" scrawled on a piece of cardboard. My heartbeat tripled when I saw a corner of the brown leather couch peeking out from behind my filing cabinets.

We crossed to my section and Jack started to work right away at moving the furniture stored in front of it. I longed to help, just to make it go faster, but with the recent shoulder injury I had to stand back and watch Jack do it.

He cleared all the stuff around until there was

nothing between us and the couch. Finally able to help, I pulled off the cushions, but there was nothing unusual.

Jack ran his hands along the seams, feeling between the back and sides of the couch on his side, and I did the same on my side.

Nothing.

My heart thumped a bit quicker, and I tried not to think about the consequences if it turned out that Mary had been lying about the gold's whereabouts all along.

Jack looked at me. "Now what?"

"Let me think. I doubt she was lying. It would have been a stupid move, because the East Germans would've found out eventually. There was no way she could have known that the office was empty."

"What if it was somewhere else in your office? Another piece of furniture, in your filing cabinets, something like that?" Jack pushed his hat off and rubbed a hand along his forehead.

"She was very specific. She said it was in the couch."

"In the couch?"

I raised my eyebrow at his tone.

"What if it's inside the couch?" At my blank look he elaborated. "Inside it. It would have to be somewhere that it wouldn't be noticed. Shoving it under the cushions wouldn't make sense; you could accidentally find it and ruin all of her and Clive's plans. She'd have to stash it somewhere that it wouldn't be found."

"And that would be where?"

He didn't answer; instead he moved to the front of the couch and crouched down. I stood on the opposite side, and he motioned for me to move out of the way. He heaved the couch onto its back, and I winced at the rough treatment of my part-time bed. Curious and more than a little hopeful, I rounded to where he stood and looked at the underneath of the couch.

The bottom frame was wooden, and a thick mesh fabric stretched across the base of it. I noticed that one corner of the mesh was torn, and even as I pointed it out to Jack he was there, shoving his fingers into the little hole and ripping it further. I winced at the sound of tearing fabric, but Jack tore the whole side of it right off. I got down onto the floor next to Jack and peered into the cavernous interior of my furniture. It was too dark to see, so side by side, Jack and I felt the sides for anything unusual.

My hand jammed against something hard and my breath caught. Jack heard the hitch in my breathing and turned to me. Our gazes locked. Neither of us moved for a second. I ran my hands along the edges of the object, and I realized it was propped along the side of the wood frame on a piece of bracing. I grabbed hold of it and yanked it off its perch and out into the dim light of the warehouse.

In my hands was a fabric bag with a drawstring top tied tight. Using my nails, I worked at the knots for several seconds until I heard a click, and Jack slid a knife beneath my hands and cut through the knots in one slice.

I nodded at him, then pulled the bag open. Inside was a black box. It had a hinged lid, and the front was closed with brass clasps. I sat back on my haunches.

"This could be it."

Jack nodded but didn't speak. Taking a deep breath, I turned the box toward me and lifted both clasps.

Chapter 40

HOLDING MY BREATH, I flicked open the top of the box. I leaned back so Jack could see too. Inside were several items bundled in cloth. I picked one at random and slowly unwound it. As the strip of cloth came off and got closer to revealing what was at its center, I felt a sense of peace settle over me.

A corner of gold shimmered at me, and I threw caution to the wind, unrolling the last bit off with no finesse at all and letting the golden object tumble out into my hand.

It was an earring. About three inches long with dangling ends of hammered gold. It was beautiful, and it was exactly what we were looking for. I turned to Jack. "Let's check them all out." I handed him a roll of fabric slightly bigger than the one I held and pulled out another one for myself. I laid the earring I'd already uncovered on the lid of the black box.

Jack and I worked in silence, taking a few seconds to look at each piece before moving on. I saved the biggest bundle for last. From the pictures I saw when I looked at the FBI file, I had a pretty good idea what this object was, and what it would look like. It held a significance all its own. I closed my eyes for a moment before unraveling it.

It was the diadem. Forged to fit the brow of a queen, the glittering headdress was the centerpiece of the Helen of Troy collection. It took little imagination to picture Helen, the Spartan queen of myth, whose beauty had caused nations to war, wearing the heavy gold band across her forehead, with the long golden chains dripping down around her ears. I had an intense desire to try it on, to see how the weight felt on my own head. Would I feel the weight of nations, of an entire society pressing down, or would it feel no heavier than the gold it was comprised of? Could the weight of Helen's Gold be measured in ounces, or was it measured in millennia and destiny?

I laid the diadem down next to all of the other treasures we'd uncovered. There were eleven pieces in all, not including the two already in the FBI's possession.

I leaned back and surveyed our accomplishment. We'd done what we'd set out to do. I hadn't known at the outset how much this quest would cost. Two lives had been lost in the search for the gold. I wondered how many more lives had been sacrificed for it over the millennia.

Shaking off the melancholy thoughts, I turned to Jack. "I guess we did it."

"We did. You are quite the P.I., Miss Fortune. You more than live up to the legend."

I wanted to squirm at the praise. The end of our road was in sight, and I suddenly wasn't ready for any of it. I picked up one of the cloth strips and began repacking one of the pieces. It was so hard to believe that this gold, this little box of treasures, had held the dreams and longings of so many. Including mine. Now that I'd seen the pieces for myself I wondered if it was really wise to hand them over to the FBI.

I had a contract, saying that the FBI would get me the information on David, but what assurance did I really have? A few scraps of paper? They were the FBI, for goodness' sake. They could do whatever they wanted. The minute I handed over the gold to them was the minute I was at their mercy.

The thoughts rolled through my mind as I rewrapped all of the gold. Jack didn't help me with the repacking; instead he sat back on his heels and watched. I had the feeling that he knew my thoughts.

"Maybe I should hold on to this until the FBI has the information for me. Once it's ready we could make a straight trade." My voice sounded high, bright. Artificially so.

Jack said nothing; he just sat in silence.

"I mean, it's not like I have any real guarantee that I'll get what I was promised at the beginning of all this. It's probably just good business sense to hold on to this until I have what I want."

Jack leaned forward, put both his hands on my shoulders, and waited until I was completely still. "Allie. The FBI is just a company, a collection of faceless people who have made you a promise. But I am not faceless. I am not a company. I am Jack O'Connor, and I have made you a promise. You will get your information. I'll make sure of it."

I looked at him, into his normally easy-going features, but now, there was no hint of a smile, only Jack asking me to trust him. Completely. With everything that mattered to me. I wondered for a second if he had any idea how much he was asking, but I saw it in his eyes. He understood exactly what he was asking of me. And he was waiting for me to make my choice.

I held his gaze for several long seconds before breaking away. I closed the top of the black case, flicking the clasps shut. Tucking it under my arm, I stood.

Jack stood too.

I turned to him. "It's been a pleasure working with you O'Connor."

"And with you Miss Fortune."

I reached under my arm and handed the box to him. "Just Allie. Call me Allie."

Chapter 41

SINCE THE RECOVERY of the gold and the newspaper story that had gone along with it, my phone had been ringing off the hook. Somehow the papers had gotten hold of the P.I. Princess nickname, and I was now a minor celebrity. Of course, my mother was mortified. The very idea of her daughter being involved in such sordid investigations made her pale in horror. My father had said nothing, but he couldn't have missed it as he read the paper back to front every day.

The publicity was more of a nuisance than a help for me, as I already had more cases than I could handle. When reporters called, I told them I had no comment, and eventually, after more than three weeks, the furor started to die down.

I was sitting in my newly painted, successful-looking office, shuffling paperwork and clearing the piles from my desk when he walked in. I hadn't seen him since I'd watched him drive away the night we'd found the gold.

"Jack." I lost my breath when I saw the large manila envelope in his hand.

"I'm here to deliver on my promise." He didn't smile; he seemed to realize that paralyzing terror had struck me mute.

"Have you looked?" It was all I could get out.

He shook his head. "It wasn't my place. This is your news. You should be the first one to see it."

He wasn't going to let me take the coward's way out.

"You came to deliver it. I guess your job is done now." I forced a smile so bright it made me wince. "I guess I'll see you around then." It was a curt dismissal, and we both knew it.

Jack readjusted his hat. "I'd better be going. I'll see you around, Fortune."

I nodded, not caring that his back was already to me.

He'd laid the envelope in the center of my desk, on top of the files I'd been working on. I reached out a shaking hand to pick it up, but couldn't bring myself to touch it. Instead, I brought my hand back and just stared.

The sun had long since faded, and I hadn't bothered with the light. In fact, I hadn't left my chair since Jack had brought me the file that would change my life. I'd just sat in my chair, too afraid to open it.

Shadows lengthened and stretched into full darkness, and only my desk lamp kept me from sitting in the pitch black.

I took a deep breath, reached out my hand, but couldn't make myself pull the envelope toward me.

I propped my head in my hands and tried to convince myself that it was time to find out.

A knock at the door made my heart stutter. I shoved myself to my feet. "Who is it?"

There was no answer, but the silhouette on the other side of the newly replaced frosted glass was huge. The doorknob rattled, and the door swung open.

I couldn't see a face, as the light on my desk was the only bit of illumination in the place. The man walked toward me, moving across to the desk. "I see you haven't opened it yet."

My breath came back. "Jack."

"Mind if I keep you company for a while?"

I nodded, then sat back down and looked around the room. I remembered the night I met Mary Gordon. The night I'd come to the office in the middle of the night to look at another envelope. To look at a picture of a dead man. It hadn't been a face I recognized that night, but maybe tonight would be the night that ended my search and I would finally come face to face with irrefutable proof that David Rubeneski was really dead.

Maybe.

But this time, unlike that night, I wouldn't be alone.

Jack sat across from me, waiting patiently. For

once he didn't fidget or even move. He didn't speak or try to give me advice. He was just there. He'd known I needed someone, and he'd come.

I took a deep breath. "I think I'm ready now." I reached out, surprised to see that my hand trembled only a little. I grabbed the envelope and was surprised by how light it was. Tearing open the sealed flap, I prayed silently. Prayed for strength, for wisdom, and most of all that I would finally know.

I reached into the envelope and pulled out its contents. One sheet of paper. Holding it under the light of the desk lamp, I started to read. It was a personnel file. The top corner of the paper was emblazoned with the crest of the Central Intelligence Agency. Large sections of the text were blacked out, but my eyes hit the one and only line that counted.

"David Rubeneski posted 1942–present. Official status: Missing in Action. Actual status: Covert."

I'd been right all along.

Jack leaned forward in his chair. "What does it say?"

I took a deep breath and said the words I'd longed for years to be able to say. "It says he's alive."

Center Point Publishing
600 Brooks Road • PO Box 1
Thorndike ME 04986-0001 USA

(207) 568-3717

US & Canada:
1 800 929-9108
www.centerpointlargeprint.com